The Library of Southern Civilization
LEWIS P. SIMPSON, EDITOR

MY YOUNG MASTER

ꙮMYꙮ
YOUNG MASTER

A NOVEL BY
OPIE READ

With an Introduction by
WAYNE MIXON

Louisiana State University Press
Baton Rouge and London

Louisiana State University Press gratefully acknowledges
the support for this publication provided
by Mercer University.

10   9   8   7   6   5   4   3   2   1

LIBRARY OF CONGRESS CATALOGING-IN-PUBLICATION DATA

Read, Opie Percival, 1852–1939.

My young master.

(The Library of Southern civilization)

I. Title.   II. Series.

PS2679.R6M9   1987   813'.4   86-27443

ISBN 0-8071-1380-8

ISBN 0-8071-1395-6 (pbk.)

CONTENTS

PREFACE AND
ACKNOWLEDGMENTS

If Opie Read is remembered at all today, it is as a magazine humorist and platform speaker. The serious fiction that he wrote had been virtually forgotten well before his death in 1939 at the age of eighty-six. Seldom has a writer so interesting been so thoroughly lost to American cultural history. Read's refreshingly iconoclastic treatment of many things southern—most of all, racial conventions—should have made him a more important figure in the study of the South's literature than he has been. I should point out, however, that the social significance of much of Read's writing was usually lost upon his contemporaries as well. In particular, *My Young Master* was not properly appreciated upon its original publication. Readers today may well be more alive to the novel's essential meaning than were those ninety years ago.

Although I have devoted a good many years to the study of southern writing, I knew almost nothing of Read until I was invited to contribute a chapter to the recently published *History of Southern Literature.* I am grateful to Louis D. Rubin, Jr., the general editor of that volume, for asking me to participate, and to my section editor, Rayburn S. Moore, for his assistance.

The essay that constitutes the Introduction herein was first presented in a shorter version at the annual meeting of the Southern Historical Association in 1984. I wish to thank Lucinda Hardwick MacKethan and Willard B. Gatewood, Jr., for their perceptive comments on the paper. Other scholars have read and offered helpful criticism of the essay as well: Fred Hobson, Lewis P. Simpson, Eric J. Sundquist, and my colleagues at Mercer University, Carlos T. Flick and Henry Y. Warnock. I very much appreciate their assistance. I am especially indebted to Professor Simpson, the editor of the Library of Southern Civilization Series, for the confidence that he had in this project. William F. Holmes, who suggested to me the idea of reissuing *My Young Master,* also has my sincere thanks.

Wilbur E. Meneray of Tulane University library and librarians at Duke University and the University of North Carolina at Chapel Hill provided help at various stages of my work on Read. Throughout the project Dumont Bunn, Lora Burns, Valerie Edmonds, and Elizabeth Hammond of Mercer's library staff were unfailingly efficient and courteous in their assistance. I appreciate also the support of a number of Mercer's present and former administrators, particularly Rollin S. Armour, Sammye Crawford Greer, Robert J. Hargrove, and Rex P. Stevens. Bessie Killebrew skillfully and cheerfully typed innumerable drafts of the Introduction. A generous grant from Mercer helped make possible the publication of this volume.

It has been a special pleasure to work with the editorial staff of Louisiana State University Press. I would like particularly to thank Beverly Jarrett, executive editor and associate director, Catherine F. Barton, managing editor, and Catherine Landry, copy editor, for their gracious assistance.

For the encouragement they gave me, I am grateful to Dewey W. Grantham, Jr., Don Higginbotham, Daniel W. Hollis, Louis D. Rubin, Jr., George Brown Tindall, and, most of all, my children, Phillip and Eleanor, and my wife, Fran.

INTRODUCTION
OPIE READ TAKES ON JIM CROW

Surveying culture in the South about 1920, H. L. Mencken, in his inimitable way, described the region as the "Sahara of the Bozart" and found precious few writers there that merited serious consideration. Fifty years later, a student of southern intellectual history called the region in the 1890s "a literary wasteland." In the years between those assessments, literary scholars referred to the period from 1890 to 1920 as the "forgotten decades" and the "dark night" of southern literature illumined only by "the pale phosphorescence of decay."[1] Although these judgments are too harsh, the writing of the period often failed adequately to reflect regional experience. The strength

1. H. L. Mencken, "The Sahara of the Bozart," in *Prejudices: Second Series* (New York, 1920), 136–54; Bruce Clayton, *The Savage Ideal: Intolerance and Intellectual Leadership in the South, 1890–1914* (Baltimore, 1972), 109; Louis J. Budd *et al.,* "The Forgotten Decades of Southern Writing, 1890–1920," *Mississippi Quarterly,* XXI (Fall, 1968), 275–90; C. Hugh Holman, "Literature and Culture: The Fugitive-Agrarians," in *The Roots of Southern Writing: Essays on the Literature of the American South* (Athens, Ga., 1972), 188–89; Holman's essay was originally published in 1957. As exceptions to the barrenness of southern writing of the nineties, Clayton mentions the work of Thomas Nelson Page and Ellen Glasgow. Yet the work for which Page is best remembered, *In Ole Virginia*, was written in the eighties, and Glasgow published only two novels in the nineties, one of them anonymously. Conspicuously absent from Clayton's assessment are George W. Cable, Charles W. Chesnutt, Kate Chopin, Joel Chandler Harris, and Mark Twain.

of the legend of the Lost Cause that idealized the Old South and the Confederacy, and of the New South creed that optimistically and mistakenly proclaimed the triumph of a new industrial order—romantic myths that curiously reinforced each other—made it difficult for southern writers at the turn of the twentieth century to view their region with a critical eye. Moreover, if their works were to sell in the heyday of sentimental romance, these writers were bound to heed readers' demands for a genteel literature that encouraged escape into either a romantic past or an idealized present. Yet despite tight constraints, some writers of fiction tried on occasion to free their work from sentimentality and to challenge convention. One such writer was Opie Read.

The author of at least fifty-five books, some twenty of them novels with southern settings published between 1888 and 1906, Read enjoyed wide acclaim around the turn of the century. Like William Gilmore Simms earlier, he wrote too much too fast, "not with the fury of composition," as the critic Vincent Starrett observed, "but with the fury of imperative haste." All too often, as Burton Rascoe said, Read seemed to have been "two sticks behind the printer." According to Read himself, he wrote *The Jucklins*, a story of Carolina mountaineers that sold a million copies and was published in 1896, in two weeks.[2] Working fre-

2. Vincent Starrett, "Opie Read and the Great American Novel," *Buried Caesars: Essays in Literary Appreciation* (Chicago, 1923), 159; Burton Rascoe, "Opie Read and Zane Grey," *Saturday Review of*

quently in the genre of popular romance, he was first
and foremost a storyteller, not a social thinker; nevertheless, many of his novels contain significant social
commentary.

As a boy growing up in Gallatin, Tennessee, in the
1850s and 1860s, Read displayed a trait that was much
admired in that time and place—grit. Never, it seems,
did he run from a fight. As a man in the 1890s, living
in Chicago and writing about the South, he took on
Jim Crow, the guardian of the color line, and fought
that formidable opponent with considerable craft in
his novels.

Literature, November 11, 1939, p. 8; Opie Read, _I Remember_ (New
York, 1930), 230; Maurice Elfer, _Opie Read_ (Detroit, 1940), 58.
Elfer's book is primarily a collection of interviews with Read.
Scholarship on Read is scant. He is often omitted from surveys, an-
thologies, and reference works that concern southern literature.
See, for example, Jay B. Hubbell, _The South in American Literature,
1607–1900_ (Durham, N.C., 1954); Richard Beale Davis, C. Hugh
Holman, and Louis D. Rubin, Jr. (eds.), _Southern Writing, 1585–
1920_ (New York, 1970); and Louis D. Rubin, Jr. (ed.), _A Biblio-
graphical Guide to the Study of Southern Literature_ (Baton Rouge,
1969). Robert L. Morris' biography, _Opie Read: American Humorist_
(New York, 1965), contains some interesting readings of Read's
works, but only one-fourth of the text deals directly with his fiction,
and Morris fails adequately to put Read in wider context. Much
more satisfactory is Reed McColloch Baird, "Opie Read (1852–
1939): A Study in Popular Culture" (Ph.D. dissertation, University
of Michigan, 1966), which presents Read as a realistic romancer
who performed the useful service of elevating the taste of the reading public. Baird's dissertation contains a thoughtful chapter on
Read's portrayal of blacks. See also two articles by Baird: "Opie
Read: An American Traveler," _Tennessee Historical Quarterly,_ XXXIII
(Winter, 1974), 410–28, and "Opie Read (1852–1939): An Introduction," _Mark Twain Journal,_ XIX (Winter, 1977–78), 11–13. The
biographical material in my essay is based primarily upon Read, _I
Remember,_ and Elfer, _Opie Read._

What moved this white man, raised in what Read described as an aristocratic town in the Tennessee Bluegrass, to question conventional views of the black man and race relations? Living outside the South from 1887 on made that task easier, but mere residence in the North does not account for the genesis of Read's attitude. Instead, the circumstances of his upbringing and his career, along with a compassionate nature, provide much of the explanation.

Read was always something of an outsider, a wanderer with a zest for life and a refreshing irreverence for Victorian convention. As a young man, he could, as he said, "chase the wild Gypsy, grab her, splash her in the giggle of the humorous moon."[3] As a middle-aged man, he could drink too much, gamble too much, and even, on one occasion at least, watch Little Egypt dance burlesque. As an old man, he could compose a manuscript with the title "Satan's Side of It: The Autobiography of the Devil as Dictated to a Sinner." He could, in short, have far more fun than polite society was accustomed to allow.

But Read's iconoclasm could also be serious. He once wrote that the invention of the wheel was "one of the first great things that man accomplished . . . because the wheel rolled him away from his neighborhood prejudices."[4] In his youth, Read defended his father's right to voice Unionist views in a county heav-

3. Read, *I Remember*, 104.
4. *Ibid.*, 303.

ily Secessionist, causing him to oppose community values, at times violently. In the 1870s, following the trade of compositor and newspaper reporter, he never lived in any place long enough to forge strong bonds with the community. Later, in Arkansas, where he worked as a humorist and took humor seriously, his gibes at the pretensions of would-be aristocrats, the excesses of demagogic politicians, and the foibles of Ozark rustics generated much resentment. Fifty years' residence in Chicago never made him part of Chicago because much of his time was spent traveling the lecture circuit and because his imagination remained rooted in the South, concerned to a great degree with the lives of black people.

What is striking about Read is the high degree of sympathy and compassion he displayed toward the Negro at a time when radical racism, with its brutal oppression of blacks, was ascendant. In his reminiscences, Read recorded that his first recollection was of a slave sale that separated a mother from her children, which he had witnessed as a boy in Gallatin. In a series of interviews given shortly before his death, he repeatedly declared his love for the black woman who had been his childhood nurse and said that when he learned of her death, although he was far away, he rode a railroad boxcar home to visit her grave. In the same interviews, the subject to which Read devoted the most attention was the Negro, demonstrating at times in his remarks a traditional paternalism but also a deep appreciation of the resourcefulness and courage of black people. It is in the fiction Read wrote, though, rather than in the facts of his life that his unconventional attitude toward the black man is most evident.

Read did not begin writing novels until after a fifteen-year career as a journalist in Tennessee, Kentucky, Ohio, and Arkansas. In Arkansas, where he lived for ten years prior to his move to Chicago in 1887 at the age of thirty-five, he made a name as editor of the *Arkansaw Traveler,* a humor weekly that he helped establish in 1882 and that enjoyed a circulation of eighty-five thousand within three years. Under Read's editorship, the columns of the *Traveler* sometimes contained sketches of darky humor that depicted blacks as either wise "uncles" or pretentious "new issue." In certain of his novels, too, black stereotypes appear, but Read often portrays such figures in a way that demonstrates an awareness that their behavior derives more from their knowledge of white expectations than from their own character.[5] At the

5. Kintchin in *The Starbucks* (Chicago, 1902) and Dominion in *The Harkriders* (Chicago, 1903) are such characters. Most other southern writers of the time did not show a similar understanding of black behavior; see Sterling A. Brown, *The Negro in American Fiction* (1937; rpr. New York, 1969), 62. Of Read's novels, *An Arkansas Planter* (Chicago, 1896), one of his poorest works, contains the most conventional treatment of race. The Negro is presented largely as the tool of designing white men. There are no significant black characters in the novel. In treating the black man in the aggregate and as a symbol rather than as an individual, Read abandoned art for argument.

same time, his novels that include racial themes present much strikingly untraditional treatment of blacks and race relations.

From an early novel, *Up Terrapin River,* published in 1888, through *The Harkriders,* published fifteen years later, Read fashioned situations that undercut racial conventions. In postbellum Arkansas, a black man and his crippled daughter live in the same house with two respectable white men under equal conditions. Black characters openly protest demeaning treatment by whites and question their integrity. On two occasions a black man threatens to whip a white man, and once a black orders a white to shine his shoes for him. A black serves as moral guide to a white, giving advice regarding his romantic relationship. A white character recognizes that a black character's servility is nothing but affectation. A white man apologizes to a black for having offended him. Two genteel whites associate with a black minister on terms approaching equality. Upon being introduced to a former slave, an upper-class Kentuckian treats him as a social equal by shaking his hand. A group of white men saves a black stranger from punishment by other white men. A white planter kills another white man to avenge his mulatto mistress.[6]

6. This paragraph is based upon my readings of the following Read novels: *Up Terrapin River* (Chicago, 1888), *A Kentucky Colonel* (Chicago, 1890), *Emmett Bonlore* (Chicago, 1891), *A Tennessee Judge* (Chicago, 1893), *The Wives of the Prophet* (Chicago, 1894), *Bolanyo* (Chicago, 1897), *The Starbucks, The Harkriders,* and *My Young Master* (Chicago, 1896).

Read challenged racial convention not only through the presentation of incident but also through the creation of black characters who play major roles in some of his novels. Old Alf, a former slave in *Up Terrapin River,* is intelligent, compassionate, and courageous. A white character says, "He has feelings finer than many a man would ascribe to one of his color" (75). Washington Smith, a black minister in *Bolanyo,* is a college graduate and a man of sensitivity and discernment, who enjoys the respect and confidence of the leading whites in the Mississippi town that is the novel's setting. None of Read's black characters breaks the mold of conventional black portraiture in postbellum southern fiction more forcefully than Dan, a mulatto slave in one of Read's best novels, *My Young Master,* published in 1896.

Set primarily on a plantation in the Kentucky Bluegrass shortly before the Civil War, the story is told from a vantage point after the war and outside the South. The protagonist is ostensibly Bob Gradley, the young master of the title, but actually it is Dan, Bob's manservant, who occupies center stage throughout the tale. That position is assured by Read's adopting the first-person focus of narration and using Dan, who is not only an observer of the action but a participant in it, to tell the story.[7]

7. It is important to emphasize the significance of Read's making Dan, not Bob, the "I" of the story, which allows Dan to assume the role of protagonist. According to Joseph M. Flora, readers at the turn of the twentieth century "were more prone than are contem-

Constant companions from early childhood on, Bob and Dan develop a close bond. When Bob goes away to school, Dan accompanies him and secretly studies with him. His formal schooling completed, Bob returns home to read law and to master oratory, again allowing Dan to study with him and planning, upon setting up practice, to make Dan a silent partner.

Meantime, Dan, hounded for most of his life by Dr. George Bates, the widower of Bob's sister Lou, kills Bates in self-defense. Believing that Dan will hang despite the circumstances of the case, Bob tells the authorities over Dan's protests that it was he who killed the doctor to save his own life. With Bob's summary exoneration, life on the plantation resumes its normal course as Bob falls in love with Jane Potter, a neighboring belle, and Dan with Titine, the beautiful mulatto servant of another of Bob's sisters.

Then the war comes, dividing the Gradley household. Bob's father Guilford remains loyal to the Union; Bob joins the Confederate army. Dan marches off to accompany Bob and remains with him until young Gradley dies in battle just before the war ends. Dan then returns home to be told by the dying Guilford that he is Guilford's son. Titine, having rebuffed Dan earlier, now admits her love for him. They move to Ohio, where, according to the story's brief epilogue, Dan is elected to the United States Congress.

---

porary readers to equate author and protagonist." See "From Virginia to Poictesme: The Early Novels of James Branch Cabell," *Mississippi Quarterly,* XXXII (Spring, 1979), 224.

Although a summary of the plot makes the situation seem extraordinary, Read develops the story line capably and generally makes it believable. True to the postbellum tradition of plantation romance, Read portrays Bob Gradley as a southerner who serves the Confederacy not so much to perpetuate slavery as to defend the South's right to self-determination. Yet, musing upon the coming of the war, Read's spokesman Dan refers to the doctrine of states' rights as a "beast-headed fallacy" and avers that "Hamilton was the wisest man that saw the birth of our nation."[8] Reflecting from time to time upon the ethos of the Old South, Dan describes it as "almost incomprehensible . . . absolute despotism in free America," as "that strange democratic absolutism," and as, in part, "beautiful and romantic, but filled with an inflammable gas" (49, 60, 132–33). Another sympathetically drawn character, Clem Gradley, Guilford's younger brother who had moved to Illinois and adopted antislavery views, says that the "whole trouble [between North and South] comes from slavery" (221).

As Read's rendering of the politics of sectional conflict veers from the convention of plantation romance, which ardently defended the southern position, so does his assessment of slavery. Because he presents the Old South's peculiar institution in the best possible light, Read attacks it all the more forcefully. The physical circumstances of Dan's life are

8. Read, *My Young Master*, 242. Hereinafter page references to this novel shall be incorporated parenthetically in the text.

hardly onerous: he lives in the master's house; he is
allowed, after a fashion, to obtain an education; seldom is he seen working.[9] Generally, as Bob sometimes
tells him, his lot is easier than that of many whites.
Even as a boy, though, Dan perceives little things that
underscore his sense of being different: sleeping on a
low lounge while Bob has a high, canopied bed (13);
being barred from the big house and sent to the slave
quarters when Bob's sister is ill (21); participating
in certain family activities, but only at a distance (48,
53, 133).

That one of Read's primary purposes is to show the
dark side of slavery is evident throughout the novel.
Early on, Dan wonders why "I should have been created a piece of property, while one, nearly of my own
color and whom I could fling upon the ground, should
possess me" (12). On other occasions later in the story,
the knowledge is again brought home to Dan that despite his good treatment he is fundamentally a piece
of property. When Guilford Gradley refuses George
Bates's request that Dan be given to him, reminding
the doctor that Dan belongs to Bob, Bates replies, "I
didn't know but you gave him away as a man sometimes
gives a colt to a boy—merely to claim" (28). When Bob
rejects an offer from Jane Potter's father to buy Dan,

9. Unlike most other southern states, Kentucky did not enact a
law against teaching slaves to read. See Victor B. Howard, *Black Liberation in Kentucky: Emancipation and Freedom, 1862–1884* (Lexington, Ky., 1983), 1. Nevertheless, the kind of education that Dan
received would hardly have been countenanced by most white
Kentuckians.

Potter responds: "Owned one about like him once. Swapped him for a woman and a child" (213).

Unfortunately for his peace of mind, as Dan grows up he develops a sharp sense of irony, which makes him pensive and melancholy. He perceives how futile his striving is and reflects bitterly upon how "hopeless everything was determined to appear. Abetted by the kindest of men I had stolen into the field of thought, was preparing to become an out-lawed advocate of the law, a sneak-thief behind the bar" (172).

Toward the end of the story, Read unleashes his most caustic attack upon slavery. Having declared his love for Titine, Dan is stung by her rebuff. She tells him that he must not ask her "to go through with a mock ceremony, the sentimental joke of a plantation, and pretend that I am your wife" (236–37). When Dan protests that nature has matched them, Titine erupts: "Nature intended me for you, indeed. Nature doesn't know you, simpleton. If she should meet you in the road she would say, 'who's your master, boy? Oh, young Mr. Gradley, eh? Tell him with my compliments that he possesses a very fine piece of yellow property.' Then what would you do? Tell nature that you wanted to marry another piece of yellow property? She would laugh at you and tell you to black your master's boots" (253). Titine is right; Dan is a piece of yellow property. But as he points out, "So is gold" (268). He is, in sum, a good man, the physical, intellectual, and moral equal or superior of any other character in the story.

Not only is Read concerned to show the essential malevolence of slavery, but also, through the characterization of Dan and in other ways, he issues a strong challenge to the ideology of white supremacy. In an arresting exchange at the dinner table, Clem is voicing antislavery sentiments when Hanna, Guilford's wife, objects. "Why, it wouldn't astonish me," she exclaims, "to hear you say that a negro is as good as a white man!" (222). Read handles the scene quite realistically by not permitting Clem to respond.

As a boy, Dan shows his mettle by his refusal to let Bob push him around and his perceptiveness in a question he asks Bob. After the death of Bob's sister Lou, Dan, pondering what heaven is like, asks, "If a nigger angel beats a white angel flying, there'll be trouble, won't there?" (27). At school Dan, the superior scholar, helps Bob over rough places. When Bob instructs Dan to spy on Dr. Bates, Dan questions the honor of such an act. Bob mistakenly thinks that Dan is doubting his sense of honor, but Dan wants to protect his own honor, not Bob's (75–76). In the judgment of the Gradley men, all of whom are sympathetically drawn characters, Dan is a "noble fellow" and a "gentleman" (197, 266). The principal thematic function of the novel's implausible epilogue is to accentuate Dan's ability and worth.[10]

10. That a mulatto and former slave who had, in effect, served the Confederacy should be elected to Congress from the North goes beyond the bounds of romance to the realm of fantasy. It is interesting to speculate upon whether Dan was assumed to be white when he reached Ohio. Read gives no indication that he was.

Yet Dan demonstrates on occasion that he can be adept at deception, particularly in his relationship with the plantation mistress, a cold, mean-tempered woman. His apparent subservience in her presence is his way of outwitting her, which he does by design and with great relish. If circumstances call for doing so, he can also "put on" the Gradley men.

In his characterization of Titine no less than in his portrayal of Dan, Read undercuts white supremacy. Like Dan, who is the beneficiary of an education, Titine, in the words of her mistress, "knows as much and is a far better talker than I am" (227). Certainly Jane Potter, Bob's betrothed, compares poorly with Titine. As Bob's fiancée, Jane is the essence of the southern lady, sweetly agreeable to her man, yet Bob is hardly cold in his grave before she marries a Union officer. In contrast, Titine, forthright and honest in her early rejection of Dan, waits for him throughout the war.

Finally, the undermining of white supremacy reaches its apogee in a remarkable passage wherein Dan does the unthinkable—he passes judgment on a respectable white woman in language that is laden with sexual overtones. Riding home with Bob and Jane after Bob's bar examination, Dan reflects upon Jane: "I was so close that when she leaned back once a wayward wisp of her hair swept across my face, more like a breath than a tangible touch, it was so silken and soft. I studied the almost imperceptible grain of her pink, plush skin, I was so near her, and yet to me she was so strangely unreal. . . . I could not have felt for her the surging passion of a human love" (208). Jane's being white is not the reason, however, that Dan feels as he does. Rather, as he says, "She was wanting in heart" (208). That a white southerner wrote such a passage in 1896 is little short of astonishing.

In addition to the explicit attack upon the evils of slavery and the usually implicit but nevertheless effective challenge to white supremacy, another major theme of *My Young Master* is the dilemma of the mulatto. Because Dan is both black and white, he is neither. Sometimes his statements reflect the white influence in his life. He calls the Gradley mansion "our . . . house" (12). In the finest fashion of southern paternalism, he refers to the plantation blacks as "our people" (23). He models his behavior upon that of his master. Yet he is saddened, not made vain, by the jealousy and resentment that the plantation blacks harbor for him. He refuses to flaunt his superiority to the other slaves, which results more from opportunities brought by his lighter color than from that color itself. Moreover, he feels both the pathos and the vitality of the black experience. In the novel's most lyrical passage, Dan, worried over the imminent return of Dr. Bates, walks alone over the plantation at sunset. He notices a black man "blowing a melancholy reed," the black children playing, the black women milking cows (175). He describes his reaction thus: "My spirits rose out of their nervous lassitude; I felt a strong and almost unnatural sense of exhilaration"

(175). Later he refers to black people as "my down-trodden race" (281).

Painfully aware of a divided identity, of ability equal to that of the white men who control his life, of the restraints placed upon his aspirations, Dan nevertheless refuses to escape slavery, even though he could do so with relative ease were he to accept Clem's offer to pay his way to the North. His affection for Bob is so great that only his love of Titine could induce him to run away, and she refuses to join him. Not only does Dan reject the alternative of escape, but when war comes, he chooses to accompany Bob, who fights for the Confederacy.[11] Why does Dan contribute, albeit indirectly, to a cause designed to perpetuate his enslavement? It is certainly not because he fails to realize that freedom lies with the Union; he shows that he so realizes. Nor is it because blood binds him to Bob; Dan does not know he is Bob's half-brother until the very end of the story.[12] Bob believes that Dan acts as he does because he is a "faithful friend"; Dan instead

11. By war's end the Union army had enlisted more than twenty-five thousand slaves in Kentucky, according to Howard, *Black Liberation*, 82. Dan's act, then, is hardly typical, but it is plausible. John B. Boles points out that "there are true tales . . . about the personal slaves of white military officers who served their Confederate masters in combat with courage and fidelity, even to the point of bringing their wounded masters home." Then, Boles writes, "duty having been done [these slaves returned] to the front to join the Union troops." See *Black Southerners, 1619–1869* (Lexington, Ky., 1983), 183. Had Bob fallen earlier, Dan might have done likewise.

12. Upon learning that Guilford is his father, Dan indicates that he has suspected that such was the case all along (301). At no point earlier in the story, though, does he reveal such a suspicion.

describes himself as a "grateful slave" (266). Bob's explanation is more apt than Dan's. Unquestionably, gratitude composes part of Dan's motivation; yet he is a slave only in the eyes of the law. Even after Bob declares him free, Dan remains at the side of this man who was always much more his friend than his master. To Read, gratitude and fidelity are estimable traits worthy of a free man whose heart can transcend what society has done to him. Finally, then, Dan acts as he does not because he must but because he wishes to, not because of the bonds of slavery but because of human ties of a kind that, Read implies, can exist only between equals.

Like George W. Cable's *The Grandissimes* and Mark Twain's *Adventures of Huckleberry Finn* and *Pudd'nhead Wilson*—novels by white southerners written after the war, set in the antebellum South, and concerned with race—*My Young Master* might have been read for contemporary applicability, for what it had to say to the South of the 1890s.[13] Should the South humiliate someone like Dan by passing laws to segregate him? Should it deny the ballot to such a man? Should it seal the door to opportunity against an entire race? *My Young Master* can be seen as an endorsement of Cable's idea that the color line, heedless of merit, tended to equal-

13. The one review of the novel that I have found, which dealt with other Read novels as well, failed to see the relevance of *My Young Master;* see "Opie Read's Southrons," *Godey's Magazine,* CXXXV (October, 1897), 443–45. See also Morris, *Opie Read: American Humorist,* 146. Major literary journals such as *Atlantic Monthly, Harper's,* and *Scribner's* did not review the novel.

ize all whites on one side and all blacks on the other, thereby blocking the road to full achievement by capable blacks.[14]

The significance of what Read did in this novel can be fully appreciated only in the context of the times. That slavery had been wrong was a truism among influential southerners at the turn of the twentieth century. Unlike Read, however, most of them focused not upon the immorality of slavery but upon its impracticality, not upon the harm done to blacks but upon that done to whites. Moreover, in the fiction of the plantation romancers, the slaves were sublimely happy. It is a far cry from Read's Dan to Thomas Nelson Page's Sam in "Marse Chan," published in 1884, and F. Hopkinson Smith's Chad in *Colonel Carter of Cartersville,* published in 1891, both of whom describe antebellum days as the best times they had ever seen. At a time when the literature of remembrance dominated southern writing, *My Young Master* placed Read squarely among the few writers who made up what Fred Hobson has called "the school of shame and guilt." At a time when an increasingly virulent racism was being reflected in the "black brutes" of Thomas Dixon and other southern writers, Read's sympathetic portrayal of the black man and his undermining of white supremacy were all the more ex-

14. Cable's idea is set forth in his essay "The Freedman's Case in Equity," in *"The Silent South," Together with "The Freedman's Case in Equity" and "The Convict Lease System"* (1885; rpr. New York, 1907), 34–35.

ceptional.[15] At a time when the mulatto was viewed by science as degenerate and effete and when he was often presented in fiction as decadent and treacherous, Read created Dan.[16]

15. Fred Hobson, *Tell About the South: The Southern Rage to Explain* (Baton Rouge, 1983), 10–11. I. A. Newby, *Jim Crow's Defense: Anti-Negro Thought in America, 1900–1930* (Baton Rouge, 1965), 3–16, and Joel Williamson, *The Crucible of Race: Black-White Relations in the American South Since Emancipation* (New York, 1984), 119–24, demonstrate the intellectual respectability of racist thought at the turn of the century. C. Vann Woodward, *The Strange Career of Jim Crow* (3d rev. ed.; New York, 1974), 67–109, and Williamson, *Crucible of Race,* 109–323, describe the pervasiveness of extreme racism in the South from 1890 to 1915. According to John W. Cell, segregation was perceived as a moderate solution to the race problem by the "better element" among southern whites, who propounded such an arrangement to counter those extremists whose policy might foment race war; see *The Highest Stage of White Supremacy: The Origins of Segregation in South Africa and the American South* (Cambridge, Eng., 1982), 175–91. Dixon is the best known of the literary extremists because of the wide popularity of his novels *The Leopard's Spots* (New York, 1902), *The Clansman* (New York, 1905), and *The Traitor* (New York, 1907). Other southern writers, however, also created black beasts, among them Thomas Nelson Page in *Red Rock* (New York, 1898) and John Trotwood Moore in *The Bishop of Cottontown* (Philadelphia, 1906). Blatant racism was also evident in national literature of the time. See Thomas F. Gossett, *Race: The History of an Idea in America* (Dallas, 1965), 198–227.

16. On the prevailing view of mulattoes among whites at the turn of the century, see George M. Fredrickson, *The Black Image in the White Mind: The Debate on Afro-American Character and Destiny, 1817–1914* (New York, 1971), 247, 321, and Joel Williamson, *New People: Miscegenation and Mulattoes in the United States* (New York, 1980), 94–95. Among southern writers, Mary Johnston created a notoriously malevolent mulatto in Luiz Sebastian of *Prisoners of Hope* (Boston, 1898), as did Dixon in Silas Lynch of *The Clansman.* One of Ellen Glasgow's early novels, *The Voice of the People* (1900; rpr. New Haven, 1972), 246, contains a reference to a degenerate mulatto. In an essay defending lynching, the aspiring Georgia novelist Corra Harris savagely attacked the mulatto; see Mrs. L. H.

Read did not believe that the so-called "Negro Problem" would be solved immediately, and he understood the anxiety of white southerners who feared "Negro domination." Occasional references in his novels to race instincts and racial traits generally compare those of blacks unfavorably with those of whites.[17] Yet a good heart and the alchemy of art transformed his racial assumptions. Most of Read's novels that treat race demonstrate clearly that he was one of only a few white southerners who, as Joel Williamson has said, "had the sensitivity and imagination necessary to put themselves in the place of black people and to understand something of the burden that color carried in the South."[18] On balance, Read's fiction shows that he believed the condition of the black man was far more the result of social environment than of racial characteristics. Virtually all of the most admirable white characters in his novels that include race as a theme hold enlightened views of the black man. In sum, the work of this forgotten writer, with its high regard for

---

Harris, "A Southern Woman's View," *Independent,* May 18, 1899, pp. 1354–55. Although it was not George W. Cable's concern to denounce mulattoes as such, nevertheless a villain of his novel *John March, Southerner* (New York, 1894) is the deceitful mulatto Cornelius Leggett.

17. Among white southern writers of the time, even George W. Cable, who was the foremost advocate of better treatment of blacks, "tended to see virtue in hierarchy of color, with the darker race inferior to the lighter." See Louis D. Rubin, Jr., "Southern Local Color and the Black Man," *Southern Review,* n.s., VI (October, 1970), 1025.

18. Williamson, *Crucible of Race,* 488.

the resourcefulness, fortitude, and honor of blacks, and its criticism of their mistreatment by the white South, merits comparison with the writings of George Cable, Joel Chandler Harris, and Mark Twain, which presaged the sympathetic treatment of the black man evident in the Southern Renascence. Moreover, in *My Young Master* Read created situations that his better remembered contemporaries did not fashion. A brief description of blacks being compelled to fight for the entertainment of whites foreshadows Ralph Ellison's graphic, extended depiction of the protagonist's battle royal in *Invisible Man.* The use of an educated slave narrator by a white writer probably does not occur again in southern fiction until William Styron's *Confessions of Nat Turner.*

Read's sensitivity to the plight of blacks was part of a broader awareness of the South's ills. Among other shortcomings that Read criticized were the region's bombastic politics, its suspicion of learning, its strident boomerism, its sometimes artificial gentility, and its stifling defensiveness. Yet despite its flaws, which long residence both inside and outside the region permitted him to see clearly, Read felt a deep, abiding affection for the South as a place where honor still counted and as a kind of pastoral alternative to the materialistic North. His relationship with the South, like that of some other southern writers then and later, was one of love and anger.

*   *   *   *   *   *

When Read was growing up, his father cautioned him never to let any boy near his size whip him. Read became a large man—six feet, three inches, and more than two hundred pounds. He was big, he was strong, and he was game. But Jim Crow was just as big, just as strong, and much younger. *My Young Master* was no match for *Plessy* v. *Ferguson*.

Even so, the damage done by that Supreme Court decision sanctioning racial segregation, which was handed down the same year that Read's remarkable novel was published, began to be repaired half a century later. Like Read, leaders of the civil rights movement abhorred injustice, insensitivity, and ignorance. As Read observed in an interview on his eighty-sixth birthday, "Supreme ignorance always thinks that it is favored by the Lord. . . . I honestly think that we should never be governed by anyone who has not known the influence of great books. . . . Profound leadership comes from the man who has in his mind the influence of noble literature." [19] *My Young Master* cannot be called a "great book" in the conventional sense of that term, but it is undeniably "noble literature."

19. Elfer, *Opie Read*, 35–36.

MY YOUNG MASTER

MY YOUNG MASTER

A NOVEL

BY
OPIE READ

Author of "The Jucklins," "On the Suwanee River," "A Tennessee Judge,"
"A Kentucky Colonel," "The Colossus," "Emmett Bonlore,"
"Len Gansett," "The Tear in the Cup and Other
Stories," "The Wives of the Prophet."

CHICAGO
LAIRD & LEE, PUBLISHERS

Facsimile of 1896 Title Page

MY YOUNG MASTER.

CHAPTER I.

This is the story of a master, told by his slave.   As I
sit now, after the flight of so many years, and gaze at
the pictures in the fire—the hills and the valleys of my
boyhood, so bright, so glowing—I am oppressed with
the fear that my rude hand can but ill execute the work
that I have undertaken.   And yet, I feel the force that
truth alone can lend, for although my transcript may
be crude, I know that in the years now far away but
which are coming toward us, my history will be read
by the thoughtful man who seeks to portray the
strange social conditions that once existed in our
country.

I was born in the State of Kentucky, on the blue-
grass farm owned by Guilford Gradley.   Many
changes may have taken place, but in my day the
northern boundary line of the farm and the southern
corporate limit of the town of Litchford here came
together; and I think that one of my earliest recollec-

tions is of a Sunday morning, when my young
master and I got on the ground and parted the long
grass to search for the line. I know it must have been
on a Sunday, for the church bells were ringing, and
Old Master and Old Miss (as we always called his wife)
passed us on their way to town. Old Master was one
of the most prominent men in the State (had been a
general in the militia), and this influence was felt even
by the humblest negro on the place, for to belong to a
great man was of itself a social prominence not
enjoyed by the bondman of the ordinary individual.
Why, I remember seeing a little negro boy weep bitterly because a playmate had taunted him with the
humiliating fact that his master lived in a log house.
Ah, those old days, by turns a sad and a happy freak
in the history of man!

Old Master had three children, Miss Lou, who had
married a doctor; Miss May, about twelve years old,
when my story begins; and Mars. Bob, about my age.
The doctor that married Miss Lou was a neat man, all
the time picking at himself and cleaning his finger-
nails, it seemed to me, and I had thought that he must
be a great man, being a doctor and wearing so white
a shirt, until one day I heard Old Master tell Old Miss
that he wasn't worth the powder and lead to kill him.

And after that I noticed that he didn't amount to much, and I firmly believed that Toney, the yellow blacksmith on our farm, could throw him down. Miss Lou was a handsome young woman, with beautiful eyes; and even now her voice sometimes comes to me at twilight, singing, 'I have no mother now.' The song always made me cry, for I had no mother. Old Balch, the shoemaker, used to tell me about my mother. He said that he had often seen her standing in the door of the cabin, with me in her arms, singing that song; and he said that she was a beautiful creature, with hair almost straight. And I recall that the first time he told me this, I slipped away, into old Mammy Liza's cabin, where I climbed upon a chair to look at myself in an old broken glass, to see how white I was. And it occurs to me that this must have been the day when a preacher, evidently from the North, made Old Miss boiling mad by patting me on the head and saying, "What a handsome little fellow." Mars. Bob was with me on the veranda at the time and it was a great scandal that the preacher should not have given him his first and most flattering attention. But he did not, and his stay in our house was short.

One morning, Old Master called Mars. Bob and me into his library. He sat there, smoking his long-stem pipe, with his elbow resting on a table. I had often run through the room, but this was the first time that I had ever taken a good look at it, with its innumerable books and dark busts of long-haired men. And I was staring about when Old Master said:

"Dan, look at me."

I turned my eyes upon him, not in fear, but more in awe, for I felt his greatness, not so much in his ownership of me, as in the searching light in his eye and the rumbling depths of his voice.

"Dan," he said, "your Mars. Bob is six years old to-day—you and he are nearly of an age—and I have given you to him for a birthday present." I looked at Mars. Bob and he looked at me. Old Master continued: "You are to be his, to go with him, to fight with him, and to play with him. If the time ever comes when it is necessary for you to die in order to save him, do it. Bob."

"Yes, sir," said Mars. Bob.

"Whose boy is this?" (looking at me).

"Mine, sir," Mars. Bob answered proudly.

"What are you going to do with him?"

"Take him with me wherever I go."

"And if anyone tries to whip him, what are you going to do?"

"Kill the feller that tries it;" Mars. Bob answered fiercely; and Old Master leaned back and laughed. "You musn't kill anybody if you can help it," he said. "Now run on."

We ran out into the yard and tumbled upon the grass under a tree.

"You belong to me, don't you?" said Bob.

"Yes."

"Are you glad?"

"I don't know yet."

"But you'd rather belong to me than to your Mars. George, wouldn't you?" he asked, meaning the doctor.

"I wouldn't belong to him," I replied. "He ain't worth the powder and lead to kill him. I'd fight before I'd belong to him."

"You musn't say that, Dan — but, so would I." And, after a silence, he said: "If anybody starts to whip you, don't make any difference who it is, come and tell me, won't you?"

"Yes, and we will both fight him, won't we?"

"Yes, but I can whip you when I want to, can't I?"

"Yes, but nobody else shall."

"I know that, but I can, can't I?"

"Sometimes, but not all the time."

"Yes, I can."

"No, you can't."

"I'll whip you now if you say much."

"Much!"

He struck me and I struck him; we clinched and I threw him, and the next moment I was snatched into the air by the doctor. "You little scoundrel!" he shouted, "I'll wear you out." And he was proceeding to do it, with a riding whip, when Bob jumped upon him like a mad cat; and there we had it, both of us biting him, when Old Master ran out and frightened us all nearly to death. Old Miss came out, too, and declared that I ought to be given a hundred lashes, but then came Miss Lou. She took me by the hand and said, "No, you must not whip the poor little fellow." And at this Old Master turned upon her. "Who the devil's going to whip him, I'd like to know? George Bates, don't you touch this boy again."

And now Old Miss bristled up. "Guilford, you are always showing partiality for that little imp. You let him take the place. I won't stand it for one."

"Madam," said Old Master, putting me behind him, "he may be what you call him, but justice should be shown even to an imp. Boys that have any spirit at all will fight and you can't help it, and by—" here he swore a terrible oath that made us all stare. "I say,

if Bob can't defend himself, he must take the consequences. Boys, run off down yonder and play, now.
Madam, do as you choose. George Bates, attend to
your own affairs. My daughter, come with me."

Miss Lou was hurt at the way Master had spoken
to her husband, and as he took her hand to lead her
into the house, she put her face upon his bosom and I
heard her say, "Please don't talk to him that way,
father."

He kissed her. And then he turned to the doctor,
who hung about abashed. "George, I beg your pardon, sir. I was a little hasty and I admit it. There,
it's all right. I'll make you a present of that clay-bank
horse you admire so much. Get him and take a ride,
sir."

"Oh, father," Miss Lou cried, "you are the best man
in the world."

"No, I'm an old pepper-box. Look out, you're
tramping all over my feet. You boys go on down the
creek and catch some fish or I'll whip both of you.
Madam," he added, turning to Old Miss and handing
her a roll of bank notes, "go to town and do your
shopping."

CHAPTER II.

It seemed that on this very day my eyes were opened with a new intelligence, and not only my spiritual but my physical surroundings became clearer. I saw our great stone house as I had never seen it before, the wooded hill-sides, deep with grass, stretching far away; the white-washed cabins, quarter-circling the spacious yard, the broad garden and the weeping-willow trees whereunder Old Master's father and mother were buried; the village street which came abruptly to our big gate and there stopped in a fringe of clover. Through our place a bright creek ran, as many toned as a pack of hounds; and far to the right the turn-pike lay, white and glistening in the sun. Yes, my eyes were wider opened on this day, and a half-frightening glimmer of reason shot across my mind. I wondered why I should have been created a piece of property, while one, nearly of my own color and whom I could fling upon the ground, should possess me. This thought stung me, but there came a balm in the reflection that if I wore fetters at all, they were bright and lined with velvet. Of course, at this age I did not thus reason with myself, but I had the feeling, the substance of the thought, and the dressing of it must have come long afterward.

Bob and I slept in the same room up-stairs, he in a canopied bed, I on a low lounge. Old Master and Old Miss slept in a large room just across the hall; and now it seems to me that many a time at midnight, a stray fancy, wandering throughout the world of space, looking for entertainment in a human mind, would come to me as I lay in that little bed—come to me and rob me of sleep—compel me to lie there and listen to Old Master's slippered feet, slowly pacing up and down the long hall. One night, and it must have followed the day when I had been given over as Bob's exclusive property, I awoke to hear the old man's distressful shambling up and down the hall. The night was so dark, all the household was so still save those restless feet, that a strange pity came upon me. I heard Old Miss call him, and I heard him reply, "Go to sleep and pay no attention to me." But he seemed so lonely out there walking alone, that I found the courage to open the door and peep out at him. A dim light hung from the ceiling, not far from my peeping place, and as he turned about he saw me.

"What are you doing, Dan?" he asked, halting and turning to me.

"Will you please let me come out and walk with you?" was my bold reply.

"Walk with me?   What could have put that into your head?"

" 'Cause I thought you must be tired of walking by yourself."

"Well, run along back to bed."

"General," Old Miss called, "who's out there with you?"

"Do you see anybody?" he asked, looking hard toward her door.

"No, but I hear you talking."

"But isn't it possible for a man to talk to himself? Please go to sleep."   Then he came back to me and said: "Go on to bed, Dan.   And, see here," he added as I turned about, "don't get up any more when you hear me walking."

I hesitated a moment, looking at him, and then I asked: "Master, did you kill a man?"

He leaped toward me.   "Who told you that?   Come back here!"   I had started to run away.   "Come here to me.   I'm not going to hurt you."   He laid a tight hand upon my arm. "Why? Who said anything about my killing a man?"

"I don't know, sir," I answered honestly. "I don't know who said it, but I thought you did. I believe I dreamed it. Did you kill a man?"

I can see him now as he stood in the dim light, tall, frail, majestic, his old eyes bright, his white hair glistening. He cast a swift glance toward his bed-room door, and then leading me with him, stepped into my room. I heard the window curtain rustle—he was feeling about in the dark for a seat—and then he sat down upon the window ledge. I stood beside him, pressed close against his knee.

"Don't ever speak of such a thing again," he said, "but I did kill a man—in this room. Are you scared?"

"No, sir," I answered. "Tell me about it."

It was some time before he spoke again. I heard Bob's gentle breathing.

"Have you ever noticed deep marks on the stairs out there?" he asked.

"Yes, sir."

"The prints of a horse's shoes?" he said. And then after a silence, asked: "Do you think that I have been drinking to-night?"

"No, sir."

"Little liar you, you know I have."

"But tell me about the man and the marks on the stairs?"

"Hush! was that your mistress calling me?   Wait a moment."   I waited for him to continue, scarcely able to keep from trembling against his knee.   "Would you think that a man could ride up those stairs?" he asked.

"No, sir."

"But a man did.   I had said that I was going to horse-whip him, and one day when I lay sick in bed, he came, drunk, and rode up the stairs to my room— this room—to make me eat my words.   I heard a terrible racket, and the next thing I knew a horse's head was poked through the door.   I thought the devil had come.   But the next moment I saw my enemy, standing in his stirrups, looking down on me. He held a pistol in his hand and he snapped it at me. I rolled out of bed, just as he fired, and grabbed a gun and killed him.   He fell forward, and his horse took fright and wheeled about for the door.   The man—his name was Solomon Putnam—fell to one side as the horse plunged, but his foot caught in the stirrup, and he was dragged away—dragged to his own gate.   The law cleared me, and I know that I was right, but sometimes I see that man, hanging to the stirrup, with the

blood streaming out of his mouth. I'm not afraid
—I'd do it over again. But I can't sleep when I see
him."

The door creaked. "General!" It was the voice of
Old Miss.

"Madam, what do you want?"

"What are you doing in there?"

"Talking to myself. Go on and I will come in a
moment."

"I told you not to drink that brandy—I knew how
it would be."

"Yes, you knew how it would be and I know how it
is, so we are about even. Go on, and I will be there
in a moment."

The door creaked again, and I heard her footsteps
as she went away. Old Master got up. "Dan," he
whispered, "if you ever say a word, I'll whip you. Do
you hear?"

"Yes, sir."

"I have told Bob. But you musn't talk about it
even to him. There, now, go on to bed."

"And will you go to bed too?" I asked.

"What's that to you, nighthawk? Go to bed, and **if**
I catch you up again to-night, I'll whip you."

CHAPTER III.

Early at morning, Bob and I were summoned by
Old Master to go squirrel hunting, to walk round the
trees, and turn the squirrel into range of his long rifle
and the deadly squint of his sharp old eye. It was
spring-time and the squirrels were nipping the hickory buds; it was sunrise and the bold cock-partridge,
his feathers ruffled, strutted up and down the top rail
of the fence. We had not proceeded far before we
came upon a neighbor, 'Squire Boyle, sitting upon a
log, picking at the lock of his gun. He hailed Old
Master and bade him wait a moment. And both men,
seated upon the log, fell into an argument that lasted
till the sun was high. We heard the blowing of the
breakfast horn, we saw the smoke rise in the fields,
where the women were burning the old corn-stalks;
we saw the men breaking up the tobacco land, but Old
Master and the squire sat there and talked, and sometimes I was afraid that they were going to fight, so
fierce were their gestures and so loud did they lift their
voices. Bob and I were impatient, and occasionally

Bob would say, "Come on, pa." But the old man heeded him not, until finally he turned about with anger in his eyes, and cried out as if in pain: "If you don't quit nagging at me, I will box your jaws. Go on to the house, both of you. 'Zounds, I can't budge but these boys are dogging my foot-steps. Go on to the house and if I catch you following me again, I'll whip you both."

We fell back a short distance and hid behind a clump of briars and sat there watching, fearful that the two men were going to fight. But their guns were thrown aside and they were walking up and down the length of the log. "I tell you," Old Master cried, "that this step will kill him. The people of this State will not put up with it. It is well enough to talk about justice and human sympathy, but if Henry Clay openly advocates the freeing of the slaves it will kill him. I don't understand how he can be so untrue to the principles of his community, but, 'Squire—" Here he halted in his walk and shook his fist fiercely—"but, 'Squire, I can understand you, sir. You are not a Southern man and you have never owned a slave. Ah, but you are an American. Yes, I grant you that, but the real defender of this country is the Southern man, sir. What's that you say? Would I break up the Union rather than lose the slaves?　No, sir, I would not; and there will never be such an issue." Here he looked about and caught sight of us lurking behind the briars. "Boys!" he cried, taking up his gun and pulling out the hickory ram-rod, "if you don't march off home, this minute, I'll wear you both out." And as we had tasted that hickory and knew its flavor, we scampered away.

"Do you know what they were talking about?" Bob asked, when we had reached a safe distance.

"Something about making the black people free," I answered.

"They are free enough already," he replied, looking sharply at me as we walked along the path.

"I'm not free," I rejoined. "I belong to you."

Then he looked at me proudly. "Yes," he said, "and we will have lots of fun. When we get big, we'll get some great long guns and go out and kill Indians, and if anybody tries to shoot you, I'll shoot him. Won't I?"

"Yes, and I'll shoot anybody that tries to shoot you."

We had crossed the bars where the cows stood at evening waiting to nourish their calves, and were going toward the stone spring-house, when we met Old Miss.

"Robert," she said, "run and find your father, quick! Your sister Lou is sick."

Bob turned to go back, and so did I, but she called me. "Dan, you are not going. Go over to Aunt Mag's cabin and stay there until you are sent for."

I sat in the cabin door and watched the old woman spin. She gave me a bowl of bread and milk, and she told me that whenever I was mistreated to slip into her house and hide under her bed. "I'm treated all right," I remember to have replied. And I recollect also to have declared that I fought when they did not treat me well. "You'se er monstus brave little man," she said, pausing at the door to pat me on the head. "Fo' gracious, whut's de matter up at de house? Look at de folks all runnin' er roun'? Go up dar an' see."

I was afraid to go in, believing, and not without cause, that Old Miss would tap me on the head with her big store-room key, and I hung about the door that opened out upon the long veranda. Everything was quiet save the mocking-bird in his cage hung in the hall. But a moment later I heard the well-known feet of Old Master, pacing up and down. I peeped in and saw Dr. Bates walking toward the door, and I ran

away and went back to Aunt Mag's cabin. Old Silvy,
the cook, took down the long horn, with a snake and
a deer's head carved upon it, and blew a blast for dinner, and then the men and the plow horses came
through the big gate, with trace-chains jangling. I
wondered what could have become of Bob. It was
rare, indeed, that we were so long separated. Aunt
Mag gave me another bowl of bread and milk, and I
sat there on the doorstep, watching the sun-mark
slowly moving round the house. The men went back
to work. I dozed off to sleep and was aroused with a
shake. I looked up and saw a girl hastening up the
path toward the house. Old Aunt Mag was standing
over me. "Dan'l," she said, looking down upon me,
"po' Miss Lou is gone—she died jest now."

The goodness and the sweetness of that fair young
woman rushed upon me, and I could not see for the
tears that gushed to my eyes. In a moment I
recounted her kindness and her winsome smile—she
had never spoken a cross word to me. I had lost a
protecting friend. Under a tree I lay with my face
buried in the grass, sobbing. An arm stole about my
neck. I looked up. Bob lay beside me.

This was my first grief. And oh, the awful sadness
of the funeral. Everywhere the negro's mellow song

was hushed, and the trace-chains no longer jangled. The sun was bright, the rose was fresh, the stiff-neck tulip was proud, but the creek which yesterday went laughing through the pasture was mourning now. The horses stood looking over the fence, the frisky colts were surprised, and turning from their play, stretched themselves out upon the clover. Old Aunt Mag dressed me, with the tears shining on her black face. "Her speret is praisin' de Lawd dis mornin'," she said. "You kin go ter de house now. All de black folks is gwine ter look at her."

I stood at the parlor door, with my knees trembling. Old Master came out to walk up and down the veranda. He saw me looking wistfully at him, and he halted to speak to me, but his chin shook and he walked on. Miss May came to me and told me to come with her. I stepped into the room and my heart leaped into my throat at the sight—Miss Lou lying on a bed of roses. Slowly our people came in, as silent as the pillow of white roses holding that beautiful head, and stood there, awe-struck. From a distant room came the broken lamentations of Old Miss. An old black man, a giant who preached for the negroes, stood at the head of the rose-shroud. He gazed with the tears in his eyes, and turning away he said: "De Lawd neber called home er mo' beautiful speret." Old Master came in, and the two men put their hands upon each other and wept.

There was no hearse, no carriages. Through the garden gate they bore their beautiful burden, and slowly the throng of neighbors followed, the negroes chanting mournfully. A white man spoke of the resurrection and the light, and the old negro giant prayed, with his knees in the clay. Old Master led Old Miss home to the dead hush of the great house; and at midnight I heard the old man's feet pacing up and down the hall. It seemed a crime to let him walk out there alone. Once I thought I heard him stop at my door, and I got up and went to him. "Marster," I said, "won't you please let me walk with you?"

He said nothing, but he sobbed, and then I knew that he would not drive me away. And so I walked with him until daylight was come. "Run along now," he said. "Be a good boy and you will go—go where she has gone."

CHAPTER IV.

The days grew hotter, the green corn waved on the hill-side, the wheat was ripening, but the deep mystery of death was over it all. The boy goes about his play, he shouts and has his daily contentions, his quarrels and fights, but darkness comes, and as he goes to his bed, his mind reverts to a soul that has recently taken its flight. Older people have the consoling prop of religion or the forceful brace of philosophy, but in the boy's nostrils lives the scent of the roses that lay upon the breast of mystic death; a fear possesses him as he peeps in at the parlor door. Ah, many days must fall upon a sad memory before it is sweetened. They told me that my young mistress was in Heaven. I asked Aunt Mag if she would be my mistress there, and she said no, that there was no mistresses in Heaven, no slaves, but all white and the angels of God. And with the flash of iconoclastic reason that comes to youth, I asked her why God made black people belong to white people on the earth and afterward made them all equal in Heaven. The old woman turned from her spinning wheel and held up her hands in fright. "Chile," she said, "you musn't talk like dat. Whut de Lawd do it ain't fur us ter question, an' ef you wan't so young you mout git struck wid lightenin' fur sayin' dem words. Run off ober yander in de yard an' play. I'se er feered de lightenin' mought strike at you anyhow."

That night as Bob and I lay in our room, he in his high canopied bed, and I on my low lounge, I asked him if he knew that all the black people would be white in Heaven. "Yes, of course," he answered. "It would be a funny Heaven with a lot of niggers standing about, grinning."

"But they wouldn't have to grin."

"No, but they would."

"And you won't own me there, will you?" I said, after a moment's silence.

"No, you'll belong to God."

"But don't I belong to God now?"

I heard him turn over. "Yes, but you belong to me, too. And when I get through with you God may have you. Get over in my bed and I'll bet I can throw you out."

"No, Old Miss might hear us. But do you think," I asked after musing for a time, "that we'll know each other up there and talk about the time when we were down here?"

"Yes; why not?"

"But you'd tell me that I used to belong to you and God wouldn't like that."

"Well, then, we won't say anything about it, but we'll think about it all the same."

"Yes, we'd keep it to ourselves. But if a nigger angel beats a white angel flying, there'll be trouble, won't there?"

"There won't be anything of that. God won't let the nigger angels out-fly the white ones."

There came a tap at the door—a house-maid come to tell us that if we did not stop talking Old Miss would come in and whip us. We whispered and giggled a long time, and then Bob fell asleep, and I lay there thinking of the white roses that had scented the parlor. It must have been very late for the lights were out everywhere, when I heard voices on the walk just below my window. I looked out cautiously and in the moonlight I saw Old Master and Dr. George Bates. Master was walking up and down, but the doctor stood still.

"I want you to understand this," said the old man. "You are at perfect liberty to stay here as long as you choose—and I will feed you and clothe you, but you must have nothing whatever to say about the running of my affairs. You are constantly meddling with things that don't concern you."

"General, it is not my intention to interfere, I assure you."

"But you do," said Old Master, making an emphatic motion. "You seem to think that I ought to divide my property with you. Get that out of your head as soon as you can."

"It has never been in my head, General. I merely suggested that if you would give me Dan I would take him and go South."

"Give you Dan! Confound it, haven't I told you that he belongs to Bob?"

"Yes, but I didn't know but you gave him away just as a man sometimes gives a colt to a boy—merely to claim."

"I don't give things that way, sir."

"I know, but your wife—"

"There, that will do."

"She said that she thought that you might be induced—"

"Didn't I say that would do?"

"Yes, sir, but let me finish, if you please. Of course

you know that my wife's share, whatever it may amount to, will fall to me?"

"Yes, if I so desire it, sir."

"But I know you well enough to feel that you won't refuse me."

"Now you are presuming upon my kindness, sir."

"No, sir; I am paying a tribute to your sense of justice. And now this is what I have agreed to do: to take Dan and wait until you are ready—"

"You have agreed with whom, sir?" Old Master broke in.

"Oh, I don't know that it was exactly an agreement. I had a talk with your wife, and—"

"Infamous puppy!" Old Master cried, shaking his fist in the doctor's face. "Didn't I tell you that you'd gone far enough in that direction?"

"General," said the doctor, stepping back, "you have insulted me."

Old Master snorted. "Oh, I have insulted you, have I? Then I have done something that I thought must be impossible. Listen to me. You came here a beggar, with a doctor's sheep-skin under your arm; you are of a good family—that I will not deny. But I say you came a beggar, and you won my child—how, God only knows. You told me that you would practice medicine on the plantation after you were married, but did you?"

"Why, yes, sir; I have attended many a case. You know one very well."

"Oh, you have? Did you get out of bed when they sent for you one night to see old Aunt Mag? Didn't you complain that you were too sick to get up? And that very night, sir, didn't you slip away and play poker over the creek?"

"Somebody has lied about me," the doctor declared.

"I admit, sir, that lying has been done, but you did it."

"General, I insist that you must not talk to me this way. I'm no dog."

"If you were, sir, I would be more considerate of you."

"Keep on and you'll say something that you may regret."

Just at that moment Old Master had turned to walk down the path, but he wheeled about. "What's that? Say something that I may regret? I don't know about that, sir, but I may say something that you'll regret. I may tell you to get off this place, and I won't regret it, but you will."

"That would be a scandal, General."

"Yes, a disgrace—to you." The old man walked down the path, tall and gaunt in the moon-light. He turned, and coming back, stepping slowly, he said: "But it is our duty to avoid anything in the nature of a rupture. So now, I'll tell you what I'll agree to do. I will give you Sam and money enough to go South, and when the time comes to divide the estate, you shall have your share. Now, I ask you if that is not fair?"

"Yes, General, it is perfectly fair, but—"

"But what, sir?" Master snapped impatiently.

"But I don't want Sam. I want Dan—want to make a race rider of him."

"What good will a race rider do you? You've got no horses."

"I can get the horses."

"But you can't get Dan, sir, so let the matter rest. Bates, I don't want to get mad, and I should think, sir, that in the light of our recent affliction—"

"I understand, General, and we'll let the subject drop, but if Bob should agree—"

"Stop, there, sir. Bob is not old enough to entertain a business proposition." For a time the old man walked up and down, with his hands behind him and then turned upon the doctor. "I believe, sir, that you are an evil-minded man. For a long time I thought

that your laziness was an indication of good nature—
the lazy dog is rarely vicious—but now I am of the
opinion that you have an active quality, that of rascal-
ity, sir."

"General," said the doctor, "I can't stand everything. You forget, sir, that I am a gentleman."

"Oh, do I forget it?" the old man spoke up. "There
is a difference between forgetting a thing and never
having known it. Bates, I have endeavored to like
you, I have striven to crush what I hoped was merely
a prejudice, but I can't. I don't think that we have
ever held an agreeable conversation. There is something about you that antagonizes me. When you are
away I am determined to like you, but when you come
back, I find that my resolve is weak. I don't want to
drive you off—I would stand most anything rather
than face a neighborhood scandal, but don't you think
that it would be a good idea for you to go away and
stay away for a long time? I say, don't you?"

"You can drive me off, sir."

"Ah, the very thing you want me to do—you want
to put my name into the mouths of the gossipers."

"General, you have called me a scoundrel and now
you are trying to prove it. I can stand a great deal,
but I can't put up with everything—even from you. I

have told you that I am a gentleman, and while a gentleman respects age, he cannot permit age to humiliate him. I know that you've got nerve enough to shoot a man who rides into your room—"

"Another word of that, Bates, and I will knock you down."

"You have gone too far," Bates replied in a tone that made me shiver. The moon shone upon his half upturned face and I fancied that I saw the glitter of his evil eyes. Master, who was now standing some distance from him said something which I did not catch and Bates, with his hand upraised, made a stride toward him. At my elbow, on a stand near the window, was a heavy glass tumbler. Indeed, I had long held it in my hand, and when Bates strode forward, I threw the tumbler with all my might. I heard it strike, and leaning out, I saw the doctor lying on the ground. I heard Old Master shout for a light, and now thoroughly frightened, I ran to my lounge and lay there with the cover drawn over my head.

CHAPTER V.

Early at morning Old Master came into our room.
I was awake but Bob was still asleep. "Dan," he said,
"I want to ask you something and I want you to tell
me the truth, and if you don't, I'll whip you within an
inch of your life, sir." He always said sir when he
strove to be emphatic. "Were you at the window last
night when the doctor and I were standing down in
the yard? It was you or Bob, I don't know which,
and as you are a night-hawk, sir, I believe it was you."

"Yes, sir," I answered promptly. And then I trem-
blingly asked: "Is he dead?"

The old man turned from me and strode up and
down the room. He went to the window, looked out,
and with his hands behind him, came walking slowly
toward me. "Dan," he said, "I told you to be a good
boy and that you would one day—you remember what
I said. But now I must ask you to tell a lie. You
must say that you were trying to put down the window
and knocked the tumbler off. Do you hear me?"

"Yes, sir."

(34)

"All right. After breakfast I will send for you and Bob to come into the library."

He went out and I thought that he tip-toed as he went down the stairs. At breakfast I stood behind my young master's chair, until the meal was over, and then I went to the kitchen to eat with the house-maids. Presently I was told by a spinning woman that Old Master wanted to see me in the library. "An' he's ez mad ez a ho'net," she said. "Mars. George wuz badly hurt las' night an' da gwine fin' out who done it, too, I tell you."

Old Aunt Mag stood in the door. "But whut da want ter sen' fur dis po', muderless chile fur?" she spoke up. "Da's questioned all de rest o' de niggers, an' now da gwine put him on de hot griddle. Dat ain't no way ter act, snatchin' up er little boy an' cuzin' him o' knockin' er big man down. But run er long, Dan, an stan' square up. Ricolleck dat you ain't no common nigger—ricolleck dat you doan b'long ter de Smifs ur de Bucks nur de Brizzentines. You'ze er Gradley an' b'longs ter folks, I tell you."

In the library were assembled Old Master, Old Miss, young Miss May, Bob and 'Squire Boyle, who happened in about breakfast time. I looked about as I entered the room, and I saw the doctor, lying on a sofa, with his head tied up.   Old Master's head began to shake with anger as soon as he saw me coming in. "Dan," he said, "last night your Mars. George and I were standing in the yard under the window of your Mars. Bob's room, and this tumbler, sir—" here he reached back and took a tumbler from a desk—"this tumbler, sir, struck him on the head and cut him badly. Your Mars. Bob doesn't know anything about it.   Do you?   Come, no lying, or I'll whip you within an inch of your life."

"He ought to be skinned alive," Old Miss declared, giving her head an emphatic nod.

"Just wait and I'll take care of him," said Old Master.   "What do you know about it?" he repeated, looking at me savagely.

"I went to put down the window, sir, and knocked it off," I stammered.

"Do you hear that?" Old Miss exclaimed.

"Yes, I hear it," said Old Master, quivering with rage.   "You went to put down the window?   And why did you want to put down the window, sir?"

"I thought it was going to rain."

"Hump!" Old Miss grunted, "the yellow imp has turned out to be a weather prophet."

"Madam," said Old Master, "let me manage him, if

you please. You thought it was going to rain?" he went on, turning to me. "And what made you think so?"

"I thought I heard it thunder."

"Oh, you did? Well, you shall hear it thunder. Madam, give me your cow-hide."

I don't know that I ever saw my old mistress spring up with such agility. She snatched the cow-hide out of some mysterious hiding place, handed it to him and said: "And, for pity's sake, see that you give him enough of it."

"You shan't wnip him!" Bob cried. "If you whip him you've got to whip me, too."

"Robert!" Old Miss shouted, "I'll give it to you in good earnest if you don't keep quiet. Your father knows what he's about. Sit down there."

Bob was forced back into his seat and Miss May, beautiful and tender creature, began to beg for me.

"Hush, everybody!" Old Master thundered. "Has it come to a pass when I am not permitted to manage my own affairs? Come with me, Dan."

He took me by the collar and led me into the store-room. "Take off that coat!" he shouted, and as I was obeying him he said in a low and kindly tone. "Now you must yell as if I were cutting you in two," and with that he fell afoul of a sack of coffee and with the cow-hide laid the lash on furiously. I yelled at the top of my lusty voice, and during the intervals when my ears were not submerged by the torrent of my own outcry, I heard the revengeful step of Old Miss, up and down the passage-way.

"Now go!" Old Master roared, "and the next time you hear it thunder, let tumblers alone."

I came out buttoning up my jacket and Old Miss gave me a smile of welcome. But Bob and Miss May stood in the library door, crying; and to this day it is a dear memory that Miss May ran to the dining-room and brought me a sugared biscuit. Old Master and 'Squire Boyle strode out into the yard, and I saw Old Master lean upon the gate and laugh.

During all that day I was the object of a pitying regard. "Po' little feller," was heard about the cabin door-ways and upon the sward, and there was many a sullen muttering and the shaking of nappy heads. Bob was furious, having come out of his tears into the territory of bold and resentful anger, and he blamed his mother with my unjust punishment, persisting until the old lady caught him ungently, slipped a soft shoe from her foot, and paddled him until the maudlin calves in a distant enclosure heeded his cries with bleatings of sympathy. And when he found himself free of his mother's avenging clutch, he ran to me and blubbering, said: "Come on, Dan. We'll go down to the creek and drown ourselves." This suggestion was in harmony with my sorrowful view, for now I felt worse than if Master had cut the blood out of me, and together we set out for the swimming-hole at the edge of the walnut grove. At times we halted to bid farewell to objects that were dear to us, the great oak from which the big gate swung, the smooth rock where we had so often sat at twilight. The horses nodded a farewell and the cows lowed at us.

"It ain't our fault," said Bob, "and when they take us out of the creek dead, I want them to know it. But I don't think they'll cry very much. How can they, when they have tried to kill us?"

"It won't make any difference to us whether they cry or not," I replied. "We won't know anything about it."

We came to the swimming-hole and the water was blue and deep. Upon the grass under a tree we sat and gazed in silence into the pool. "We'll take off our clothes," said Bob, "and then when they find us they'll think that we were drowned accidentally and that will make 'em cry."

The song of a plow-man came floating through the soft air; a blue-jay above us shrieked in a fit of merriment; a cat-bird laughed at us and we looked at each other.

"Mars. Bob," said I, "he didn't hurt me much."

"But I thought he was killing you by the way you hollered."·

"Yes, but he told me to.   I'll tell you something if you'll cross your heart that you'll never tell anybody."

He crossed his heart and I told him, and he lay back and laughed.   "But you were whipped in earnest," I said.

"Yes, but it didn't hurt.   Ho, think that old shoe could hurt me!   Let's go in swimming?"

We snatched off our clothes and into the water we plunged, but a damper was put upon my enjoyment, for looking up I saw the doctor standing near the bank.   A bandage was over one eye, and with the other one he gave me a hard and evil look.

"You boys get out of there," he commanded.   Bob rebelled against his order, but I obeyed, and as I was putting on my clothes he came up, cut at my bare legs with a switch, doing so, I suppose, to leave no doubt as to his presence.   "Hurry up," he said.   "Go and catch my horse; I want to go to town."

Bob came out. "He don't have to catch your horse, Brother George. Make Sam catch your horse. Dan belongs to me."

"I have heard enough of that and I don't want to hear any more," the doctor replied. "Go catch my horse," he added, turning to me.

"I will if Mars. Bob says so," I replied.

"You'll do it if I say so."

"No, I won't."

He rushed at me with his switch, but I dodged, leaped into the water and swam to the opposite shore. Bob clapped his hands in glee, and the doctor shook his switch at me. "I've had my eye on you for some time, you impudent scoundrel," he shouted, "and the first thing you know, I'll skin you alive. You can keep out of my way for a while, but not always. See this?" he cried, tapping his bandaged head. "I know —and I'll make you pay for it."

CHAPTER VI.

I hid about the place during the day, sometimes peeping at the doctor from the hay-loft, sometimes dodging behind a cabin to keep out of his way, constantly wishing that Old Master might come; and late in the afternoon I saw him walking in the garden with his hands behind him. The doctor was not far away, and I knew that he would discover me if I should dart out from my hiding place, but I did finally and he yelled at me, but I ran to Old Master, looking back in fright as I approached him.

"Tut, tut, there!" he cried. "What are you running about this way for, tramping down everything? First thing you know I'll give you another whipping within an inch of your life!"

"Marster!" I cried, clinging to him, "the doctor is after me!"

"Well, he won't get you. Turn me loose. Hang about near me, but don't let your mistress see you. The doctor's going away to-morrow to be gone some time. Here he comes now. Go on to the house."

I passed the doctor, skirting far into a flower bed to give him plenty of room; he glowered at me and said nothing. But I knew that he would let slip no opportunity to harm me, and that night Bob and I barricaded our door. He had an old horse pistol that wouldn't shoot, and I had a broken saber, and we took turn about standing guard behind our breast-works. "You've been there long enough. Come on and lie down and let me stay there awhile?" he would say; and he never failed to add: "And you must pretend like you're asleep."

At morning I awoke in bed and found Bob asleep behind the barricade. I aroused him, and he jumped up and declared that he had stood guard all night, and hadn't slept a wink. I pretended to believe him, and he rewarded me with a crock marble and a biscuit covered with sugar.

Early that morning I had the satisfaction of seeing my enemy, the doctor, leave the plantation, and then followed a day of happiness, playing up and down the creek. At the house one other enemy was left, Old Miss, but I did not hate her, for her dislike of me could be none other than a divine right, something which I would not permit myself to question. She was cold and proud, and rarely did she give way to the affection which she must have felt for her own children. It was said that she could trace her origin back to great warriors, and this gave a reason for her pride and her coldness; but Old Master's forefathers also were great fighters and statesmen, and yet he was warm-hearted and sympathetic. Aunt Mag told me that Old Miss had refused to marry Henry Clay because he was poor, and had always regretted it, but I could not see why, for surely my master was as great as Clay.

The evening after the doctor left us, I was lying on the ground near the stone steps leading to the broad hall, when I heard Master and Old Miss talking. They were sitting on the portico and did not see me.

"I told him," said Master, "that he might draw on me for what money he actually needs, but that I would put up with no extravagance. Of course, he has a sort of a claim, but I don't intend that he shall embarrass me in any way."

She cleared her throat with a rasp that always made me shudder. "He surely has a claim," she replied.

"Well, that's what I said, didn't I?"

"Yes, but you seem to think that it is not much of a claim."

"I don't seem to think anything of the sort. He

shall have everything that is due him. **But, madam,**
the truth of it is, he is of no account."

"He is a gentleman."

"In what way?" I peeped up and saw him look
hard at her. "In what way has he shown himself a
gentleman?"

"He was born a gentleman," Old Miss replied.

"Born one, yes. His father and mother may have
been good stock, but I tell you that he's a scrub. Still
I will give him what's due him."

"Oh, I know that."

"Then there needn't be any further discussion about
it."

"No," she said, "not so far as I am concerned."
And after a pause she asked: "What's your object
in sending Bob over to school at Layfield?"

"To learn something, of course."

"But why can't he go to school at home? Can't he
learn something here?"

"We have had a teacher for him here and he has
done no good."

"Yes, but can't you send him to school at the Academy in town?"

"I could do it, of course, but I would rather have
him go away. It will make him more important in

his own estimation—will give him more confidence in himself."

"Is Dan going with him?"

"Oh, I knew what you were driving at. Yes," he almost shouted, "Dan is going with him."

"I don't see why. Why not send Sam with him?"

"Madam, is it necessary to explain to you that Dan is the property—property—"

"I know all about that. But they are too much like companions, and will study together."

He looked hard at her. "Study together? And what of that?"

"I don't want a child of mine studying with a negro. He has no business to study. He knows enough already! Educate him and he will be of no account on the face of the earth. I never knew it to fail. Mason had an educated negro, and what became of him? He ran away and went north and told a pack of lies about the people in this State, about the cruelties he had suffered, and the abolition papers are still harping on it."

"Yes, that's all true enough," said Old Master, "but in Dan's case it will be different. He is not likely to pick up much learning, and besides he's grateful. He'll never run away."

"I have been thinking," she said, "that we might—"

"Might do what?" Master snapped before she had finished.

"Well, you know how much the doctor desires that boy. Why not let him—"

"Madam!" Master thundered, "don't you know that the boy belongs to Bob? How long will it take you to learn that? Must I keep forever dinging it into your ears?"

"Well, you needn't get mad about it."

"That's true, and I beg your pardon. But just let me manage it, if you please. I believe you said yesterday that our carriage is getting too old for you to ride about in?"

"Yesterday? I have talked about it for the past year!"

"Yes, so you have. Well, you may go to Louisville yourself and select one to suit you."

That night I told Bob that we were going off to school together, and we grabbed each other in our glee.

CHAPTER VII.

The next day we were bundled off to school, distant more than thirty miles, driven by the family coachman. Old Master and Old Miss walked with us as far as the big gate that opened into a street of the town. I say, walked with us, but they walked with Bob, I keeping close pace behind, constantly afraid that my mistress would turn upon me with her stout parasol, yet too discreet to fall farther back, lest I might by this show of caution call her wrath upon me. At the gate, when the driver got off his seat and stood by the open door of the carriage, Old Miss put her arms about Bob, with more of affection than I had ever seen her show, and bade him be a good boy and keep his mind on his book. She kissed him time and again and then she turned to me, Old Master standing there waiting for the end of her part of the ceremony: "Dan," she said, "I want you to black his shoes every morning." This, with the tears in her eyes, and with sorrow in her voice, touched a foolish sense within me and I giggled, dodging wisely as I did so; and it was

well that I did, for in a fury she struck at me with her parasol. "The infamous imp!" she cried, "standing there laughing at me. General," she demanded, stamping the ground, "wear your cane out on him. I won't be treated in such a manner—I won't put up with everything from that ape."

My impulse was to run, but I killed it with a gentler resolve; I dropped upon my knees in the dust of the road and humbly begged her pardon. This act of grace was most effective. This humility, done, I fancy, with some show of gallantry, won her for the moment, and bowing to me she said: "I know you didn't mean it, Dan. There, go on and be a good boy."

We bade them good-bye and were rolled away, and hour after hour, amid the changing scenes of that charming country, a vision of that woman stood before me, bowing, and my heart was warmer toward her than it had ever been. Strange, and now almost incomprehensible life — absolute despotism in free America.

The Layfield school was set among romantic hills. As a seat of learning, it was unpretentious. The main house was of brick, with dormer windows and green blinds; the other buildings were cottages, mostly of logs, scattered along a shaded avenue, leading down to the banks of a green river; and I remember that the first sight of this great stream (it must have been fifty feet wide, but it was an Amazon to me, fresh from the little creek running through the pasture) thrilled me with a mysterious delight. Upon a near approach though, I was disappointed, not at its size, but at its quietude; for if our creek could sing, why did not this river shout? And it gave no sound save a low murmur almost as still as silence.

The master of Layfield Academy was an old man with long, white hair. He received us most kindly and himself went with us to the cottage we were to occupy, together with a number of boys, sons of wealthy men, many of them attended by the unmistakable mark of Blue Grass gentility—the favored slave. And it was not without a feeling of pride that I heard a young fellow say, "Gradley's got the best-looking nigger in the crowd." My master and I occupied a small, but comfortable room, that is, comfortable for him, but with regard to me, the line was closer drawn than it had been at home, for instead of sleeping upon a lounge, I was assigned to a rug upon the floor. Bob did not like this, and he grumbled to the Master and was told very emphatically that he must not seek to interfere with the time-honored regulations of that great educational household. I soon found that my life here was not to be altogether peaceful, for the spirit of rivalry existing among the young masters extended to the slaves. And of a Saturday those blood-loving spirits would match their "niggers" against one another like cocks in a pit and bet on the result. My master was too young to be a leader, but he was forced to take a part in the sport, and it redounded to my credit when I bloodied the flat nose of a black fellow who strove to knock me out of a ring. This made Bob an important factor, gave him a new bearing, and I remember that I lay down upon my rug with a feeling of pride.

"Oh, we'll show 'em what's what," Bob declared. "And after I whip Saunders, we'll be way up."

"But do you think you can whip him?" I asked.

The moon was shining into our room and I saw him rise up in bed. "Why, of course I can. And the fight is set for to-morrow."

"He's bigger'n you," I remarked.

"Yes, but he hasn't got the blood. His people don't amount to anything. You just wait."

I had to wait, but it was not with any great confidence, for Saunders was a lusty youth. I expressed

no further fear, however, and early in the morning I
rubbed my master down with a coarse towel and with
him set out for the battle ground. Saunders was
already there, with a party of boys about him, feeling
the muscles in his arms. The affair was conducted
with great secrecy, and each warrior had to promise
that in case his teeth were knocked out he would swear
that he had fallen down. I was nervous. The negro
boys looking at me, shook their heads. The line was
drawn and the combatants stationed. The word was
given and I looked away. Then followed the sound
of quick blows—then came a shout, all before I looked
toward the ring. And when I did look, I saw Saunders on the ground. I threw up my hat and shouted,
whereupon a yellow fellow who belonged to Saunders
struck me. Well, when we went back to our quarters
my master and I both were heroes. And now, having
established his standing, Young Master was permitted
to enter upon his studies. This had all happened
within a week.

It was here that a desire to learn first took strong
hold of me. Of course I did not presume to own a
book, or to study one except at night, when Bob and
I were alone. In a negro any show of intellectual
ambition was looked upon as a rebellion against the

unwritten law of society, and thus to steal the mind-mysteries that made the white man great was doubly sweetened. I kept so good a pace with Bob that in me he sometimes found a helper over rough places, and I even now recall with pride that one night he looked at me admiringly and said: "Dan, it's a shame that you ain't a white boy."

At the end of the fourth week, Old Master and Old Miss drove over in the carriage. The president of the school met them with great ceremony and would not let them rest until he had shown them through his establishment. Bob went with them and I was permitted to hang behind, upon the implied condition that I was not to hear anything that was said. But I did hear and I remembered. In one corner of the main recitation room was a globe and shelves holding numerous books, to me the most learned spot in the world; and here the company halted.

"These books," said the president, "are kept here in constant view of the student to stimulate his ambition, to force upon his mind the power and the importance of thought. He has heard of the earth's great minds, and here he finds the fruit of those minds. I do not believe in shutting books in a stuffy room, sir; they ought to be where the sun-light, the companion of learning, can constantly fall upon them. Ah, and I am sure that as time passes your son will draw many a draft from this well. Won't you, Robert?"

Bob looked at him, while his parents waited for his answer, and said: "I like books with pictures in 'em."

"Ah, quite a shrewd remark," declared the president, putting his hand upon Bob's head. "His thought turns upon art, no mean branch of learning, I assure you. Of course, he is as yet too young to be consulted, General, but have you thought upon any profession for him?"

"The law," Old Master answered.

"The ministry," said Old Miss.

"Maw, what's that?" Bob asked.

"I want you to be a preacher," his mother replied, drawing him toward her, buttoning his jacket and then unbuttoning it.

"I don't want to be a preacher. They don't have any fun!"

"Hush, sir," she said. "Your grandfather was a preacher."

"But he didn't have any fun."

"Hush, I tell you."

"I will, but did he have any fun?"

Old Master chuckled and Mistress gave him a sour

look. The president coughed. "Both the law and the ministry are learned professions," he said, "and I have no doubt that our little man would grace either calling."

"Bob," said Mistress, "show me your sleeping room. You needn't come with us," she added, speaking to the president. "We will not presume to take up any more of your time—you've been so very, very kind, I assure you."

I think that the president would have urged his attendance, but that he was afraid to show how much time he could spare, so he bowed and said: "I thank you for the confidence you have reposed in me, placing your son in my charge, and I assure you that I shall do my utmost by him. Now, make yourselves perfectly at home."

Old Miss turned up her nose when she entered our room. "Whew, it smells like a bear's den," she said, and Old Master's spare frame shook with laughter. "And for pity sake, what have you got in this cup?" she asked, looking at a tin can on a table.

"Fish-worm oil," Bob spoke up rather proudly. "We dug the worms and roasted their oil out. Rub it on my legs so I can run fast."

Master snorted and Mistress turned to me. "Dan,"

she asked, clearing her throat with a dry rasp, "isn't this one of your negro superstitions? Didn't you put him up to it?"

"Madam," said Old Master before I could reply, "the knowledge of the efficacy of angle-worm oil comes down from the ancients and I am astonished that you should impute it to negro superstition. Leander, before trusting himself to the torrent of the Hellespont, rubbed himself with it, and if you read closely, you will find that Byron went through the same performance before tempting the same feat. Haven't you read of the angle-worm oil bearer at the Olympian games?"

He slyly turned his face away to laugh, and Old Miss, like all pretentious persons, afraid of the weapon of wisdom, was willing enough to change the subject. "I am glad to see that you are learning," she said to Bob, "but I don't want you to learn things that will be of no particular use to you. By the way, General, I don't want you to school him into the notion of becoming a lawyer or a doctor."

"Surely not a doctor," Master replied. "We have one doctor in the family and he is quite sufficient— unto himself. What's that in the Bible, 'sufficient unto

the day is the evil thereof'? That's it. Well, it suits
him any way."

Old Miss sat down, gathering her skirts that they
might touch nothing. "General, that's no way to
talk," she said. She looked about and cried suddenly:
"Why, is that a poultice there on the mantle-piece?"

"Boxing glove," said Bob, and Old Master roared
again.

"General!" she spoke up in sharp reproof, "I do
wish you wouldn't stimulate disrespect by your constant tittering and teheeing. One would think that
you had sent the boy here as a monster joke. To send
a child away from home is no jest, I assure you."

"Madam," said Master, winking at us, lifting the
tails of his long coat and seating himself on a corner
of the table, "it makes me young again to come into a
place like this, and being young I must be foolish.
Well," he added after a pause, "do you want to stay
here to-night, or shall we stop on the road?"

"We might as well go," she answered, getting up.
"There's nothing to be done here. Bob, you must
write to me every other day. And Dan, I want you
to see that his shoes are blacked every morning."
And here, remembering the disrespect that I had
shown her in the road, she seized her parasol as if to

strike me.   But with hypocritical gallantry (shrewd rascal that I was) I dropped upon one knee, caught her hand impulsively and assured her that my young master's comfort and good appearance should be the study of my life.   And in her eyes there was a light of real kindliness.   "There, get up," she said.   "I am glad to see that you are improving.   General, we may make a respectable servant of him yet."

When the carriage had rolled away, Bob and I ran back to the room, locked the door, rubbed our joints with the fish-worm oil and wrestled with each other in ecstasy,

CHAPTER VIII.

How hallowed and sun-glinted that school life now seems to me. Many a grave has been opened and closed, the roots of many a greenbriar is embedded in the ashes of a heart that was once alive with fire, the fierce passion of life. The sun is still shining, and the arch of God's many-hued lithograph is still seen in the sky, and hearts have fire shut within them, but I wonder if the sun is as bright as it was in the long ago, if the rain-bow is as purple, if the fire in the heart is as glowing. Ah, and I know that my grand-children, in the far-away years to come, will lean feebly upon the gate and wonder if the world is as full of light as it was. Every emotion you have felt you may know has been felt by other men. It is this that makes nearly all poetry seem old; it is this that sends true poetry to the human heart.

I will not linger over those days at school. I have sought thus far to picture my early life, not that it held incident, but that it revealed a condition. Time has been so sweeping, the hot blast that blew from the North was so scorching, and left such dried and brittle stems where green memories grew, that the youth of to-day can scarcely bring himself to comprehend that strange democratic absolutism which once existed in the South. And I wonder now that it could have lasted so long, though for years the wonder was that it could so soon have been broken up. How odd now it would seem to point out a man and say, "He once owned, in this land of freedom, a hundred human beings—owned them in body, but Christian-like yielded to God the direction of their souls."

During the regular sessions, until he had reached his eighteenth year, my young master attended the Layfield Academy, and then he was entered at Center College. I had kept well up with him, a dead secret between us, for Old Mistress had more than once made him promise that I should be kept down upon the servants' proper level. But the secret was discovered and once it was held threateningly over me.

Bob and I were home to spend the Christmas holidays. On the plantation was an Ethiopian Lothario, named Steve, and one evening in his cabin he asked me if I would write for him a letter to a mulatto girl who lived on a distant farm. "I want you," said he, "ter fling in jest ez much sweet pizen ez you kin, caze

I lubs dat lady an' her head is monstus high. I yered
de white preacher say sumfin dat he 'lowed wuz frum
de dead language. An' kain't you dash in er little o'
dat dead talk? I know it'll fetch her caze dat preacher's dead talk fotch me."

"How do you know I can write?" I asked, for I had
curbed the pedantic instinct of the negro blood within
me and except to a few trusted friends had dropped no
hint that I could even read.

"Oh, I 'lowed dat ez smart er boy ez you gwine off
ter school an' college wid his young marster oughter
larn how ter do dat. Will you write de letter fur me?"

I wrote him a screed that made his eyes snap when
I read it to him. It was a mixture of cold Latin gram-
mar and warm persuasion. "Ah, Lawd," he said as he
sat, tallowing his Sunday shoes, "ef dat doan fetch her
she ain't ter be fotch." He folded the letter, and when
he had put it into his pocket he turned upon me. "Oh,
yas, you goes off ter school an' l'arns dead talk an' de
rest o' us hatter sweat in de fiel'. An' de fust thing we
knows you'll be crossin' de Ohio riber ter make
speeches 'mong dem 'litionists. I'm gwine tell Ole
Miss."

"What!" I cried, "after I have written a letter for
you?"

"Oh, I kain't hep de letter. Dat wuz er—wuz er matter o' fack. But it ain't er matter o' fack dat you'se been trying ter put yo-se'f up 'mong de white fo'ks, er turnin' up yo' nose at us caze you'se whiter an' got mo' dead talk den we has."

"Steve," I pleaded, "please don't tell her. I couldn't help learning something, and I pledge you my word that I don't know much. Why, there are hundreds of negroes all about here that can read as well as I can and their masters think nothing of it."

"Doan you fool yo'se'f 'bout dat, honey. Dar's er heap said erbout it. Da reads dem little flat books ter de uder niggers an' da gits whupped fur it, too. And de fust thing we knows you'll be readin' trouble on dis plan'ation. I'm gwine ter de house in de mornin' an' tell Ole Miss."

"Yes, and if you do, I'll have you whipped. Young Master won't put up with such an interference with his affairs. I belong to him and not to Old Miss."

"Ah, hah, but whut Ole Miss say comes mighty nigh bein' law sometimes. I'se had my eye on you fur er laung time, an' I'd like might'ly ter see you out yander in de fiel' er brilin' er laung side o' me."

I argued with him, threatened him, but it was of no use. He shook his head and declared that he would tell Old Miss. And the next day he proved his mean nature. I kept a close watch on him and saw him start toward the house just as Old Miss stepped out upon the veranda. I can see him now, wool hat under arm, bowing to her. I knew that he expected a reward and I wondered what it would be. She listened, and greatly to my surprise replied: "Well, I hope he'll learn enough to behave himself."

"But goodness me, Ole Miss, ain't you gwine gib me suthin' fur all dis?" the rascally tell-tale pleaded.

She took out a small piece of money, tossed it to him and said: "There. And now I want you to remember one thing—don't come to me with any more stories."

She saw me as I dodged behind a corner of the dairy, and called me to her. "Dan," she said as I came up the steps, "I thought you had more sense than to create jealousies by exhibiting the crumbs of knowledge your master has permitted you to pick from under his table?"

I looked at her in surprise; surely the idea was not her own, but in her expression of it there was almost a majestic rebuke. I can see her now as she stood, her gray eyes fixed upon me, her silver-streaked hair parted flat, a bunch of authoritative keys hanging from her girdle. I gave her the all effective knee-bend of submission, and recounted briefly the manner in which the black rascal had snared me. This amused her and she laughed with a cold cackle, but she did not strike me with her keys, as I had feared she would, though the memory of that feelingless laugh lived with me longer than the ache of a blow would have lasted on my head. Old Master came walking slowly out of the hall, with his spectacles on and with a letter in his hand. "Madam," he said, "Doctor Bates is coming back. Dan, saddle the sorrel horse and bring him round to the front gate."

I hastened to the stable, musing upon the return of that trouble-brewing man. He had been home a number of times while Bob and I were off at school, but I had not seen him. More than once I had half suspected that he sought to marry Miss May, to fasten another grip upon the estate, but it did not seem possible that so gentle a woman could marry so hard a man. Yet, I was wise enough to know that we can never tell. A woman's heart is like a bird, beating upon the window at night, dazzled by the promise of a warmth within a glowing room, and seeing not an icy cruelty sitting beside the fire, lying in wait for a tender victim.

While I was holding the horse, waiting for Master to mount, he paused, with his hand on the horn of the saddle and said: "Dan, when your Mars. George gets here, I want you to treat him with the greatest respect. Do you hear?"

"Master," I replied grandiloquently, "I might fail to hear it thunder, but I cannot fail to hear what you say."

He looked at me and remarked: "Look here, you are getting to be a good deal of a d—d fool." But I saw him chuckling as he turned his head away, and I knew that he was pleased. Masters liked the flattery of their slaves, and this is the reason that there is so much cozenage, even in the negro of to-day.

"Do you know why he is coming back?" I ventured to ask.

"Coming back because this is his home, sir. And I don't want you to presume to ask such questions, sir. Well," he said, noticing that I was still holding the bridle, "are you going to let me go, or must I stand here until you are ready to release me?"

"I beg your pardon," I replied, stepping back.

"All right," he said as he rode away, and looking back he added: "Remember that I want you to treat him with the greatest of respect."

CHAPTER IX.

Doctor Bates came two days later and I saw him at breakfast as I stood behind my Young Master's chair. I was surprised to see that the years had touched him so lightly. Indeed, he appeared but little older than at the time I had thrown the glass tumbler at his head. And this set me to a study of all the faces about me. How slowly they had aged while Young Master and I had grown so fast! The doctor was dressed beyond any former mood of neatness, blue broad-cloth coat and ruffled shirt; and Miss May was beautiful in a long, beflowered gown. There had been a heavy frost, and a low, cheer-giving roar came from the logs in the great fire-place. Outside the negroes were singing and dancing in the crisp air. The looms and the spinning wheels were hushed; it was a time for music, for feasting, for jollification—a whole week of "colored freedom." The talk at the table was full of jest, for in the midst of the company was a great bowl of eggnog. And even the steely eyes of my old mistress snapped with pleasant mischief.

"Doctor," she said, "Dan has become quite a student, and he writes Latin love-letters for black Steve."

"In Latin to show that Steve is dead in love!" the doctor roared, shaking his ruffled shirt with his mirth. "But I should think," he added, "that a woman who could love him must be color-blind."

"Or still worse, blind to all sentiment," suggested Young Master.

"Or left alone by all lovers," Miss May declared.

"But," said Old Master, "being so ill-favored he may be faithful."

"The ugly are not truer than the beautiful," Miss May spoke up.

The doctor bowed to her. "I am glad that you assert your own fidelity," he said, and Young Master looked up at me. Miss May blushed, and Old Mistress said: "Daughter, that was a charming compliment, quite worthy of a Southern gentleman."

"And accepted by a Southern lady—with blushes," spoke my young master, and I felt a strong impulse to grasp his hand.

"Ah, Bob," said the doctor, "you are improving. You give real evidences of a thoughtful mind, and I have no doubt that you will make a great lawyer." Here he looked at Old Mistress.

"Yes, lawyer," she replied, "for I have given up the hope of his becoming a minister. He does not take to the church."

"Except to get out of a shower of rain," Bob spoke up, and his mother's gray eyes stared at him in reproof: "Why, Robert, I am astonished at you." Old Master put by his egg-nog cup, tittering down in his stock collar, and Old Miss turned upon him.

"Such encouragement on such a day!" she said.

"Upon days of merriment it is meet that we should laugh," Old Master replied.

"And not bread that we should be sad," said Bob.

At this Miss May laughed a stream of music, clear and rippling; but Old Miss rebuked both Bob and his sister by declaring that it was easy enough to make a wise remark appear foolish. Old Master had begun to laugh at everything, for up to the great yellow bowl in the center of the table his cup had been passed many times. His face glowed with good humor and he joked with the doctor. "Really glad to see you back again, George," the old man said, blinking a newly-felt welcome. "We never know how much we think of a fellow until he's gone. By the Lord—"

"Why, General," Old Mistress cried in surprise.

He looked at her. "Why, what did I say? Said I

was glad to see him, didn't I, and I am. You know it, Hanna, as well as I do. Said I was glad to see him, and you don't seem to believe it. Dan, see that a hogshead of egg-nog is served to the negroes."

"Oh, not that much!" Old Miss protested.

"Hanna, I said a hogshead," he persisted, blinking at her, "and I can't forfeit my word. Go out there, Dan, and tell them that they are to have a hogshead."

That night, after a day of feast and an evening of good-natured riot, Bob and I sat in our room, he listening, and I reading aloud "The Count of Monte Cristo." During the day and the evening, amid the gaiety of the negro quarter, my young master had laughed with as loud a haw-haw as the lustiest buck on the plantation, but I had seen that at times his face was sad; had heard a melancholy note sounding under the jig tune of his revelry.

The hour was late, the fire was growing gray. I put the book aside and raked the chunks together. "We have drunk the warm light and now we'll drink the cooling dregs," he said. And looking at him I replied:

"You are a boy but sometimes you talk like an old man."

"And act like a fool," was his quick retort. He got

up quickly, overturning his chair, and without stopping to right it, strode slowly up and down the room. He walked for some time, with his eyes cast down, half theatrical, treading the forum, for his reading had a deep influence upon him; and then he halted and turned to me.

"Do you see that chair?"

"Yes, sir."

"Why don't you take it up?"

"Pardon me, sir," I replied (at times we were stiffly formal) and then I placed the chair back against the wall. He resumed his walk muttering something, and suddenly his stiff forensic bearing became lithely natural. "Dan," he said, "do you know what I believe?" and before I had time to reply, he continued: "I believe that wolf is trying to marry my sister. And I want to say this, to go no farther, that if he wins her, I'll cut his throat. Mean it?" he cried, his eyes aflame, "I mean it just as sure as there is a God in Heaven. I have always hated that man. I never told you my first recollection of him. I was playing alone in the yard, sitting under a tree. I was very young, I know, but I remember it well. He came along with a bone which he threw to his dog, and then he bent over me and wiped his greasy hands on my head. I howled in anger, and someone came; my words were so few that I could not set forth my resentment." He strode to the door and then hastily came back. "He is a snake, and May is a bird, and he perhaps can charm her, but if he does, I'll let the blood out of his throat. Father always hated him; of late it seems that he is giving way. But I won't give way."

"Mars. Bob, you know what I think of him. One night I tried to kill him, and—"

"Hush!" he cried, glaring at me fiercely. "You are old enough to hang."

"Flattering growth, looking toward a hopeful majority," I replied.

He shot a keen glance at me. "Dan, sometimes you are inspired with a scythe-like wisdom."

"My association with you, Mars. Bob—"

"That will do. You still have the negro's flattery. But it is an infamous shame that you are not white."

"I am, nearly."

He stamped his foot hard upon the floor. "Fool, there is no such thing under social law as nearly white. One drop of negro blood would Africanize humanity."

"Then one drop of unfortunate blood would make the whole world unjust."

"That will do," he said. "If I let you go on you will preach me an abolition sermon."

I bowed and he sat down, drawing his chair near to the dying fire and placing his slippered feet against the chimney. He mused for a long time, and then he said, without looking at me. "I have been reading an old man's book, and it impresses upon me the glorious appreciation of youth. To be young and to place the proper estimate upon it—how magnificent!"

"But isn't there a danger in such early ripeness?" I asked.

"Sir Sage," he said, shifting his feet and crossing them. "Yes, there may be, and you give evidences of it."

Another silence fell, and the candle as well as the fire was dying. "Dan," he said, "I have done enough scanning and soon now I am going to take up the study of the law. You know that it is my ambition to be a great orator, and something within me says that I shall be. I talk to you as I could talk to no one else; with some degree of literal truth, you are a part of myself—I own you." A shadow fell black upon the wall and he looked round at the struggling candle. For a moment the light revived, and he continued: "I believe that one day I shall stand in the Senate, and the storm that rages within my breast will sweep over the land."

"The hope of every young Kentuckian," I ventured to say, determined not always to be a negro flatterer.

The light was nearly gone, but I saw his anxious face turn toward me.

"A streak of lie and a stripe of truth," he replied. "And why do all young Kentuckians have that hope? Because Kentucky has produced so many orators? Oh, I know that we don't take account of the failures. The failures come largely from the plow, from lack of advantages, but I have advantages, and I have fire and ability. Do you believe that?"

"Mars. Bob, I know it."

I wondered what there was in the tone of my voice to impress him so, whether it was a sadness on my part or a sudden and moving conviction striking deep into his own mind, but I saw his feet fall from the chimney, saw him cover his face with his hands—and then the light was gone save a dim glow in the gray fire; no sound in the house nor from the cabins—the boundless night was dead.

CHAPTER X.

It must have been nearly a week later, for I know that the holidays were drawing to a close, when my young master said to me: "Dan, I must ask you to do something which may not seem to be very honorable, but which must be done. I have told you that if Bates wins my sister I will cut his throat; I have reconsidered that threat—I will not cut his throat, but I will give him a chance to shoot me, and if he avails himself of it like a man, all shall be fair, but if he does not, I will shoot him. Do you understand?"

"Yes, sir, but what is it you want me to do?"

We were in the stable at the time this conversation took place. He peered about cautiously to see if any one were within hearing, and then he said: "As I said, it is not very honorable, but it must be done. I want you to sneak—I don't know of a softer word, Dan—I want you to sneak about and—and as best you can listen to what he says to her."

"It is not for me to make an objection by asking

(74)

such a question, Mars. Bob; but do you think it is an honorable thing to do?"

He was looking at me over the partition of a stall, and his eyes snapped. "Did you say something to me about honor?" he asked quietly, but to me his soft tones were louder than a shout.

"Not of honor on your part, but on mine, Mars. Bob."

"A fine shift. Well, I'll attend to your honor and mine, too. I am doing this to save my sister and the honor will come in my giving him an opportunity to defend himself."

"Don't you think you'd better speak to Old Master?"

"No," he snapped. And then he added: "Will you do as I bid you?"

"I am your property, Mars. Bob?"

"Rascal, you disarm me. Listen to me a moment. Has a father ever taken more care of a son's education than I have of yours? Compare your condition with that of every other slave in Kentucky, and then form an estimate of my treatment of you."

"Mars. Bob, I don't have to compare; I already know, and I appreciate. So far as I am concerned, I don't care—I would crawl after the doctor and listen to all he says, but I am afraid that after a while you may think less of yourself for sending me."

"Very thoughtful, I'm sure; but you need have no such fear. I am making a bright justice of a black necessity, and if there should be any repentance, I shall be the one to repent. Will you do as I tell you?"

"Yes, sir."

He took my hand, something he rarely did, for although sociable, familiarity was by him held in quiet abhorrence. I went straightway to the house, leaving him in the stable, and as best I could, entered upon the discharge of my distasteful duty. I heard the doctor's voice in the library, and I was hanging about the door opening out into the large hall, when Old Miss spied me.

"What are you doing here?" she asked, coming forward with one hand resting upon her great bunch of keys.

"I am waiting for my Young Master," I replied. "He said that he would meet me here."

"But you can be better employed than by standing round here. Take out that library rug and beat it."

I ventured to remind her that the Christmas was not quite over and that all work was by custom supposed to be suspended. At this impudence, she lifted her keys and I know that she would have struck me had I not hastened to obey her order. While I was folding the rug, making more than necessary work of it that I might listen to the Doctor and Miss May, I saw him step back from a window, where the two had been standing, and then I heard him say to her: "I am going to town, but will be back this evening," and then in a still lower tone, he added: "And may I have the promise of a talk in the parlor with you to-night? I have something that I wish to tell you."

"With pleasure," I heard her say as I went out with the rug. And long before the coming of night my dangerous plan was formed. In the parlor, usually some distance from the wall, was a large, old-fashioned horse-hair sofa. I decided to get behind this piece of furniture and lie flat upon the floor. There was a strong chance of discovery and a certainty of punishment should I be discovered, but to my young master I had given my word and I was determined to take the risk. Just before supper I laid out my plan to him and after a thoughtful moment, he said: "It's as dangerous as the deuce, but it is the best thing you can do. Wait a moment. I will do it myself."

"You shall not, sir," I was bold enough to declare, and he looked at me admiringly. "All right, Dan, but be careful. Just before supper is over, slip out, and if anyone should ask for you, I will say that I have sent you off."

Old Master had passed through a moody spell since, with so free a hand, he had dipped into the egg-nog, and just now his rusted spirits were brightening. "What, wine at supper, George?" he said, looking at the doctor.

"Our gracious lady's blackberry cordial," the doctor replied, with a wave of his hand toward Old Miss. "Won't you have a glass?"

"Not unless I have lost my senses, and I don't think I have," Old Master rejoined, shrugging his thin shoulders. "When you want to drink, take whisky, for all those side drams are vicious pretenses."

"The percentage of alcohol—" began the doctor, but Old Master shut him up with a loud "Tut, tut. I don't give a snap for the percentage of alcohol," said he. "Take the lowest percentage, drink a little too much, and then see where you are. So I say that if a man wants to drink, it is better to take the shortest route."

"That is, if he wants to get drunk," said the doctor, "but I don't see why any man wants to do that. I don't, I'm sure; I never was drunk in my life."

"There are better men, sir, who cannot say as much," was Old Master's reply, and the doctor pretended to laugh, but I could see that the remark so truthfully delivered by Old Master cut him deeply. I was waiting for the conversation to become earnest, so that I could slip away unobserved, but the talk began to lag, and Mars. Bob must have divined my thoughts for he strove to enliven it.

"Father," said he, "I am ready now to take up law at any time you may suggest. I think that I have had enough of miscellaneous training—I have read nearly every book in your library."

"Take your degree, sir; take your degree," Old Master replied.

"That, sir, is a mere matter of form."

"And a form to be observed, sir—to be observed."

"Yes," said Mars. Bob, "but my reading teaches me that an orator can be trained down to a point too fine —it may weaken his passion, dim his fire with too much judgment, hem him in with too much criticism and compel him to dodge. I think that it was Greek art, sir, that kept Ben Johnson from creating great characters. The perfection of Greek form rendered it impossible for him to give us anything save talking moralities."

"Sophistry!" Old Master shouted, and upon the young man he turned with such a storm that I found my opportunity to escape.

In the parlor the light was dim, the flame in the fire-place not yet having enveloped logs recently put on, and in my eagerness to get into my hiding-place, I overturned a chair. It struck the floor with a deafening noise, I thought, and as I put it back into place I listened for approaching footsteps, but heard nothing save Old Master's loud-toned talk upon the necessity of observing all beneficial forms. I could not understand what he said, nor did I halt long enough to try, but leaping behind the old sofa, stretched myself out upon the floor. Of course every sound about the house was now increased to new volume, and of course my heart beat so hard upon the floor that I was afraid that someone might hear it. A cat came in and purred against the legs of the sofa, a yellow, hateful creature that all previous coaxing had failed to induce to come near me; and I scolded at her under my breath, but she rubbed against me, and mewed as if to invite dis-covery of my shame. I knew that I must get rid of her, and I think that once I felt in my pocket to find my knife to cut her throat, but by a slight noise was frightened out of this cruel intention. I did not parley with her, though I picked her up, clambered over the sofa, raised the window and as she clawed at me, threw her out. And I had just time enough to hasten back to my hiding-place when I heard foot-steps in the hall. There was no opening through which I could see what was passing, for my peeping-place commanded but a view of the hearth and the rug spread in front of it. Presently upon the parlor carpet came the doctor's footsteps—I knew them well—and the soft rustle of skirts. For a few moments the doctor stood on the rug, and the skirts, which I could just see, showed me that Miss May had sat down in a rocking chair. I fancied that the doctor was lighting a cigar, and about the time I thought he must have it going, he sat down not far from Miss May. For a long time they talked of neighborhood happenings, parties, marriages, deaths—she as artless as a child, frank and cheerful; but he, sly and insinuating. He told her of his adventures, with race horses in the East and with gamblers on the Mississippi River, and her exclamations from time to time told me of the effect the recital had upon her; and I could well understand it, for indeed the rascal interested me. Sometimes I thought that he had wandered so far from the subject which had on his part induced this communion that I did not see how he was to approach it, but somehow he found his way back, though not with perfect ease, for I saw my young mistress move her chair in her embarrassment. "And May," he said, "during all these years, while you were growing and blooming, my mind dwelt upon you— and but for you, I don't think that I should have cared to live—"

"Why, Brother George," she broke in, "what are you saying?"

"May, listen to me a moment. Don't call me brother—call me George. Wait a moment, please." There was a flouncing of her skirts and I thought that she must have been getting out of the rocking chair. "You look frightened when, indeed, this should be as quiet as the time when you say your prayers. May, I am no longer as poor a man as I was—"

"But, brother, has anyone reproached you with your poverty?" she asked.

"There you go, calling me brother again. Not lately, but in the past, yes. I have eaten the bitter bread of the dependent—"

"Don't say that," she protested. "Did you invite me here to tell me this? Tell me more of your adventures?"

"May, you are not a child."

"Well, no," she laughed. "I am really getting along in years. I am much older than Bob, and you know he is nearly a man now."

"We are all getting along in years," he replied. "Time is cutting the pigeon wing. But now let me talk seriously to you. Your memory of my devotion to your sister Lou must still be fresh, and God knows I loved her, but May, my love for you is greater, passes all understanding, and I ask you to be my wife."

He was leaning toward her, for his hands came down within the sweep of my vision. It was some time before she replied, and I lay there waiting, my heart beating loud. He had so impressed her that she was seeking to frame a graceful answer. Could it be that she was thinking of accepting him? She got out of the chair and her skirts whisked about as if she had turned toward the door.

I lost sight of the doctor's hand and I saw his feet move. "May, please don't go!" he pleaded.

"Doctor Bates," she said, "you insult me and the memory of my sister. I am going to marry a man that I love and that you hate, although you have seen him but once."

"You don't mean John Marston, of New Orleans?" he almost cried.

"Yes, I do. I am going to marry him."

"May, if you do I will shoot him."

She laughed. "Oh, you might kill him if called to attend him, doctor, but you will not shoot him."

"I will pass your insults, Miss. One more moment, please? Does your mother know about it?"

"I have honored you first, Doctor. See what confidence I have in you? I have made my own choice and have consulted no one. Perhaps it might have been better if my poor sister had done the same."

"You shall not insult me this way. I'll call your father."

"Do, puppy."

She whisked out of the room, and I felt myself rising from the floor, so strong was my impulse to spring upon the scoundrel and choke him, but when I straightened up, he was no longer in the room. I hastened to my young master, whom I knew was waiting for me up stairs, and I almost flung myself into the room. There he sat near a table with two pistols lying upon it. He strove to control himself, but he was biting his lip as he looked up at me.

"Well," he said.

"It is well," I replied.

"Out with it—tell me. What did she do?"

"She called him a puppy," I replied. And then I told him all that had passed, and he listened, motionless, with his hand lying across the two pistols.

CHAPTER XI.

Early in the morning I arose and kindled a fire and sat beside it, waiting for my master to awake. The day was still and cold, and what was unusual with us, a dark fog lay low on the land, like the skeleton of night left hanging in the air of dawn. Master turned over and I looked round at him. He did not notice me; he lay upon his back with one arm under his head, his great brown eyes wide open, a graceful curl of hair upon his classic brow. A piece of poplar kindling snapped— and he looked at me.

"Dan," he said, rising up, and propping his shoulders against the head-board, "what was it you said last night about John Marston?"

"I repeated what Miss May said; that she was going to marry him."

"Why, he hasn't been here very often."

"But that doesn't seem to have made much difference," I replied.

He smiled at me. "Love comes once and is ever present afterward," he said, half musingly. And then rousing himself he added: "I am so much pleased to know that she is beyond the artifices of that nimble wolf that the prospect of her marriage with anyone else seems almost a blessing. But I wonder what father will say. I don't know but that he may look at it very much as I do, though I don't suppose he had an inkling that Bates was striving to win her."

"And how about your mother?" I asked.

I was looking straight at him, and I thought that his face darkened. "I could never understand her liking for him," he said.

"Neither can we understand a woman's liking for any man," I ventured to suggest, and he laughed as he got out of bed. He pulled off the snow-white counterpane and wrapped it about his shoulders, and stood before me a Greek poet, ennobled with the pride of a conquered prize.

When we went down to the breakfast table, Dr. Bates was not in his accustomed place, but Miss May was there and her face was as bright as if nothing had happened. "I wonder why the doctor doesn't come on?" said Old Miss. And then she turned to me: "Dan, step up to his room and tell him that breakfast is ready."

"I object," Young Master cried, setting himself back

from the table, and Old Master gave him a sharp look. "Robert, what do you mean, sir? Object to what?"

"Pardon me, sir," said Young Master, bowing. "I was thinking of something else and didn't really know what I was saying. Yes, Dan, go tell the doctor to come to breakfast. But here he comes now."

The doctor came in smiling. "Glad to see everyone looking so well," he said, sitting down opposite Miss May and beside Young Master. "General, you appear to have enjoyed a good night's rest, and madam, (speaking to Old Miss) to look at you always takes me back ten years. I met old Tom Marshal not long ago, and he told me that at one time you were the most bewitching woman in Kentucky; and with captivating graciousness he added that in one hand you might carry the cares of the present, but that with the other you held up the glowing lamp of the romantic past. And I must be permitted to fancy that Miss May stands as a reproduction of your earlier days. Bob, how are you this morning?"

"A great man has said that one can be below as well as above flattery, and I am one or the other; I shall not say which," Young Master answered. Miss May smiled, Old Master pretended not to hear, but Old Miss heard, and I thought that the wrinkles on her brow grew deeper.

The doctor laughed. "Let us say above, Bob."

"All right, sir; if you desire to be very near the truth."

"But," the doctor added, "let us not agree that you are above truth itself. General, don't you think that his shrewd sophistry more than ever fits him for the law?" And before Old Master could reply, Young Master spoke up. "The law has kept abreast with all human advancement, but I know of a profession that lags in disputatious ignorance, wagging its head at a Harvey and denouncing a Jenner—bleeding the already bloodless patient—"

"Robert!" Old Master cried, dropping his fork with a clang upon his plate, "if you find it impossible to be agreeable, leave the table, sir."

But Young Master was not to be thus driven away. "If I am disagreeable I beg your pardon."

The doctor was laughing. "His words may be disagreeable to some ears, but not to mine," he said. "There is truth in what he says, and that is one of the reasons why I have practically abandoned my profession."

And then Old Mistress spoke. "And I am very sorry you have," she said. "To heal the sick is the

most noble of all arts—one that our Saviour practiced."

"Greatly to the insult of the recognized medicine of
His time," Young Master declared.

Old Miss cleared her throat and was going to say
something but the doctor cut in ahead of her. "Yes,"
said he, "but it was the lawyers who condemned Him
to death."

I stepped back, expecting to see Young Master
spring up in wrath, but he didn't; and he was quiet in
his answer: "And it was oratory that spread the great
news of redemption—the native force of Peter and the
cultivated grace of Paul. Yes, the men of the text
book condemned Him to death, but borne upon the
eloquence that flew from the heart of impulsive man,
His name was carried to the ends of the earth."

I thought that the doctor gave him a look of admiration, but it might have been a trick of his hypocritical
nature. But Old Miss looked at him proudly, and I
saw a warm light glow in Old Master's eye; and this
show of respect for the young man influenced the
doctor to change the subject. "I am going to town
this morning," said he. "Has anyone a commission
to give me? Miss May, can I bring you anything?"

"No, I thank you. I am going myself after a while."

"When did you stop calling her May?" Old Mistress inquired.

"I don't know when and I don't know why," the doctor made answer, looking at the young woman. "I suppose it was when I discovered that she had lost her sisterly regard for me, though I don't know exactly when that was."

"Wasn't it last night?" Miss May asked, giving him a straight look. But not in the least was he daunted by it. "Last night? Let me see," he went on, pretending to muse. "Oh, I don't know but it was. We had a little dispute then," he added, turning to Old Miss. "But it was not serious."

"What is it?" Old Miss asked, looking up at a house-maid who had just entered.

"Mr. Marston is in the parlor," the maid answered. Miss May jumped up and ran to her room to adorn herself for his reception, and the doctor, following her with his eyes as she ran up the stairway in the hall, could not conceal the dark bitterness in his heart. Old Master looked on and was silent until Miss May had quite disappeared upon the upper landing and then coming out of his muse with a sudden jerking of his hand which lay upon the table, he said: "It appears to me that his visits are becoming frequent, Madam."

Old Miss smiled, as I had seen her smile some time before when it was incidentally mentioned by someone that the man Marston owned a large sugar plantation in Louisiana. "Yes," she replied, "and for one, I must say that I am pleased." And thereupon the doctor turned his head slowly and gave her a searching look. "I mean it," she said, smiling at him. But he did not smile in return; he rattled his fork upon his plate and sat in silence. My young master was turned about so that I could see his face. The sullen discomfiture of the doctor was pleasing to him, and with a sudden motion of his hand, a forensic gesture which was now unconscious with him (so surely was oratory taking possession of him) said straight at Old Master:

"I don't see why so much import should attach to a few visits. One might suppose that my sister had been living apart from social influences when the fact is that young men have for years ridden from the valleys and the knobs to call upon her. I hope you do not wish to get her off your hands?"

Old Master was rolling a bit of bread between his thumb and finger, a habit with him. And he looked up, still rolling it, and with a mischievous light in his eye, asked if anyone had seen his daughter posted for sale.

"I won't put up with such talk as this," Old Miss declared. "Robert, you and your father would make me out a heathen. Offered for sale, indeed. General, I am ashamed of you."

The old man rolled his bolus of bread and chuckled softly. "I don't know," he said, his eyes blinking, "that anyone has tried to make you out a heathen. In fact, I think you give strong evidences of an advanced state of civilization. The heathen mother would be caught by feathers and paint but it takes a sugar plantation to sweeten your smile."

Young master roared and was still laughing when Miss May passed the door on her way to the parlor. Old Miss was so furious that she would not trust herself to say anything; her face changed from one hue to another, and her eyes looked young with fire, but she held her peace, with her teeth set upon her thin lip. It was now time for the doctor to say something, and with the sympathetic smile of the scoundrel he turned to her. "Nothing is too sacred to escape a man's joke," said he. "Of course, the General meant nothing, but it gives me the opportunity to say that of all mothers I have known, I think you are the noblest."

Young Master looked at him. "My mother needs

no one to defend her against a pleasantry uttered at her own board," said he.

"Tut, tut," Old Master cried, slapping his hand upon the table. "It was all nonsense and should have been taken as such. Dan, tell Sam to get my leggings and bring my horse round. I'm going to ride."

During the forenoon, though the air was sharp, I saw Mr. Marston and Miss May walking about the place, along the banks of the smoking creek, in the woods, where the cold birds fluttered; I heard them laugh, and I saw him leading her by the hand as they strolled down the lane. Only twice during the day did I catch sight of the doctor, once as he stood leaning moodily against a tree in the yard, and later as he walked to and fro near the stable, lashing his leg with a riding whip. Old Master rode abroad and remained long away, and when he returned just before the dinner hour, I heard negro Sam tell him that the doctor wished to speak to him in the library. I know not what passed at the interview, but I remember that as I went through the hall I heard Old Master say, "It is a matter, sir, that should concern you very little. You may regard yourself as a member of the family, but I am at the head of the household, sir." I imagined that the doctor was advising against Marston and that Old Master had thus shut him up.

That night Bob and I were in our room, studying an immortal oration, when there came a tap at the door. The young man frowned at the interruption and putting aside his book, went himself to the door. "Come in," he said, stepping back stiffly. And the doctor entered. It was the first time for years that I had seen him in that room and all three of us felt the embarrassment of the visit. "Sit down," my master invited, placing a chair for him. He took the seat, leaned for a moment toward the cheerful blaze, then straightening up, remarked upon the coldness of the night. Master said something in reply and I knew that they were skirmishing; that something must soon follow— through their politeness I saw a deadly hatred.

"How long does that man expect to stay?" the doctor asked.

"What man?" master spoke up, with an air of surprise.

"Marston, of course."

"Why of course?"

The doctor turned nervously, looked at me and said: "Will you please move a little?" motioning with his hand, "You are too close to me."

"Dan," said master, "sit over there."

I went over to the window, the place where I had

stood one night and looked down upon a quarrel
between Old Master and the doctor.

"Why of course?" master repeated.

"Thought you knew the man I meant."

"He and almost all other men had passed out of my
mind, sir," said the young man, leaning with his elbow
upon the table. "There are times when I don't think
of man, but of what man has said."

The doctor coughed. "Don't you thing there's just
a little pretense in all that—this learned abstraction?"

"If there's any pretense at all it is just a little. I
know men who have more than a little pretense."

For a time they were silent, listening to the crackling
of the fire. "But I didn't come to bicker," said the
doctor.

"Didn't you? Have the revivalists brought about a
change of heart?"

"I have come to tell you good-bye," said the doctor, graciously overlooking my master's remark.

"Oh, to tell me good-bye? When do you expect
to go?"

"Possibly to-night—surely in the morning."

"Expect to be gone long?"

"I may never return."

"You expect to be gone then some time?"

They looked at each other. "It would seem so," said the doctor. And then he added: "I am going South."

"That's all right," said master. "It really makes no difference which way you go."

"You are getting old enough to pass from annoyance to insult," the doctor replied.

"Yes," said master, "one is supposed to progress."

"True," replied the doctor, "but premature progress argues premature decay. Kentucky is full of the dusty shells of young hopefuls. Sometimes at nineteen a boy gives promise of becoming a great orator; at twenty-five he is a haggler—at forty, forgotten. I have known it to be the case."

"Yes," said master, leaning heavier upon the table, "some men change while others are always the same—with low instincts and only the sharpness that appears to be the inheritance of the scoundrel."

I stepped forward. Master noticed me and motioned me back to my place. The doctor did not even wince. He sat gazing into the fire. "I came to make you a proposition," said he.

"All right. Let it be a short one."

"It will not take long to state it."

"Longer to get to it, I presume?"

"It's this," said the doctor. "You are going into the law and I have no doubt that you will make your mark. I don't believe that you are ambitious to acquire wealth, but I feel that you would like to hold intact your father's estate. A part of the estate, you must know, will fall to me. I don't suppose there will be money enough to satisfy my claim, without a division of the land, so to avoid this, I will agree to take a small amount in ready money as part payment, and Dan as the remainder."

A cold shiver ran over me, not that I was afraid of the issue, but because that man's determination to possess me was freezing my blood.

Master did not change his position, neither did he look up. He made this simple answer: "When the time comes, you may take what belongs to you, even to the estate itself. I will keep Dan."

"But I have consulted with your mother and I act upon her advice."

"You may take the estate when the time comes, but I will keep Dan."

The doctor got up. "Bob Gradley," said he, "when you were a child, you toddled into my way, and now that you are nearly a man, you persistently obstruct my path."

Master sprawled flat upon the table and laughed.

"Well, if this isn't gall!" he cried. "I was born on my father's plantation to stand in your way." He got off the table and laughed as he walked up and down the room. "Toddled into your way? And didn't my mother apologize, and didn't my father try to make excuses for me, doctor?" he said, facing about. "Doctor, the first light of reason that fell upon my mind brought the knowledge that I hated you. Once I cut my finger and looking at the blood, wondered if your blood were not black instead of red. And I'd like to satisfy myself upon that point now. Here, (tossing a pen-knife upon the table) prick yourself and let me see if the ooze is not black. I'll bet it is, and what a proclamation the devil could write with such ink, and with a pen made of a lizzard's claw!" This idea brought back his mirth, and laughing he walked up and down the room, the doctor's eyes following him with a sullen gaze. After a time master came back to the table and sat down. "I am much obliged to you for this entertainment," he said.

"Make the most of it," the doctor replied.

"Oh, I will; I have been known to make much out of poor material."

"And you have been known to make too much out of a negro that ought to be in the corn field."

"Yes, more out of him than could have been made out of some white men."

"Look here, sir; do you mean to draw a comparison between me and that negro?"

"Oh, no; not at all, and I beg your pardon for inadvertantly producing that impression. I wouldn't go so far as that."

"I should hope not," said the doctor.

"Oh, surely not," master replied. "I am sometimes wild but I am never frantic. I wouldn't compare you with Dan. I have too high an opinion of him "

"I will not stand this!" the doctor cried springing to his feet. "No gentleman in the State of Kentucky would put up with it and you'll have to take it back or—" He took out his watch and glanced at it. "That was the worst insult I have ever known, Bob Gradley, and I will give you just five minutes to take it back."

"What time have you?" master asked, taking out his watch.

"Fourteen minutes of ten, sir."

"You are just a little slow. I'm fifteen. Fortunate that my derringers are loaded—don't believe I could load them in five minutes." He pulled open a drawer and took out two pistols. "And now," said he, "in the event that I should drop off to sleep, wake me up when the time is out."

"Braggart," muttered the doctor.

I heard Old Master walking in the hall. Once he halted at our door—I heard his hand upon the knob. I hastened to the door and opened it and the old man stepped into the room. Young Master gathered up the pistols and put them into the drawer, and the doctor snapped his watch which he had continued to hold open in his hand. The antipathy that lay between Bob and the doctor was felt by every member of the family, and I saw the old General stiffen with surprise upon discovering the doctor in the room, but he gave no mouth to his astonishment; he sat down upon the chair which his son sprang up to give him, looked from one to another of us, and rubbing his thin hands said that he had a piece of news for us. The doctor, as if he already divined the news and did not care to hear it uttered in words, hastily quitted the room; and then Old Master, paying no attention to the abrupt departure of his son-in-law, told us that he had given his daughter to the man from Louisiana.

CHAPTER XII.

I was up and abroad upon the plantation early the next morning, Old Master having sent me to look for a colt that had been missing for several days. In a wild bit of thicket-land I found the colt in a sink hole and was rejoiced to discover that it was not hurt. But it was weak and when I had helped it out, it trotted off with its knees knocking together. I followed along to drive it to the stable and was putting up the bars after seeing the hungry creature stumble into the lot, when someone accosted me. I looked up, pausing with a bar in my hand, and there stood the doctor muffled to the ears. "I want you to drive me to town," he said.

I finished my work of putting up the bars before I answered him, and this apparent sullenness smote upon his sense of resentment, for when I turned toward him he was gazing hard at me. "Did my Master say that I was to drive you?" I asked. I was looking down and I saw the frozen ground grinding under his heel; I glanced at his face and his countenance was aflame with wrath. With both hands he tore the muffler from about his neck; he looked about and appeared to stand harder on the ground—all this before he spoke again, and when he did speak his voice had a hissing sound. "You yellow dog, I ought to cut your liver out."

"But I am sure that my master did not tell you to do that," I was bold enough to reply. He leaped toward me. I was strong enough and skillful enough to have given him an unmerciful beating, and my blood burned to knock his teeth down his throat, but judgment had not deserted me, and putting one hand upon the top bar, I leaped lightly over, leaving him swearing on the other side. Had he made a motion to pursue me I would have run away, but I saw Old Master coming, so I stood my ground. The doctor saw him, too, and turned away, muffling his throat as he went. Breakfast was over and I hastened straightway to my Master's room. He was writing as I entered, but he looked up pleasantly and asked if I had eaten, and when I told him no, bade me go at once to the servants' hall.

"I had better not go now," I replied. "I met the doctor out in the lot and he ordered me to drive him to town, and—"

"That's enough," he broke in, and putting down his

pen, went to the front window and looked out. "I wonder if he is gone yet," he said, speaking more to himself than to me. "I repented of my action of last night, but now I wish I had kicked him down stairs. I wonder how long God wants me to put up with that fellow."

"If I am allowed an opinion, sir," I replied, "I don't think that God takes him into account."

He looked at me with a smile. "You are allowed that opinion and I will help you entertain it," he said, and a moment later he added: "Come down with me and get something to eat."

The front hall door stood open and as we turned the bend in the stairs we saw the doctor driving off from the gate. Old Master came up the steps from the hall. "I see he's gone," said the young man.

"Yes, thank God," Old Master replied. "There's only one way that Bates has given me pleasure and that is to see him driving away. But I don't think he's as bad as he used to be. He used to worry the life out of me with trying to buy Dan when he might have known that it was against my principles to sell a slave."

"It's not against my principles to sell anything that annoys me," said Old Miss, coming out with her keys jangling. "As for you, General, you are always willing enough to get rid of white men but you stick close enough to your negroes. Dan," she added, "I want you to take up the sitting-room carpet and beat it."

"Mother," Young Master interposed, "he has had no breakfast. And besides, that is not his work."

"Any work that I tell him to do is his," Old Miss replied, drawing her thin lips together. I gave her a bow of most humble obedience, not that I felt any reverence for her, but that I would protect Young Master against all spiteful upbraiding. "Dan," she said, "tell Tilly to give you something to eat, and then I want you to beat that carpet."

I looked at Bob and he nodded assent, gracefully enough, but I could see that he was not at all pleased. I was turning away when his voice arrested me, though his words were addressed to his mother. "At times I have an odd fancy," said he. "When I am making a speech in my mind and a coldness chills my words, I imagine that the chill is an inheritance from you, mother."

Old Master laughed, and pressed his bony fingers till his knuckles cracked. But Old Miss did not make a laughing matter of it; perhaps she felt the sting of its truth. "It's a singular thing," she replied, "that so cold a mother should bring up so warm a son. General, I wish you wouldn't grin at me that way!"

"Which way shall I grin?" he asked. "If you know of any better way, just show me, and I'll adopt it. But come, madam, don't be put out. You must remember that an old man's humor dries with his advancing years."

"Humor!" she said. "You haven't a vestige of it, and even if you had, you—" Her lips trembled and the corners of her mouth went down. "I have seen trouble enough—"

"There, now," said the old man, his voice soft with tenderness. "Robert, you ought to be ashamed of yourself for speaking that way. Your mother is not cold, sir," he almost stormed, "and if ever I hear you intimate it again, I'll thrash you, I don't care how old you are. You ought to be ashamed of yourself, sir."

"I am," said Bob, and swiftly crossing the floor he kissed his mother. She put her arm about his neck and said that she knew he did not mean it; and then Old Master turned upon me. "Go on, sir," he cried, "and don't stand there gaping like a fool. Confound it, you think you ought to hear every word that's spoken on the place."

I hastened away, wondering what she meant by saying that she had seen trouble enough. Surely she would permit no conversation to be wholly agreeable, certain it was that her manner invited no affection.

The news of Miss May's engagement had spread among the negroes, and many a nappy head was thrust forth seeking a look at the man as he walked about the grounds. I learned from Bob that the wedding was soon to take place. The journey was long, and the man had said that he would not return home without his bride. I had passed him many times in the hall, in the woods, in the road leading to town, but not until one evening when I was summoned to mend the parlor fire did I get an estimating look at him. I had put on a log and had turned about to go when he asked my name. I told him, and he asked laughingly if I were a descendant of the Daniel who was cast into the lion's den? I told him that I was a Daniel who had come to many a judgment and been found wanting.

"Dan belongs to brother," said Miss May, "and they read the same books. Brother thinks a great deal of him."

"Evidently," Mr. Marston replied. He was a trim looking man of medium size and with black whiskers. His teeth were very white and his brow was broad and smooth. He was easy in manner and was quick to perceive, for noticing my almost instantaneous measurement of him, he looked at me sharply and said: "Well, I suppose you have no objection to my marrying your young mistress?"

"No one could object to her choice," I replied, pleased with myself, and Miss May, smiling sweetly, said: "Thank you, Dan. Shut the door as you go out."

I took this as a dismissal, whether she meant it or not, and it cut me. But my mind was soon made to feel at rest for as I was going up the stairs she came out and called me softly: "Dan," she said, "I didn't want you to talk very much to Mr. Marston. He is from the far South and thinks that a negro that can read is a great danger to the community, and after I had indiscreetly told him that you and brother read the same books, I thought that it was time for you to go— I didn't want him to say anything to hurt your feelings. I want you to like him."

This simple act of kindness brought the tears to my eyes. Ah, through the misty years I can see her now, standing in the hall with upturned face, sweet and beautiful.

Preparations for the wedding were hastened forward, and one day the negroes peeped through the parlor door, as we had peeped, long ago, at an array of flowers, Miss Lou lying among them. But now there was no black man to lift his faltering voice in grief—he was gone long years ago and lay sleeping under a dead apple tree; there were soft words of love; and at night there was feasting, the sounds of quick feet, and the spirit of the fiddle was borne upon the air.

CHAPTER XIII.

One morning at breakfast there came an unexpected interruption, the arrival of Old Master's half brother. I knew that he existed, for on occasions at least a year apart, I had posted letters addressed to him and directed to some town away off in Illinois; but a sense of his unreality was so strong with me that I often smiled to think that Old Master would send a letter to find a shadow. But in came the man that morning at breakfast, strikingly real, brown-bearded, tall, loud of voice, and I thought rather roughly dressed for a gentleman. He was much younger than Old Master. Some one, I don't know who, had told me that years ago he had wandered away in consequence of a disappointment in love, though to look at him now I could not believe that he had ever given entertainment to so tender a sentiment. No part of the landed estate fell to him, so, with a small settlement of ready money, he set forth, swearing that never again would he put foot upon that accursed blue-grass spot. He had never been a drag upon Old Master; indeed, he had been a man of exceeding thrift, had made fortunes but had lost them. I well recall his first words upon stepping into the room. Amid the surprise and the bustle caused by his sudden appearance, his loud voice arose:

"Don't want anybody to get scared. Sit down, Guilford, and you, too, Hanna, (nodding at Old Miss). Ah, and this is the one you call Bob? All right, got no objections to that, either. Dropped my baggage out there on the porch. Have someone take it up. Not now, plenty of time. Don't want anybody to get scared; I'm not a pauper. Shall insist upon paying my way. Here, girl, bring another plate; I'm as hungry as a prairie wolf. Look here! (and now he turned to me). Don't want you to call me master. Won't have it; call me Mr. Clem. Long time since I went away, but nothing has changed. Hurry up, there, with that plate. Confound it, don't be put out so, everybody. How are you getting along, Guilford?"

All this was rattled off before anyone else had a chance to say a word. Old Master was glad to see him and the tears ran down his wrinkled cheeks. He tried to tell him much but could tell him nothing except that he was welcome to make his home there.

"What's board worth?" Mr. Clem asked, and Old

Master cried out, "Good Lord! Did I ever hear anything like that? Clem, is it possible that you—"

"Mean to pay my board as long as I stay here. You'll have to take the money, Hanna. If you don't, agree I'll grab my saddle-bags and put out. I'm from a place where every man is expected to pay his way. Wish you'd all quit your everlasting sniffling. What are you doing, Bob?" Old Master was now helping his plate. "Another slab of that meat, Guilford. What are you doing, young feller?"

"Preparing myself for the law," Young Master answered proudly.

"All right, no particular harm in it. Good job for a lazy man. Hanna, you hold your own pretty well. Not as old as I expected to find you; and Guilford is a marvel of youthfulness. Don't know how I happened to come back—Just took the notion one night and I was on the road before daylight the next morning. That's the way we do things in Illinois. Pass me some more of that egg-bread. Hanged, if that ain't Kentucky up and down. Old aristocracy still on its mouldering throne, eh? Good thing for some people while it lasts, but it will tumble over pretty soon."

"Clem, you musn't talk that way," Old Miss interposed.

"All right, I'll shut it off; thousands of things to talk about. What's board worth in this neighborhood?"

"Clem," said Old Master, leaning upon the table and looking at him, "I don't know that I ever heard of a gentleman paying board in this neighborhood."

"Hah! By the hoofs, I never heard of a gentleman refusing to pay board in any neighborhood," Mr. Clem replied. "Come, how much am I expected to pay? Can't get board here, board somewhere else."

"Oh, that would be a scandal," Old Miss cried.

"Then let us avoid scandal. Find out what is customary and let me know. Guilford, devilish glad to see you. Wish I had come before. Bob, got a horse you want to trade for a better one? I've got a nag out there that's a beauty. Let's go and look at him?" he added, throwing down his knife and fork and shoving his chair back.

"Not now, uncle Clem," the young man replied, laughing.

"Uncle! That's good—like to hear it; gives me a sort of anchor. I think you and I will get along all right. Guilford told me, I don't know how long ago— got the letter somewhere—that it was your ambition to become an orator. And I can give you a few points, for I have lived for years in a hot bed of free speech, and without free speech, there is no real oratory. Round here they think that Marshall and Clay were great orators, and they were in a way, but you ought to hear Abe Lincoln."

"I never heard of him," Old Master spoke up.

"Oh, no; but you will. He can squeeze mirth and tears out of the heart all at once. When he arises to speak, and even before he has uttered a word, every man in the audience says to himself, 'there is my brother.' Guilford, your polished Kentuckians speak out of the book, by note, and they may work themselves into a fine heat, but this man Lincoln cries from the fullness of a soul that the Lord has given him."

"Clem," said Old Master, bending a hard look upon his brother and rolling his pill of bread, "you tempt me to say that you are a blasphemer against the majestic voice of my State, sir. Never was the voice of man truer than among these graceful hills, and never did the heart of man beat warmer for freedom and justice."

"Ah," Mr. Clem cried, "for freedom, did you say? For slavery, you mean."

"Sir," said Old Master, "Henry Clay has spoken for the bondman."

"But was he honored for it?" Mr. Clem asked. "Do you honor him for it?"

"Clem, if you have come to sow the seeds of abolition, to disgrace my household with the mud brought from your free soil—your sink hole of iniquity—I must request you to go away."

"It is easier to drop a subject than to ride a long distance," Mr. Clem replied with a broad smile. "Got any good horses?"

"Horses native to this land and therefore the best," said Old Master.

"Got one you can't manage? If you have, I'll make him get down on his knees and beg for mercy."

Old Master looked at Bob and laughed. "We've got a great black horse we call Zeb, and our sick quarter is sometimes filled with his victims. Dan here, can break almost any piece of horse-flesh, but he's afraid of Zeb. The negroes don't call him Zeb— they call him the Devil, sir."

"And I would advise you not to have anything to do with him, Uncle Clem," said Young Master. "He cut a great gash on Andrew's head, broke Tony's arm not long ago, and laid Dan up for a week. We keep him merely for show, for he is the most graceful thing you ever saw."

"And I will drive him to town this morning," Mr. Clem declared. And getting up, he added: "Come, show him to me?"

We could but laugh at the self-confidence shown by this rugged man from the West; we felt that he had brought with him the breezy brag so characteristic of his boundless territory. But I felt a pinch of regret, for I had conceived a liking for the man and did not wish to see him humbled.

"Come on," said Old Master, leading the way, but Old Miss interposed. "You must not go near that vicious creature," she said to Mr. Clem. "Nothing would delight him more than to plant a hoof between your eyes, and I declare, General, it's a shame that you encourage such a thing."

"Come out and take a drive with me," Mr. Clem cried, gently putting Old Miss out of the way. But she shuddered at the thought and closed the door upon us as we passed out. "In one respect I am not a true Kentuckian," said my Young Master to Mr. Clem as we walked along toward the stable. "I could never find it in my heart to worship a horse."

Mr. Clem stepped in front of the young man, halted and looked at him and then at Old Master. "Guilford," said he, "can it be possible that this is your son?"

"Wait until you see the Devil, and you will deny that you are my brother," Old Master laughed, rubbing his thin hands in a sort of mischievous glee. Bob took Mr. Clem by the arm and as they walked along I heard him say: "If I had known you, I should have wished for your coming. There is something so unexpected about you that I must call you the new man—you are the very opposite of the books I have been reading."

"Yes, Bub, I am the opposite of all your teaching."

"I don't know that I like the word Bub."

"But you'll have to stand it; I'm going to pay my way, and the world, the flesh and the devil are willing to put up with much from that sort of a man."

We had now come to the stable. Through a small window we saw the fiery horse's black eyes shining. "Bring him out," Mr. Clem commanded.

"That is easy enough," Old Master replied. "It is only when you attempt to put leather on him that he shows his mettle."

"Bring him out," said Mr. Clem. "Here, boy, bring me a bridle and a set of buggy harness."

There was a great commotion in the barn-yard, and the negroes went running to and fro, amid whisperings

and the suppressed excitement of expected sport. The
horse was led out by the halter, a picture of devilish
majesty, head high in contempt, nostrils broad, eyes
afire. The harness lay in a heap upon the ground. Mr.
Clem took up the bridle. In an instant the horse had
jerked the halter from the negro's grasp, was standing
almost erect on his hind feet, and he came toward Mr.
Clem, cutting the air with his fore hoofs. The rest of
us fell back, one over the other, but Mr. Clem did not
move. Old Master shouted at him, but paying no
heed he stood, with his eyes fixed upon the advancing
beast. I was off to one side and could see his face,
hard-set and with steady eyes. "Ho!" he said, low in
his breast, and the horse's feet fell to the ground. I
don't think I ever saw so complete a picture of astonishment. The horse, cowed by that one low word,
stood there trembling, with the coming sweat glistening upon his flanks. Mr. Clem stepped forward and
touched his neck and he squatted and trembled. A
loud murmur arose among the negroes. The Devil had
been conquered with a word. He took the bit and
suffered the harness to be put upon him; he was put
between the shafts and with but one protest he was
driven about the grounds. That one protest was a
convulsive kick. Mr. Clem got out of the buggy,

walked round, caught him in the nostrils, and with a violent torsion cried, "Ho!"

That was a great day on the plantation, and before nightfall the news had spread about the neighborhood, and at evening a number of people came to welcome Mr. Clem's return to the home of his youth. The degree of fawning shown on that occasion was of great amusement to my Young Master, for he knew that had his uncle come back a great scholar, an authority upon some scientific discovery, he would have been suffered to poke about almost unobserved; but appearing as the conqueror of a vicious horse, he laid a strong hold upon the admiration of his fellows.

CHAPTER XIV.

The coming of Mr. Clem had a great effect upon our household. It was like a new breeze, blowing in from afar off where the woods are fresh. With his foot he was ever ready to press upon a tradition, and to leave off if the annoyance was too great; he experimented constantly with the sentiments and prejudices of any-one who happened to be near him. He joked with Old Miss, something ever dangerous to undertake, and at times he wrought sorely upon Old Master by arguing abolition with him. But no matter how hot might be the discussion, it was always pleasantly tem-pered, in the end, by some joke borrowed from the sturdy men who were busy with the building of a new political empire in the West. Lincoln was his hero. He had lived in Springfield, and had seen the great stump-speaker striding across a pasture land with a naked youngster on his back, and with the Galilean's smile upon his face. From his saddle-bags he brought forth newspapers with abstracts of the backwoods-man's speeches, words that rang like an axe on a frosty morning, and he never was weary of declaring that the man was inspired. "He is Peter come back to the earth," I remember hearing him say, "and upon a rock he is going to build a great church not for caste, but for man."

"If you are going to worship a man, let him be a hero," Old Master cried. We were in the library and the elder brother was walking up and down in the fire-light. I was hunting a book for Young Master and purposely made a lag of my errand.

"I don't know what you mean by a hero," said Mr. Clem, looking up from his pipe in the corner.

"A man who does something for his country," Old Master retorted, still walking with his hands behind him.

Mr. Clem smiled. "Yes, that is a hero," said he. "But what would you have a man do? Overcome a band of Mexicans and win a new territory, or save his entire country?"

Old Master halted, posing to make an impressive reply, but at that moment Mr. Clem sprang to his feet, threw open the window and thrusting forth his head shouted: "Hi, there, don't you want to swap that horse for a better one?"

He had heard the sounds of hoofs and had seen a

man riding past the gate. The man reined up and looked round. "I don't know but I might," he answered. "Well, just wait a minute," Mr. Clem shouted and turned about to leave the room. Old Master frowned. "You are not going to swap horses here on a Sunday morning," he said. "It will bring a scandal upon us."

"Now, Guilford, that's nonsense," Mr. Clem protested. And then he shouted again from the window: "Ride on down to the end of the lane and I'll meet you there."

He hastened away, and just before dinner he came back leading a trim horse, so much better than his old nag that his brother racked himself with a loud laugh. His shrewdness was indeed remarkable. He came to us on a woolly-looking plow horse, and before he was in the neighborhood two months, he was the owner of three of as fine mares as I have ever seen. The negroes looked upon him in the light of a vastly superior being, and about the fire at night they told tales of his marvelous power. He would permit none of them to call him master, and at first this told against him, bespeaking as they thought a very humble station; but their prejudice was overturned when they perceived that among the high-born he could hold his head with a lofty pride. Sometimes he talked in a way almost to chill my blood. I have often mused upon his meeting me one evening as I strolled along the shores of the little creek, listening to the music bursting with more boldness as the twilight settled down. Spring was come and I smelt the smoke of the dead grass burning in the fields. I had halted and was standing on a rock when he came up to me.

"Fishing?" he asked.

"No, sir; listening to the water."

"And yet they tell us that the negro has no soul," he said.

"No gentleman has ever told me that," I ventured to reply.

"No," he rejoined, stepping upon the rock. "The gentlemen acknowledge your soul so that the pulpit may continue to hold you in slavery. I know that you and Bob are great friends, know all that, but if I were in your place I would leave."

"Mr. Clem!" I cried.

"Yes, I would. Here, you are a young fellow of parts waiting for what? Nothing. Why, you could go North and make a man of yourself."

"I am going to make a man of myself as it is," I replied, actually trembling.

"Make a man of yourself for someone else.   Young man, the world is becoming too enlightened to permit of slavery much longer.   They tell you that God made slaves.   That's an insult to the Almighty.   I don't really advise you to leave your master, for I can see that Bob makes your bed as easy as it could well be made; but it is an infamous shame that a young man as intelligent as you can have nothing but a life of bondage to look forward to.   It is true that as compared with the others, you walk on rose-buds and sleep on feathered palm, but you are a slave for all that."

He moved up closer to me, put his hand on my shoulder and turned me about as if in the growing darkness he would study the expression of my face, the effect his words had wrought.   I trembled under the light weight of his hand, for it was as if freedom from afar off had touched me; but I could give no ear to this bold man's suggestion.   I had read many a book conceived by great minds that abhorred servility, poets that had shaken their fists in the faces of the earth's annointed, orators whose last utterances were cried aloud for the freedom of man, not the white man alone, but man.   All my life I had been tapping upon the head the ambitions that arose within me, killing them and seeing their skeletons bleach in the desert of my fancy; and with a stout and determined heart I could have turned my back upon Old Master, for his years were nearly spent; but I could not leave the young man, though the incense of freedom filled my nostrils. Not many miles away flowed the Ohio River. Beyond that stream were thousands of people who would be glad to help me, would regard it a duty which they owed to their religion; and farther away was a British domain, where all men were free—the way was clear, but in that direction I could not have stirred from that rock. My heart was my real master.

"Mr. Clem," said I, and I must have sobbed, for he turned away to hide his own face, "I may be a fool, but I cannot be a traitor to my affections. I wear a chain, but it is made of gold, and I would rather exchange it for one of iron than to know that Bob Gradley had lost confidence in me. I know that I could amount to something in the world—I feel it; I am convinced that I could go to the North and help free the wretched creatures in the far South, but I should have to speak against my Young Master and that I could not do." He caught my hand with a tight grip, and I continued: "I value your kindness; I know that it is genuine, but I must ask you not to tempt me again."

And still harder did he grip my hand as he replied: "There is a salt of the earth and it never loses its savor, and you are of that salt. If you had come to me and begged me to point out the road to freedom, I might have sent you to your Master; your fidelity and strength caused me to speak to you in your behalf. But I did not know the full measure of that strength and fidelity. I know now and I honor you. But keep to your books; the time will come."

Suddenly he broke away and turned on a trot toward the turn-pike, not far off. I heard the hoofs of a horse beating on the hard macadam, and soon I heard this queer man shout, "Hi, there; who ever you are. Hold on a minute. Believe I can give you a better horse for the one you are riding." The hoofs fell slower, and a voice replied: "That you, Clem Gradley? Don't want to transact that sort of business with you—Came in one of having to walk after the last swap. Another whet and I couldn't more than crawl."

The hoofs fell faster and Mr. Clem, chuckling mirthfully, returned to the rock. It was now quite dark and I could not see his face, but I knew that he was in favor with himself, for he had clapped his hat on the back part of his head (a good-humored bravado characteristic of him) and continued to shake with joviality.

"I think that was Lige Berry," he said. "They told me that he had nipped everybody in this county, but I guess I skinned him a little. That's the way to do, Dan. When they try to skin you, skin them. Suppose we go on toward the house? Yes, sir-ree," he continued as we walked along, "skin the skinners in a horse trade. And skin anybody else for that matter. Everything is fair in a horse trade—you've got to be slick and believe nothing. I remember starting out once on an old mule. I had owned a steamboat and it had burnt up without a copper of insurance. I thought I'd make my way to St. Louis and there get something to do. A captain offered me passage on his boat, but I told him no, that I would try the luck of going over-land. Well, as I tell you, I set out on that old mule, bought on credit for twenty-three dollars. I was a long time on the road, months, I might say, but when I got to St. Louis I drove in about as fine a lot of horses as you ever saw. And three weeks afterward I steamed up the Illinois River on a boat of my own. I swapped it for a stock of goods in old Salem—always somebody in that town ready to swap off his store, knowing that he couldn't get the worst of it—and I staid there until I went broke. I don't know why I never could hold on to anything. I am great up to a certain point, and then I go to pieces. Why, if I had owned this farm I would have made it three times as large and then lost it all. I've done most everything except to sponge on people, and I never could do that. Set up a drug store in a little place called 'Prophet's Town' on Rock River. Didn't know anything about drugs—helped a feller too liberally to something his prescription called for and poisoned him. He didn't die, but I thought it was time for me to get out of that sort of business. Yes, and I practiced law. Didn't know anything about law, but I could talk. Defended a feller and they hanged him. Of course that might have happened with anybody—with Lincoln himself, for that matter—but a prejudice was raised against me. It tickled Lincoln. Of course he didn't want to see the man hanged, but he had to laugh at me. 'Gradley,' he said to me shortly afterward, 'I want you to do me a favor. I have an enemy, a man that has always stood in my path, and I want him removed. You can do it. I will have it whispered about that he is a thief; you defend him and they'll send him to the penitentiary for life!' "

The supper bell was now ringing and I hastened

into the house to take my place behind Young Master's
chair. He had many a time commanded me to leave
off this useless act of servitude, but such a favoritism
would have inflamed Old Miss against me, so I
insisted upon a continuance of the office.

Old Master and Old Miss were Hard-Shell Baptists
and at supper there was present an old and honored
exponent of that faith, Elija Brooks. He visited us
often, but Bob and I had a stronger cause than this to
call him to mind. Once we had taken his rubber over-
shoes and made a town-ball of them and had been
severely whipped for our enterprise. The old gentleman refused to erase this, our act of meanness, from
his mind, and whenever he looked at me I felt that my
soul was surely lost. Upon this visit he was in higher
spirits. Out in his neighborhood, we were soon
informed, a man discovered to be an abolitionist had
been tarred and feathered, an example of God's avenging wrath; and the old man's mouth appeared to water
with the delicious recollection of the sight. "They
came to my house," he said as he passed his plate for a
Shanghai rooster's breast, "and asked my opinion in
case the fellow was found guilty. I took down the
good book and sought instruction, and I think that I

modified his punishment when I recommended tar and feathers. Ah, Brother Guilford, the ways of the devil are many and sly; we must keep a constant look-out for him."

"He is never idle a moment," said Old Miss with a sigh.

Old Master didn't say much. He wasn't a very strong believer in the devil, and but for his negroes and his blue-grass land, he had surely been turned out of the church for saying, in the midst of a God-loving assembly upon his own veranda, "the devil be damned!"

"What had the man done?" Mr. Clem asked, and I saw his face harden.

"Why, sir," returned Mr. Brooks, "he had openly set our institutions at defiance and proclaimed abolition. He said that no Christian could own human flesh and blood."

"Had he been in the community very long?" Mr. Clem asked.

"Several years," the preacher answered. "And there comes in a strange part of the affair," he continued. "He had lived among us for that length of time and had never been known to steal anything or to commit any sort of depredation."

"Marvelous," Mr. Clem cried, setting his cup violently upon the table. "Hadn't stolen anything! Why, sir, I expected you to tell me that he had murdered women and children."

The unsuspecting preacher was deeply moved by the earnestness of Mr. Clem, but Old Master slily shook his head as a warning not to go too far, and Old Miss cleared her throat. "It is a thousand wonders," Mr. Brooks went on, "that he had not committed murder; and now it comes to mind that certain little pilferings throughout our neighborhood may justly be laid to him."

"No doubt of it," Mr. Clem cried.

"It is at least a well-founded suspicion," said the preacher.

"He ought to be burned at the stake!" Mr. Clem shouted, and the preacher, his suspicions aroused at this outbreak of vehemence, looked searchingly at the man from the West. "I would not advise quite so stringent a measure," said he, turning his eyes upon Old Master and then directly his gaze again at Mr. Clem.

"Oh, yes," Mr. Clem insisted, "I would even go further than that. I would burn him at the stake and if he has any children I would skin them for the delight of the Sunday school. But I forget. Your **denomination** has no Sunday schools."

"Sir," said the preacher, "I will waive your sarcasm to refute your attack upon my church," and he had squared himself to deliver a harangue when Old Master struck the table with his fist. "I want an end of this right now," he snorted, shaking his head, and with his nose looking more than ever like an eagle's beak.

The preacher took no part of this reprimand to himself; indeed, he struck in with an approval of Old Master's violence. "You are scarcely expected to restrain yourself, Brother Guilford," said he. "The Lord has not asked us to put up with everything, and most of all with sentiments that seek the destruction of our country."

Is it not singular, I must stop to reflect, that only a few years ago a large part of our country believed that liberty and prosperity depended upon slavery? This old preacher I knew to be an honest man, a God-serving and a generous man. His plantation was large, his soil strong, his crops bountiful, and he gave nearly everything to the poor; but, viewing him in the broad light of to-day, his heart was narrow and his soul was blind. Such was the atmosphere in which we lived, beautiful and romantic, but filled with an inflammable gas; and one hot word would serve to set it off. I remember that at a store not far from our house a man sat on a box, reading the "New York Tribune." A deputy sheriff, standing near, discovered the name of the publication, tore it from the man's grasp, threw it upon the ground, spurned it with his foot and swore that he would shoot the person who attempted to take it up. The paper was not taken up, but the question was discussed at the polls, and the deputy was elected sheriff. Still the wise men in the East were at work quietly with the pen which soon should be supported by the sword.

Conversation that evening fell pleasantly enough, after Old Master's forceful veto, and out upon the veranda where the air was soft they sat until a late hour, Young Master with them, and I, seated on the steps. Mr. Clem sang a dolefully-comic song, "The State of Illinois," which moved the preacher to gracious laughter, and Old Master told many a humorous story. But in the height of this pleasantry Old Miss broke in with the trouble that was hers, one daughter dead and the other married and gone afar off. This I thought was to tell the preacher that it was time to pray and go to bed. And he must have accepted it as a hint, for shortly afterward he said: "Brother Guilford, let us pray!" Then came a solemn shuffle as they followed the preacher to his knees. I was included in the invitation to ask God to help me and I knelt upon the stone walk at the bottom of the steps. From a distance came the song of the ignorantly-happy negro; I heard the opening notes of a pack of hounds on a hillside far away, and the creek lifted its voice in a sweeter prayer than man could utter. The preacher implored the Lord to bless Old Master's household, white and black; to hasten the day when the holy word of the Savior should be acknowledged throughout the earth. He prayed that all evil might be stricken from the sin-inclined mind of man; that the benighted politician who strove to prevent the admission into the union of more slave territory might be persuaded to see the error of interfering with the progress of the South, and closed with asking God to bless all mankind. The hanging lamp in the hall had been lighted, and as the old preacher passed under it I could see from where I now stood on the veranda that he tottered with emotion, so fervent had been his supplication; and I thought of the prayers in another part of our country; the gray men imploring our Father to hasten the time when the chain should drop from the slave. Ah, man, self-appointed keeper of the Maker's seal, you pray that your brother may be cleansed and then you shoot him. But I will not moralize against you, for I am earthly enough to believe that war is sometimes a blessing, that the world's greatest progress has been sprinkled with blood—blood, the emblem of the soul's salvation.

CHAPTER XV.

I went with my young master immediately to his room. He was beginning already to withdraw himself from other studies and to devote all his time to the law; so taking up a sheep-bound book, he began to read aloud. Suddenly he flung the book down and leaned back in his chair. "Law," he said, "is supposed to be common sense, but I have about reached the conclusion that there is no common sense in the human family."

"So soon?" I asked.

"So late, you mean," he replied. "A boy can sometimes see what an old man has failed to discover. Now take that preacher, as good an old fellow as you would find in a day's ride, and note how pinched his mind is."

"In what way, Bob?" I asked.

He stiffened up and looked hard at me, and standing near, I bowed until my head almost touched the table. I had called him Bob, a familiarity that I don't think I had ever before ventured upon, and it fell

like a mallet. When I straightened up, he bowed to me
and not a word was spoken on the subject of my neglect to put "Mars." before his name.

"You ask in what way is his mind pinched. I might
answer by saying in every way, but I'll specify one.
He believes that he's serving God when he puts tar
and feathers on a man who has ventured to express his
opinion."

"But in this respect is he more narrow than others I
could mention?" I asked, for I could take issue with
him, argue and even quarrel with him without treading
upon ground too oozy with familiarity. "He believes
that slavery is a God-ordained institution. Don't
you?"

I shall never forget the look he gave me. I stood
with my arms folded looking down upon his handsome
face, his Greek head. A lock of hair had fallen upon
his brow, and he slowly put it back, still looking at
me, and there was a strange, thrilling music in his
voice when he spoke: "Did I teach your mind to eat
that it might gulp such food?"

"You gave me the bill of fare and were generous
enough to invite me to help myself," was the answer
I made.

"But I didn't tell you to eat filth."

"And filth I did not eat, but I swallowed many a mouthful of reason."

"But did any one of those mouthfuls tell you that I considered slavery a God-ordained institution?"

"Not you especially, but you belong to a caste."

"Still I am no fool. Who gave the slaves to Rome? Conquest. What led to conquest? Physical superiority. And wasn't there a grandeur in that? And is not a grandeur almost a sacred thing?"

Now here was an argument and it might have been prolonged, but at that moment there came a tap at the door. Master cried an invitation to come in, and Mr. Clem entered.

"What are you boys talking so loud about?" he inquired, taking a chair and putting his feet upon the table. "Didn't know but you might be trying to swap horses."

"An exchange of night mares," Bob replied, reaching over and moving his inkstand.

"That's all right, but do you make him stand up all the time?" Mr. Clem asked, nodding at me.

Bob laughed. "He can sit down if he wants to."

"Well, then, please do," Mr. Clem said, looking at a chair and motioning toward me. "It makes my legs hurt to see you standing there." I sat down and he continued: "I noticed that our old preacher rode pretty good stock over here."

"You didn't see him when he rode up," said Bob.

"No, but I took a lantern just now and went out to the stable and had one of the boys find his horse for me. Yes, sir, pretty good sorrel horse, fine shoulders, but nostrils rather small. Good bottom, though. I went to his room after I came back and found him in bed, but I got him interested in my nag, and if he ain't walking before three weeks pass he'll ride on a straight line out of my circuit. Does he hold prayers of a morning? Of course he does, though; wouldn't miss an opportunity, you know. Well, I'll join him, and afterwards put in a few petitions of my own. It's not right for a preacher to ride such a horse any way. Ought to walk; for don't the Bible say something about how beautiful are the feet of those that tread the path of righteousness? Strikes me that I've heard something of the sort. Tarred and feathered him, eh? Bob, do you know what would happen if they should dab any of their tar on me?"

"I don't believe you would submit very quietly, Uncle Clem."

"Well, I wot not. Wot's all right there, ain't it? Yes, I guess it is. They might put the stuff on me,

but do you know what would happen after they got all
through with their fun? There'd be more fun. I'd
get one of these old fashioned blunder-busses, load it
with nails and scraps of iron and scatter flesh all over
this community. By the flint hoofs of the devil I wish
they'd smear tar on me. But I musn't argue any more
with that preacher. I want his horse."

"You wouldn't cheat him, would you, Uncle Clem?"

There was astonishment in the look Mr. Clem bent
upon the young man. "Cheat him? I don't exactly
understand. Bob, there's no such thing as cheating in
a horse trade. Man tells me that his horse has good
eyes. I look at the eyes and see that they are defect-
ive. Man is a liar, but hasn't deceived me, therefore I
am not cheated. I tell a man that my horse has good
eyes. He looks and fails to see a defect and swaps.
Afterward finds out horse blind of an eye. Who's
fault? His own—error in judgment."

"That is a very comfortable way to put it," said the
young man. "But suppose you buy something and the
dealer misrepresents it?"

"I hold him accountable," Mr. Clem replied.
"Merchandising is one thing and trading horses
another. The keeper of a store is a catch-penny
figurer upon small or large margins of profit, which-

ever the case may be. Some little shrewdness is required, but above all, he must be a fawner and a man of dogged patience. He advertises that the world may, with perfect safety, take his word. On the other hand, the horse trader is a sort of adventurer, a knight with sharp judgment for a lance and with strong assertion for a battle-axe. He takes no advantage of man's necessity, but challenges him. He needn't enter the combat—he can say, 'no, thank you,' and ride on."

He took out a large plug of tobacco and with a Barlow knife, cut off a wedge-shaped piece, wiped the blade on his trousers, snapped it shut, returned both knife and tobacco to his pocket, put the wedge into his mouth and turned it about with exceeding satisfaction.

"Yes, sir," he went on, "the horse trader is a man of skill, going about sharpening the wits of society. He stirs the blood of cupidity and then teaches man a lesson, enforcing the moral that the glittering is not always the gold. He is an orator and his subject is horse. Through the horse he reads human nature. He is self-confident, never tells too long a story, and people like to hear him talk. Ladies sometimes sniff at him and say that he is horsey, but when they have been sufficiently bored by the empty prattle of the refined dolt, they return to the horseman to be entertained. Bob,"

he added, after going to the fire-place to spit, and
returning to put his feet upon the table, "there is one
type of man that I should like to see hanged—the
negro-trader."

"Nearly always a brute," Young Master replied.

"Always, Bob. And society, even in this State,
holds him in contempt, yet recognizes the justice, or I
should say, fails to recognize the injustice of the institution he serves. D— me if it ain't riling!" he cried,
striking the table with his heel. Master moved the ink
stand till further away and leaned back in his chair.
Mr. Clem continued: "The South is an exotic, living
under glass. But one day the glass will be smashed
and the cold air will blow in. What could be more
disease-breeding than our present state of affairs, one
end of the republic heating with degenerate luxury,
the other end cool with self-reliant industry?"

"Uncle Clem, they have turned you into a Yankee,"
said the young man.

"By the hoofs, they have opened my eyes and if to
see is to be a Yankee, then I am one."

"But having seen, do you now come to sow eye-
opening seeds, in fact, to scatter trouble?"

"I've got as much right in this State as any man

that lives in it; I carried a gun into Mexico and I wear the scar of a leaden missile."

"No one questions your right, and I, for one, am warm in welcome of you. But you turned your back upon Kentucky, shifted your citizenship to another State."

Mr. Clem jerked his feet off the table, went to the fire-place, spat out his tobacco, and began to walk up and down the room, with his hands behind him after the manner of Old Master.

"Bob," he said, pointing as he spoke, "there, at the north corner of the lane, where the steps go over the stone fence, I stood in my country's uniform and told a girl good-bye. She clung to me like a sweet vine, and with trembling fingers I loosened the tendrils of her love. Behind a gallant warrior I marched into the City of Mexico, thrilled not with the victory, but with the thought that my face should soon be homeward set. That night I received a letter telling me of her perfidy. She did not write—my brother's hand sent the news. I couldn't believe it—in my breast I called him a liar. But I came home with a quaking heart, to find that she had married a negro-trader. And then, in taking up my small belongings to leave the State, I swore that I would never return so long as she was in

it alive. Once that fellow came to Illinois to catch a
run-away slave. He caught the fugitive at a town
called Princeton. I chanced to be there. A noble-
hearted man named Bryant, brother of the poet, heard
the negro's pitiful story and then turned upon the
trader. 'Sir,' said he, 'the shadow of a black and
outrageous law may fall upon your case, but humanity
which is above all law, cries out for the protection of
this poor creature. Be gone from here.'

"'Not until I have had my say,' I cried. 'Bring a
rope and I will hang him.' There was an uneasy stir
among the men assembled in the little court-room.
The trader looked at me sharply. A grim smile spread
over his dastardly face. I had learned more than I
have yet told you—He held a mortgage upon the
negroes that belonged to the father of that girl and
she had married him to save the negroes, to keep them
from being taken South and sold to the heartless
drivers. This she had written and given to a friend to
send to me, but he was tardy in sending it. However,
I could not have forgiven her, although there might
have been some truth in what she said and some nobil-
ity in her act. The fellow leered at me, and turning to
the justice of the peace, said to him: 'This man ought
not to have a word to say. He hates me because I mar-

ried the girl he loved.' This set the idlers to tittering, and I got out of the court-room, frothing at the mouth. Under protection of the law, the rascal was permitted to go away in peace, but he did not take the negro, not then, but got him afterward. Bob, I'm strong enough to confess a weakness, and the man that isn't, isn't game. I'm bold enough to defend a prejudice, for prejudices are sometimes our dearest inheritance."

He resumed his walk, went to the door, halted and came back to the table. "I said that I would never come back to the State so long as that woman was in it alive, and I didn't. She died less than a year ago, and her husband is now a planter in Mississippi, and about all I ask of the Lord is that I may some time meet him—accidentally." He looked at his watch. "It's getting late and I guess you boys are sleepy. Believe I'll take another look at that horse and go to bed. Good night."

I went to bed, leaving master in his chair, settled in a deep consideration. The candle-wick fell into the socket, but the fire-light showed him still musing, his eyes wide open but dreaming. I fell asleep and awoke in the dark, aroused by the sound of the young man's voice. He was making a speech, had sat with it running in his mind while the words of Mr. Clem had fallen upon me like burning coals.

CHAPTER XVI.

"Don't make a fire," were the first words I heard at morning. I looked up and found the orator in bed, propped upon his elbow. He looked at me—his eyes were always fascinating—and I waited to attend upon his bidding.

"Do you know that what uncle said last night didn't strike me very hard until just a few moments ago?" said he. "A stream of nonsense was rippling through my mind at the time and I was too much taken up with it to feel what he said, but it hit me hard just now. He has seen trouble and I honor him for it. Know what I would have done? Shot that fellow. If we are taught to die for love we ought to kill for it." He lay back upon his pillow and after a moment's reflection, broke into a tittering laugh.

"I wonder," said he, "if Uncle Clem would cheat that preacher. But of course he would, since there is no such thing as cheating in a horse trade—By a self-soothing turn of argument his conscience legitimizes any advantage he may take over the judgment of his adversary. We'll go out and see the preacher defend himself."

In the trade that followed, if indeed one did take place, the preacher may have lost his eye-teeth for ought I know. I went down stairs that morning with full determination to see the contest, but upon reaching the hall-way, a loud voice, in the dining room, told that something of graver moment had befallen—the return of Dr. Bates. Old Master sat looking at him, and the expression on his face was not one to bespeak a pleasurable emotion. The doctor glanced up as my Young Master entered, and with a broad smile which I could see was pumped up with great effort, he got out of his chair to shake hands. Bob took his hand, though not with any pretense of welcome, said that he was surprised at his quick return, and sat down without another word, the doctor evidently waiting for him to say something more. But he waited in vain, for the young man sat gazing hard at his plate, with his hands in his pockets.

"I am glad to find the weather so delightful," said the doctor. I have just come from a place where icicles were hanging from the eaves."

"I should think that you would be likely to find places too warm," Bob spoke up.

The doctor glanced at him out of the corner of his eye. "Well, that depends," he replied, casting about for something else to say but not finding it upon demand. "Some of us are influenced by one thing and some by another," he added, still skirmishing. "But youth is often too much lacking in judgment to estimate its surroundings—the dangers that lie about, I might say. Talk comes early but sense follows very slowly along." He had evidently found something to please him for he smiled at Old Master, who, without a word, still sat looking at him. "Yes," said Young Master, "sense not being so light of foot has a hard time trying to overtake wordiness and there are cases where it does not succeed."

The doctor gave Bob a mere glance and addressed himself to Old Master. "Since I have been traveling about," said he, "and particularly when I have gone East, I have been compelled to listen to sharp criticisms passed upon Southern society. They say our life is most unnatural, our society, feverish; and they laugh at our intellectual intercourse—say that our conversation is more observant of color than of sense, and that our young men are taught to stride on sophomoric stilts. Of course I was strong in my defense, but I couldn't hide an inward acknowledgement of a part of these strictures. Our young men do attempt to stand off the ground when they talk."

"It makes no difference to me what an envious person may find fit to say," Old Master replied. "We of the South have our way of thinking and talking and are willing to grant that privilege to other men. Why the deuce don't these people come on to breakfast?"

From the rear veranda came the voices of Old Miss, Mr. Clem and the preacher. "Dan," Old Master commanded, "tell them to come on here."

I hastened away, glancing back to see Young Master boring the doctor with a look. Mr. Clem and the preacher were warm in an argument and Old Miss was standing near, supporting the views of the preacher, but was, I could see, persistent with suggesting that they give over the contest and go to breakfast. And when I stepped forward with the announcement that Old Master had sent for them, Mr. Clem said, "All right, soon as I blow out my tobacco," and ducking his head over the "banister," he snorted out his quid and swore that he was as hungry as either of the she-bears that ate up the forty children. The minister would have stayed to rebuke him for this irreverence, but being himself pinched by appetite, gave him merely a look of reproof and struck a trot for the breakfast table.

The doctor had met Old Miss and the two men earlier in the morning. He smiled at Old Miss, nodded at the preacher and addressing Mr. Clem, said that he had ever wanted to meet him. Mr. Clem made no reply until he had spread a napkin upon his knees, and then he said: "Well, sir, you see me now, not quite as good a man as I have been, perhaps, but pretty spry and ready to whet the edge of my judgment against every gritty substance I come across. What do you know about a horse, sir?"

"Not a great deal, although I have owned several racers," the doctor answered. Mr. Clem looked at him, moving back a little so that he could measure him from head to foot. And when the survey was completed to the satisfaction of the surveyor, he blurted forth his estimate: "The case of a man who hasn't improved his time very much, I reckon. But you like a good horse, pretty well, I take it."

"Well, I can't say that I'm more interested in a horse than in anything else."

"You can't? Well, sir, I don't want to throw you off hard enough to bruise you, but I don't reckon you and I can trot together. Good-bye."

"Oh, you are not going away, are you?" the doctor asked. Everyone looked up, even the preacher, who had been exceedingly busy.

"No;" said Mr. Clem, "that is, I'm not going to leave here just now. But as I have decided not to trot with you, I'm gone, so far as you are concerned." And with that he turned from the doctor and I am almost positive that not within my hearing did he ever give him another word. It could not have been that the doctor's indifference toward the horse was the real cause of Mr. Clem's contempt; I am of the opinion that the old fellow had made up his mind not to like him and to tell him so should opportunity offer, and then brought forward the horse as a pretext. I have often speculated over what might have been the result, had the doctor professed an absorbing fondness for the horse. I imagine, though, that Mr. Clem would have tried one thing after another until he had found a vital objection to the man, for as I say, he was resolved not to like him, and I remember that on this very morning, after I had followed my master to his room, Mr. Clem came in with an oath directed at the doctor.

"I don't understand how you get along with him at all, Bob," said he.

"I don't," my young master replied, turning slowly

the leaves of his sheep-bound book. "We have come near having trouble, and, when we do, it will be red trouble, I tell you. He's got some sort of a hold on father, something other than an interest in the estate. I have no idea what it is, but I know it's something. However, I don't believe that the old gentleman will put up with him much longer."

"By the flint-hoofs, I wouldn't stand him a minute," Mr. Clem swore. And then looking at me he asked my opinion of the man. I looked at master.

"Tell him," said he.

"Exactly what I think, Mars. Bob?"

"Yes, say what you please."

This was indeed a rare occasion. I was to have an unfettered say—was to talk as a man. The image of the doctor arose before me; I saw his hateful grin, his eyes full of evil and deceit—and the insults that he had put upon me freshened in my mind. Something in my manner must have foretold the temper of my speech, for they looked at me with an interest that never before had I beheld in an eye bent upon me. "Speak out!" Bob cried, and I found my tongue and found it hot:

"I hate him deeper than any man was ever hated!" I almost shouted, for my first free speech rose high. "He has done all he could to make my life miserable. It burnt his skin to see that I was not sent to the corn-field—bled him to know that I could be fitted for something better; and his enmity passes through me and touches my master. If I could choke his tongue out and see it covered with the vilest dust —if I could see his eyes mashed into the ground—" I hesitated. The flight of freedom held a threat to be too wild, and love for the man who sat staring at me told me to drive it back to mean and humble earth.

"Go ahead," Mr. Clem cried, but master was silent, looking down. "Gentlemen, I am a slave and you are American citizens," said I. "For me, there are no privileges except those granted by individual kindness. The law which I have studied page by page with my Master, scarcely touches me, except so far as I am a piece of property. If I run away, the law that I have studied will follow me and bring me back with hand-cuffs on my wrists. If my master chooses, he can put me on the auctioneer's block and sell me. I—"

"Don't, Dan," Master pleaded, lifting his hand. "Don't draw such a picture as that. You are better off than many a white man; you can think, you have been taught to reason; and you know that I would rather starve than to sell you. I am not responsible for the melancholy fact that you are a slave. You—"

"Who is?" I broke in.

"God," he answered.

"Oh, H—!" Mr. Clem shouted, leaping off the floor. "Bob, I think a great deal of you, would do anything for you—fight for you—but let me beg of you never again to give echo to that sounding rot. The greedcant of a pandering pulpit gives us enough of such answers to flatter the soul. Bob," he said, stepping forward and laying a hand on Master's shoulder, "look at me. You have a heart," he went on, looking into the young man's eyes. "The God you say made this boy a slave, made you an uncommon man. Even as young as you are, you have the brains almost of a philosopher—surely the power and the expression of an orator. You are going to make a deep mark on the page of your country's history. I believe it, I swear I do. Then, why do you care to own a man? Bob, set this boy free."

Master got out of his chair and went to the window before a word of reply came from him; he looked out upon the broad spread of green sward, flooded with sun-light, he turned back toward his uncle and then he said: "I can't. I want him, and he must stay with me. I don't want him so much as a servant as I do as a companion. Other men may be liars, but he tells me the truth. My thoughts are his and I hope that his are mine. At midnight, when the world is still and my mind is in an uproar, I do not struggle alone, but awake him and he steps gladly into the whirl-wind. Uncle Clem, I have a real affection for him, so strong that it is selfish. If I should set him free, he couldn't stay here, and besides, not yet being of age, I cannot give him freedom."

"An argument," said a voice at the door, and looking up, we saw the doctor stand there. No one spoke a word bidding him to enter, but he stepped into the room. "Well," said Mr. Clem, speaking to Master, "I must go."

"Won't you stay longer, Uncle?"

"No, I've got to go down the creek and kill a snake."

"I'll go with you," said master. "Come with us, Dan."

"May I have a few moments with this boy?" the doctor asked, looking at Master and then leering at me.

Mr. Clem had reached the door but he turned back. Master wanted to know of the doctor what business he could have with me, whereupon he said: "Oh, just a little private matter."

"But, sir, Dan keeps none of his affairs private from me."

"Indeed! A very close relationship, I must say."

"Must you? I didn't know that you felt an obligation."

"An obligation? What do you mean by that?"

"Oh, you said you must say, and must moves us to discharge an obligation.

"If a barber were as much given to the splitting of hairs, we'd never be more than half shaved."

"And if the instinct of the wolf prompted bristles to grow continuously, and if no barber cut them off, I could pick out a man whose beard would soon drag the ground."

Mr. Clem laid his hands upon the door-facing and snorted. "What ails you, sir?" the doctor asked, turning toward him, and Mr. Clem, without looking round, said: "Bob, they've got a fish over in Illinois they call the doctor. Hook one of them and you think you've got something, but pull him out and you find he's all bill. Come on and let's go after that snake."

We strode away without another word, the doctor tramping hard down the stairs just behind me. He followed us to the yard, and seeing Old Master standing near the garden gate, sheered off from our course. We strolled along the grass-fringed margin of the creek, and when we came to the rock whereon I had stood, listening to Mr. Clem's persuasive tongue, urging me to run away, the kindness and the life-long protection of my Master arose and smote me, for on that rock I had almost rebelled against him. I did not want to stop when the others halted, but Mr. Clem called me back. "Bob," said he, "I didn't always know the feeling you have for Dan, and it was here, not long ago, that I told him to run away—offered to furnish him money; but with a fidelity that I had forgotten existed among men, he refused."

Bob turned his face from us, but I saw his neck stiffen with resentment. There was something noble in his aspect, his head high, his hat off; and his hair, lying in waves, looked like the leaves of a wreath. But in a moment this was all gone and he looked as if a grief had fallen upon him. "Uncle Clem," said he, turning slowly toward the old man, "I wish you wouldn't give advice against the interest of one who is very near to me. If he were to run away, he would lose confidence in himself and his memory of the sunny days along this stream would but serve as a reproach to him."

"My dear boy," Mr. Clem replied, "if I had intended to give him further advice along the same line, I would not have mentioned it to you—would not have hinted that I had said anything. So, now, as far as that is concerned, you may rest at ease."

"All right, we'll say nothing more about it. Uncle Clem, do you think that I'm stilted in my talk?"

"Why, not any more so than the average boy in this part of the country. You know the Kentuckian is taught to talk with a flourish; it is in keeping with the pretense of his surroundings; he must be gallant with woman and lordly with man. No, you are not particularly stilted, but there is one branch of information that you are stubbornly overlooking—the horse. You have studied the orator, but I want to tell you that the horse has done quite as much to make Kentucky known as the orator. After all, oratory is nothing but talk, while there's action in a horse. And, by the way, who's that riding along the pike? Too far off or I'd yell at him. Good horse; no, little lame in the left hind foot. See, he don't move evenly."

"I can't tell from here," said master.

"Ah, hah, and that goes to prove what I say, that

you haven't given enough study to that important subject. It isn't right for a man to cultivate one lobe of
his mind and neglect the other. Man's mind, you
know, has two lobes—one embracing the horse, and
the other covering the human family and other little
things. I wonder how much longer things are going
to be as dull as they are now. Why, out in Illinois we
had something every day to interest us, up hill and
down, but here everything is on a dead level. There's
not enough ginger in the air."

"But it's full of poetry, Uncle Clem."

"Full of poetry? Well, maybe it is, but you have to
listen too close to hear it."

"Ah, but the sweetest communications come in a
whisper."

"By the hoofs, the boy's in love. Now, you take a
horseman's advice and keep out of it. It's a jolt, leaving you for a time to wonder whether you're hurt or
not, and after a while you find that you are. Yonder
come the General and that doctor. Let's sheer off
this way and go back to the house?"

CHAPTER XVII.

How the coming of one person can change an atmosphere! At one moment the breath we draw is a new and invigorating hope, the next instant the air is parched and dead—we see an evil eye, a hated face. My education was not systematic; I read as a hungry man eats; and, as my learning progressed, I began to give myself up to a speculation upon the sadness of my lot in life, my eyes becoming wider and wider opened to the fact that knowledge could avail me nothing, could but throw a lime-light upon my bondage and make it ghastly; but when the doctor returned I looked back at my state of happiness during his absence. It was true that Old Miss gave over no opportunity to humiliate me, but I had grown so accustomed to this that no longer did it sting me—I put it down as the soured whim of an old woman. But the sight of the doctor, the fact that he and I were under the same roof, was iced water constantly dripping upon my head. I was not physically afraid of him; gladly would I have fought him; in a fight I could have cut his throat and stood looking calmly upon his blood, and thousands of times had I wished that I were a white man, that I might challenge him; but morally I stood in horror of him. I avoided him, slinking about like a thief; I hid myself behind stone walls and in thickets until he had passed, but at the table I was compelled to look upon him and to hear his voice. Once when he spoke to me my Young Master saw me tremble and when we had gone forth together, the young man said to me: "Dan, don't stand behind my chair at meal time any more. It's a piece of nonsense anyway, a notion covered with mold."

I thanked him and told him that I would not, but at supper that evening, Old Mistress flouted so and made such a fuss at my absence that Master came to the foot of the stairs and called me. "It won't be for long," he said as I came down. "I don't believe that fellow can stay here much longer."

But the days wore along and he continued to remain, and though I was skillful in my avoidance of him, yet he sometimes confronted me when I least expected it. One afternoon, during the wheat harvest, I was sent to the distillery to get whisky to be served to the hands. Just as the distiller had handed me the full jug, the doctor stepped out and in apparent surprise asked me what I wanted there. I told him that Old Master had sent me for whisky.

"I believe you are lying," said he, "but take it and go, and don't fool along the road, either. Do you hear?"

I told him that I had no intention of fooling along the road. "That yellow rascal is petted until his fingers and toes stick out," said he to the distiller. "I wanted to take him and make something of him, but they wouldn't let me. But I'll get him yet."

"He'd be worth fifteen hundred if he was a little pearter," said the distiller, looking at me as I moved off.

"Yes," the doctor agreed, "and an apple tree sprout well laid on would add many a dollar to his worth."

I walked as rapidly as I could, but the doctor being on horseback soon overtook me. I wondered what new insult was fermenting in his mind. I had not long to wait. "Boy," said he, riding up, "are you sure you haven't swigged some of that liquor?"

"I have not touched it," I answered without looking up.

"Stop a minute," he commanded and I obeyed. He

looked up and down the road, and then said: "Take
out that corn-cob stopper and drink."

"It is not for me, sir," I replied.

"I don't give a d— whom it's for; you drink it."

I stood near a fence and with one arm resting upon
it as I replied: "You want me to get back drunk to
bring disgrace upon my Young Master and myself."

He kicked his horse and rode almost upon me. His
eyes were green with hate and had he thrust forth a
forked tongue like a serpent, I could not have felt surprise. He stood in his stirrups and lifted high his
riding whip. "You yellow ooze of the devil, I'll make
you drink that liquor or I'll slit your hide until it won't
hold feathers." His lips were apart, his teeth were set
and his brows were knit with the force that he summoned to his arm. Within a second this stinging blow
must fall, but I commanded him in so sharp a tone to
hold that his arm came down slowly and his whip hung
at his side. "Do you threaten me!" he hissed, thrusting his chin forward. Year after year he had eluded
the notice of age, had escaped, it seemed to me, without enumeration, but now the time he had cheated
came full upon him, wrinkling his face, yellowing his
countenance and making him hideous. He was so
close upon me, leaning forward with his sharp chin

pointed at my heart, that I could smell the fumes of
brandy on his breath. He gazed hard, trying, I could
see, to hold my attention, but I noticed that his hands
were not idle. He changed his whip to his left hand
and with his right plucked out a keen knife. I was in
a corner of the fence and the horse's breast was almost
against me. And thus he was poised like a fierce animal, waiting for my reply, hoping that it would not be
one of submission. I was not frightened, but reason
flew through my mind like a bird caught by a strong
wind. To defend myself meant the gallows.

"Doctor," said I, "you have no cause to seek my
life. You are a white man and I am what you are
pleased to call a negro. In the court-house your mere
word would be a law against my oath. You have
every moral as well as, at present, every physical
advantage. You are a man of education and are
closely connected with one of the best families in this
proud State, and now what prompts you to tread upon
me?"

My coolness drove him mad. He kicked his horse
and jammed me into the corner of the fence. For a
second his knife gleamed like the belly of a snake
circling in the air. I threw up the jug, caught the
knife and the broken blade fell to the ground—I

seized the horse in the nostrils, as I had seen Mr. Clem grasp "the devil," wrenched him until he fell upon his knees, caught up the jug which I had let fall at my feet, threw it over into the soft clover and with a spring followed it. The enraged man's oaths ripped like a saw striking a knot.

"I'll get you yet," he cried, shaking the knife-handle at me.

"You will feel better when you are sober," I said, smiling at him. I could have sliced his heart and therefore I smiled—at the happy thought. "And I want to tell you one thing. I may be hanged one mile from the court-house, but this is the last time I am going to run from you." I turned to go, but he called me. "You have threatened me," he said, not raging, but with more of quiet than I could have expected, "and on my part it would be justice to take a gun and shoot you, but if you will agree to say nothing about this affair when you go to the house, I will swear never again to molest you. The truth is I've been drinking and am not myself."

"I looked at it in another light, sir. I thought that the drink had given your true self a bold development."

"God, but you can talk, you yellow—but I say, Dan,

I mean what I say. Agree not to mention this affair and I'll always treat you civilly. I've had enough to spoil the temper of any man alive, but I'll hold it down so far as you are concerned. What do you say?"

"I agree, sir."

"All right. Now give me a drink out of that jug and I'll call it square."

"No, this liquor is not for you; it is for the harvest hands; it isn't up to your grade."

"Consideration or impudence, one of the other—but I'll let it pass. All right, now," he added, tightening his bridle-rein to ride away, "remember your part of the contract and I'll remember mine."

Old Jason, at the head of the men in the field, censured me for passing so much time on the road, and old Steve, humorous rascal, gave a broad grin as he looked upon the whisky and swore that he didn't think that I had passed anything on the road; that everything had passed me. Old Master came walking up to the clump of alder bushes under which a number of the hands had gathered to "blow" in the shade, and after making a pretense of drinking with them, told me to walk to the house with him. With what envy the black men regarded me as I strode off beside the man who held their destiny in the hollow of his hand!

Looking back I could see many a dark frown. Among the blacks the "yaller man" was never a favorite. An attempt to be refined and especially a smattering of learning invoked contempt from the sturdy yeoman of the negro quarter.

"They are not so mighty fond of you," said Old Master as we walked along. His old eyes had caught the expression of their disfavor.

"No, sir, and I am sorry, for I would give much for their good opinion."

"I'm glad to hear you say that, my boy. It is a true proof of a gentlemanly instinct. The coarse-grained man holds himself above the opinion of those far below him, but a gentleman would value the good will of a dog. By the way, have you seen the doctor to-day?"

"I think, sir, that I saw him in the road as I was coming from the distillery."

It was some time before he spoke again, walking along with his gaze bent upon the ground. "Dan"— and he looked up at me, "do you remember the time you threw the tumbler on his head?"

"As well as if it were but an hour ago," I answered.

"If you had seen him this morning you would have felt like striking him a harder blow," he said. "We had a quarrel and my old blood was so stirred that I was almost tempted to cut his throat. He made a demand on me for more money than I could really afford to give—the scoundrel, I have given him already far more than his share—and was insulting when I refused him. Your Mistress has been brought to see him in his true light and I have her consent to drive him away and I'll do it. He calmed down and apologized, but I told him that he must leave within a day or two, and he'll have to. I can't stand him any longer."

"Master, I don't see how you could have stood him so long."

"It was to keep the neighbors from talking," he replied. "Differently situated, I would have kicked him into the road long ago. He is the strangest man I ever met. He's bright, and at times he appears the perfect gentleman and is exceedingly interesting, but in a moment his nature seems changed. We were at the barn this morning when his insulting mood came on, and I looked up at a scythe hanging there and was sorely tempted to mow off his head. But that would never do."

We were walking along a fence bordering the turn-pike. Someone in a buggy called the old man and I

went onward to the house, with a regret that I had
been so long away from my law book. We had given
to our room the name of office, for Young Master had
already begun to recite his lessons to a retired judge
who almost daily dismounted from his horse to give
us the benefit of his learning. In the office I found
Bob and Mr. Clem.

"Why don't you go in with some lawyer in town and
be done with it?" Mr. Clem was saying as I entered the
room. "You are not quite old enough yet to reach the
bar, but you've got about all the law you could get at
school, and about all that remains now is to pick up the
details of practice."

"Yes, I know," said Bob, "but when a young man
goes into an old lawyer's office he is expected to do all
the work, take none of the glory and receive but little
of the pay. We'll hang on here a while longer, won't
we, Dan?" He looked up at me with a smile.

"Yes, sir; and when we go, we'll go strong."

"Dan is to be my silent partner," he said, nodding at
his uncle.

The old fellow jerked his shoulders as he replied:
"Yes, sir, and he'd better be pretty devilish silent at
that, I tell you. The leaves from so many abolition
pamphlets are fluttering in the air that anything with

the appearance of granting the negro more of equality with the white man will be resented in no uncertain way. But I'm glad to hear that Dan is to be your partner and I advise you to keep it strictly to yourselves. Heigh ho." He leaned back with a stretch. "This country is slower than tar in January. Haven't seen but two horses—horses that I'd have, you understand—go over the pike to-day. And that's rather discouraging for a man who insists on paying his way. Only two horses, and I didn't get but one of them." I thought to ask him concerning the outcome of his contest with the preacher, but he continued to talk, and I never thought of it again. Billows came to swallow the little waves.

"Yes, sir, only two horses that I would have, and yet this is the State of Kentucky, where Clay lived and died. Two horses, mind you, and I didn't get but one of them. Fellow didn't want to swap; said he was in a hurry. Might as well have said that he didn't want to live because he was in a hurry. But I got him to stop, and then I brought out the bay mare that I got the other day. She had her Sunday clothes on and I could see that she caught his eye. He got down and looked at her feet and then gathered up the skin on her shoulders; said he thought it was a little too tight. I told him that there wasn't anything loose about her; that the contract only called for enough skin to cover her. Well, we swapped, and I got twenty-eight dollars to boot, all he had. Would have got more, but he didn't have it. He was a sad sort of fellow and I didn't want to take advantage of him, without giving him some sort of a show, so I told him that he'd better not take my word for anything. But he did."

"Wasn't your mare all right?" Bob inquired.

"Oh, yes, in a measure—bad measure, I might say. She had been galloped down-hill on the pike until her shoulders were sorter stove up, and that's what made the skin too tight, and her wind ain't of the best, but she's good enough for him. I took his horse to town —just got back—and got a first rate price for him on the public square."

After a time Mr. Clem lay down and fell asleep, and I took up a book to keep the silent company of Young Master, and I read page after page without being able to grasp a single idea. How hopeless everything was determined to appear. Abetted by the kindest of men I had stolen into the field of thought, was preparing to become an out-lawed advocate of the law, a sneak-thief behind the bar. A silent partner, indeed, a mys-

terious counsellor, a dumb orator.   As supper-time
drew near, I shuddered at the prospect of meeting the
doctor's eye.   Would he keep his contract with me?
An easy matter if what Old Master said was true.
But I feared that the old gentleman would weaken
when the time came for him to be strong.   And should
that man be permitted to remain, I believed that he
would murder me.   Ought I to keep my word with a
wolf?   I asked myself time and again; and more than
once I was on the point of breaking it, but a sense of
honor held me back.   Why should I feel the fetters of
honor chaffing me?   I looked up to meet Young Master's eyes.   Ah, they, so full of soul and fire, were an
inspiration to my struggling manliness.   And his affection, though given under cover of dark secrecy, was
the most blessed reward I could receive on earth.

In the dining room I waited, standing behind Young
Master's chair, looking across at Mr. Clem—waited for
the doctor but he did not come.   Every sound without
gave me a sickening stir, a chicken on the rear veranda, a dog trotting through the hall, the wind-stirred
fox-horn tapping against a post just beyond the door.
But the man did not come.

CHAPTER XVIII.

My nerves were so wrought upon by the continuous dread of the doctor's coming that by the time the meal was over I was almost in a state of collapse. Young Master's eye noticed my indisposition, and as we turned about in the hall to mount the stairs, he said to me:

"Slip out, Dan, and take a walk in the fresh air, alone. You don't look well." I thanked him and halted, and he passed on without inquiring into the cause of what he must have seen was a pitiable dejection. A thousand well-sifted words could not have shown the delicacy of his nature more fittingly, and my gratitude followed him step by step as he went up the stairs; and when he had reached the landing I stole out of the house.

The brown veil of dusk lay upon the land, but in a hill-side thicket far away a light was shimmering to illumine the early evening festival of the gray fox—the moon was coming up. The air was still and soft, but heavy with the sappy scent from the damp grass land down the creek. On the comb of a cabin, grotesquely outlined in this dun-colored close of day, sat a negro blowing a melancholy reed, and high above him the bull-bats were screaming. In the shrubbery a hord of negro children were playing a counting-out game. I passed the cow-pens; the women were there and I heard the stream of milk spurting hard in the "piggin." My spirits rose out of their nervous lassitude; I felt a strong and almost unnatural sense of exhilaration, and this alarmed me, for we are sometimes afraid to feel an unaccountable buoyancy lest it may foretell a coming fall. I have known Christians who had prayed for sanctity in the sight of the Lord, to tremble at happiness, afraid that it might be a trap set by the devil. I skirted the shore of the creek, crossed the meadow, passed through the woods, entered the grassy lane and stood there with my arms on the fence, looking at the full moon, now high above the trees. And I thought that the foxes must have given over their dancing to scatter about for a night of mischievous prowling. I was on a knoll, and turning about I could see the lights in the cabins and the great house, a hen and her chickens squatted upon the ground, I fancied. The strongest light came from my Young Master's room, and in my mind I could see him sitting at the table with his eyes fastened upon his sheep-bound book. And the self-reproach of an ambitious thought that I was not keeping up with him started me homeward at a bound. But I had not gone far before I was stopped by a voice. A man stepped from the corner of the zig-zag fence. "Hold on!" he said, and the doctor stood before me. The moon was on his face and in the coarse lines that traced his countenance the devil's mockery was legible.

"Where are you going?" he asked, standing with his hands behind him.

"Home," I answered.

"Home!" he repeated, and vitriol was in his voice. "Is there a home for everyone but me?" He threw his head back as if motioning toward the house. "Can you go back there and sleep on a bed when I am told never to cross that threshold again? Can you?"

"I don't know what you mean, doctor?"

"I have been driven away this night. The old man has turned me out."

"But am I to blame? I am the humblest member of that household."

He did not change his attitude, but I thought that I saw his bosom swelling. "The humblest because you are the lowest down, but a snake is low down," he said, thrusting his chin toward me. "Look here, spawn. The first step you took put you in my way. Do you hear me?"

"Yes, sir, and I am much surprised to hear you say it. I didn't think you would acknowledge that I had so much force. We have not been friends, it is true, but I thought that my position kept us from being enemies. To be enemies must argue a certain degree of equality, and I have never presumed upon that. You may have stooped. And now let me beg you to straighten up and forget that I ever existed."

"I will forget that you have existed, and I will straighten up, but not until I have stooped lower. Look here. I hate the fool boy that owns you, and if I could kill him this moment, I would. I am getting old and there is nothing left for me. But I want revenge and I am going to have it, for I am going to be sensible. I never was a fool."

"Doctor, I don't understand your meaning."

"You are duller than usual. If I were to kill your master or that old imbecile, this whole county would follow me, but if I kill a yellow dog, they—" He leered at me, the moon full on his face. A chill seized

my legs and ran to the top of my head and the roots
of my hair felt cold.

"You mean that you will kill me?"

"That's what I mean. They drove me to brandy and
brandy has pointed you out."

I was perfectly calm; the chill had left me. "Will
you please let me pass?" I asked; and he stepped back,
still with his hands behind him. "No," he said.

"Have you forgotten our contract?"

"You are a fool if you put faith in it. You are not
negro enough to be put by with a kick. You are white
man enough to be killed. And when they find you in
the morning they will think that your little learning
drove you mad."

This startled me. I believed that they would think
so, if they should find me dead, but no obedience to a
social law and surely no regard for the statutes could
force me to submit quietly to the bloody purpose of
this raving man.

"Doctor, I have run from you for the last time. Get
out of my way!" I stepped aside, but he moved
toward me. Now his hands were in front of him and
I saw a knife. I had nothing. I could have turned
and run away; I could have leaped over the fence, but
hot blood was coursing where the chill had crept.

"I am going home," said I, "and I am going down this lane."

He made no reply, but with a leap and a strike he was upon me. I caught the wrist of his right arm; I threw my left arm about him. I thought that I heard his bones cracking and it gave me a thrill of mad delight. I did not strive to get his knife. I bent his head down till his cry was but a mutter; his right hand was crushed against his bosom—and I threw him upon the ground. He struggled, with one faint cry, for his face was in the grass, and I put my foot on his back to hold him down, to complete my victory over him. And I am free to confess that my soul was full of a joy that almost burnt me, it was so hot. Many a time had he stood with his foot upon my trembling heart, and the memory of those long years of humiliation swept over me and I lifted my hands and cried aloud to the God of vengeance. I looked down at my foe under my foot. And now he was so mean and shrunken that my heart flinched with a pity that pricked it. I lifted my foot with a quick jerk lest another memory might press it down the harder, and stood waiting for him to get up. He did not move. "Get up," I said, taking him by the shoulder. But he made no effort. Then I turned him upon his back and the moonlight fell upon his blood, and horrified, I looked at him, his eyes wide open, his teeth hard set with grass between them. His right hand was still upon his left breast, clutching the knife, and its blade was buried in his heart.

I dropped upon my knees, and gazed at him, now so old and wrinkled. I leaped to my feet and the air whistled in my ears as I bounded down the lane. I was struggling to run away from the knowledge that I had killed him, but it kept up with me—showed me a jail and a gallows. I halted when near the house, put my arm about a tree and stood there. The negro cabins were dark, but a light burned in Young Master's room. The hour was late. The creek was louder than I had ever heard it, a mockery, not a music. A wind had sprung up and in the tree-tops there was a cold and rasping whisper. I was striving to reach a decision as to what course I should pursue. Undoubtedly I had killed the man or had thrown him so that he might kill himself, but of this I had entertained no thought at the time, my aim being to protect myself and to humiliate him, to show him that I could turn and be his master. But I could not explain this to the authorities, therefore I held no notion of giving myself up. To run away were an acknowledgement of guilt, a brief inquiry and the rope. I could make a flat denial, if accused, but was afraid that I could not summon the nerve to maintain it. Still something must be done. I might go to Mr. Clem, tell him the truth, get letters from him to persons in the real land of the free and with his financial aid make my escape out of the country. But this was blocked by the love I bore my Young Master. I went to the well and washed my hands, although I could find no blood on them, and the windlass was so loud with its groaning that I fancied the whole world must hear it. A dog came up, sniffed at me and trotted off. Life had been stirred until I had found the sugar at the bottom. I must save myself, but I could not run away without telling my Master, without asking his advice. I would go to him. Up the stairway I stole without a noise. I was afraid that I might find Old Master pacing the hall, and I listened to hear his slippered feet, but all was still. I turned the knob so gently that Young Master did not hear me when I entered the room. He sat gazing at his book. I spoke and he started.

"Why do you come slipping in this way, Dan? You startled me. What were you doing so long? What the devil is the matter with you, boy?"

I caught at the edge of the table, dropped upon my knees and told him my story. I do not know what his face might have shown, for my eyes were cast down, I don't know what he felt, but I do know that not a sound escaped him. I got up at the end and looked at him, and his face was pale and hard.

"Lie down," he said, pointing to my lounge.

"To be pulled up by the sheriff?" I cried.

"Lie down and ask no questions, and stay there until I call for you. If anyone comes in, you are too ill to get up. Do you hear me? This is not a request; it is a command. D— you, will you do it?" he cried, stamping the floor. "You belong to me. Do as I tell you. Take off your clothes. If father asks for me, tell him I went away early in the evening. Don't say a word."

I took off my clothes, with the tears falling on my trembling hands. He watched me until I was in bed and then he put the light out. I heard the door close— heard him going down the stairs.

CHAPTER XIX.

Would day-light never come was a speculation that
lay upon my mind until it seemed to gather mold, like
a rag in a damp cellar. But why should I long for the
sun to rise to pour light upon the blood in the lane?
And to myself I said that it would be better for me if
darkness should remain forever upon the earth. But
the hours were so tiresome and the world was so
reproachfully still. I had thought that my reading had
led me away from the superstitions of my negro
ancestors; long ago I had thrown away the lucky bone
taken from the head of a cat-fish; I had ceased to make
a cross mark in the road and spit in it whenever I
found that I had forgotten something and was forced
to turn back; I did not believe that the hanging of a
dead snake across the fence, belly up, would make it
rain; I had laughed at old Steve when he told me that
a horse's tooth, ground to powder and carried sewed
up in a sack, would prevail against the tricks of the
conjurer. But now I believed in it all and trembled at
the awful consequences that a renegade scorn might

call upon me. With a cold sweat I remembered the
words of a black hag who lived in a hovel at the edge
of the town. On an occasion, not more than a month
gone-by, she had taken offense at what she termed my
uppishness; she crossed her crutches in front of me,
cut a mysterious diagram in the air and swore that
before the moon changed twice I should fall a victim
to a blighting calamity. The moon had not changed
twice and the calamity had fallen. I got up to look at
the moon, to search for a confirming mark upon it,
but through the windless night, dark clouds had
floated and the sky was black. At the window I sat
and gazed into the darkness toward the lane. A wind
sprang up and was hoarse in the tree-tops. Rain
would come and wash the blood away, but the body
and the crying wound would be there at the coming of
day. I wondered whither my Young Master could have
gone and why he should have left me. Was it that he
had gone thus early to the authorities to beg for my
life? That were useless. Law and society must have
my blood. On my side a ton of justice would be but
a thistledown, blown by a baby's breath. And I gazed
from the window toward the lane. Day-light could
not be far away; it had already fallen upon the hill-
tops, I thought. Yes, the far-off sky was turning gray;

but nearer it was black with clouds. Strange that a storm should be gathering just at this time. The lighter it grew the nearer the clouds came. They split, one in the form of a great bird, sailing away; the other was a horse galloping madly, with a ribbon, a bridle-rein of lightning, flashing at its throat. The household was stirring. I heard Old Master go down the stairs; I heard old Steve calling the hogs. There was not to be a storm. The clouds were gone and the air was sultry. The horn was blown to call the negroes to breakfast. I heard horses galloping over the turn-pike. But the body in the lane had not been found. God, I could see it, lying near the fence! I heard someone coming and I crept back to bed and covered myself. Mr. Clem entered the room.

"You boys going to sleep all day?" he asked. "But Bob's gone; where is he? Why, he hasn't been to bed. Didn't he stay here last night?"

"No, sir; he went away early on business."

"But what's the matter with you this morning? You look sick."

"I am, sir. I don't believe I am able to get up."

"I'd better send for a doctor. Why, you've got a chill."

"Don't send for a doctor," I pleaded. "Don't send for anyone; let me lie here alone."

"Well, I'm sorry you're sick," he said, turning about. "Want anything to eat?"

"No, sir. I just want to lie here until Young Master comes."

For a time he stood looking hard at me, with his hand on the door. "Hear of the row last night?" he asked. I feigned surprise and said that I had not, whereupon he continued:

"The Old General finally summoned the requisite nerve and drove the doctor off. I wasn't very close, but I heard all that passed. The doctor pleaded and started to threaten and then the old man roared. 'If you are anywhere in this neighborhood by morning,' said he, 'I will take a shot gun to you, I don't care what the public says or how close its investigation may be.' The doctor moved on off and I followed along, to see what he intended to do when the old man's back was turned, and once I got close enough to hear his mutterings and to understand him to say, 'I'll let the old fool go, but somebody will die before morning.' Just then the General called me and I went back. I don't know who the doctor intended to kill, didn't know but it might be Bob, and

I would have come in last night to tell him—saw him going up the stairs—but Bill Mason came over and said that he wanted to beat me out of a horse or two, and so I went over to his place and haggled with him nearly all night. Man of considerable worth, Mason is. Has kept his eyes pretty well open while other people have been dreaming, but he napped a trifle and I came off some time before day with two better horses than I took with me and a pretty fair roll of money. I told Bob, you remember, that I never would say anything more to you about running away, and I won't. But somehow I think that justice ought to be stronger than friendship or even blood relationship. Still, I'll keep my word with him and not advise you to run away. I tell you what I'm going to do, though. I'm going to throw this roll of money over there on the bed, and if it's not there when I come back, and if you are gone by to-night—but I promised Bob."

He threw a roll of bank notes on the bed and almost trotted in his haste to get down the stairs. I got up and walked about the room, not daring to look at the money, but my mind was not so obedient as my eyes. The means of possible escape lay there within my reach. Could any human being blame me for struggling to save my life? I went to the window and

looked out and drew back with a shudder. The body
had been found. Several persons were standing about
it, and along the lane there walked a number of men,
my young master in the midst of them and among
them I recognized the coroner of the county. They
were going to hold the inquest. I saw Old Master
and Mr. Clem walking hard to overtake them. Now
was my time. I jumped into my clothes, wondering
that no one had called me to see the dead man; I
clapped my hat upon my head—and seized the money.
I ran to the door, but to save my life I could not cross
the threshold. I stood there gasping, with that old
woman's crutches crossed before me. I threw the
money upon the bed and my love for my master arose
strong and overpowering in my heart, and with the
tears streaming from my eyes I bounded down the
stairs, out into the yard, over the fence, and tore down
the lane toward the spot where the body lay under the
stern eye of the law. I caught up with Old Master
and Mr. Clem just as they reached the place—I ran to
Young Master, and he turned upon me with a frown.
"Don't interrupt me," he cried, waving his hand. "I
know your devotion to me, but I demand silence.
Gentlemen," he said, addressing the coroner and the
jury, "I don't intend to make myself out altogether

blameless, but I was forced to kill him. I was unarmed and it was his own knife that shed his blood." And then, while I stood there gaping, he gave in minutest detail an account of the strike, the struggle and the fall. I looked at Old Master as he stood there bent forward, staring; at Mr. Clem as he gazed upon the young man who had stepped in between me and the hangman, but my jaws were locked wide open and I could not speak.

"Gentlemen," said Mr. Clem, "I demand to be sworn." He held up his hand, muttered the oath and then proceeded with his testimony.

"Last night I heard the doctor say he would kill him. He said that he would let the old man go, meaning my brother, but that someone would die before day, and I know that he meant Bob. It has been well known among us that bad blood existed between them. I—"

Suddenly I leaped forward, struck upon the head, I fancied, by the crutches of the old woman, and with a cry I fell upon my knees. "My master did not kill him;" I groaned in agony. "I killed him. Listen to me and then you may hang me. I—"

Bob sprang at me and clapped his hand over my mouth. "Gentlemen," he said, "this poor, devoted boy

would save my life—it's his way of repaying a life-long
kindness. Pay no attention to him, but let us attend
to the demands of justice. I killed this man, I have
told you why and how. And I am ready to take the
consequences. Come here, Dan." He jerked me to
my feet and led me off. "Dispute me another time,"
he said, "and before God I will cut your throat. Now
go to the house or I'll take a stick and beat you every
step of the way."

I was almost bereft of my senses as I walked toward
the house. I met Old Miss with a troop of negroes
behind her. She was wringing her hands and the
negroes were crooning a low chant. Some one bade
me stop, but I hastened on, through the yard, up to the
room; and the sight of the money lying there on the
bed, the thought that I had clutched it to run away
from the noblest man that ever breathed, drove me
mad; and I fell upon the lounge and the world was
black.

When I opened my eyes to the light, I was
undressed between the sheets and a cloth was bound
about my head. Someone was talking. I looked up
and saw a physician just taking his leave. Bob stood
at the window. I raised myself up and he hastened
to me.

"Don't get up, Dan," he said.

"Yes, I am all right now." But I was not all right. I was so weak that I could scarcely sit up in bed.

"What time is it?" I asked.

"Oh, about ten," he answered, smiling. "And I'm devilish glad to see that you've come out all right. We thought at one time that you were gone. You raved all day yesterday."

"Yesterday! No, we were deep in our books yesterday."

"Dan, you have been in bed a week."

"Is it possible?" I cried, and then I looked at him. He read the inquiry that was in my mind. "The coroner's jury discharged me," he said. "And not a vestige of blame clings to me. The neighbors all have come to give me their hands. Now if you are going to cry like a fool, I won't tell you about it. There, I didn't mean to be harsh. It's all right. They said that I couldn't have done otherwise, and no regret is expressed. Why, it has made quite a hero out of you. Fame whirls her cloak in the air and we never know how soon it is going to fall. Don't look at me that way. Oh, yes, you may take my hand if you want to. There, now, don't blubber. Why, don't you know they would have hanged you long before this time? But we won't talk about that. We didn't bury him in the garden," he went on after a slight pause, "but in the grave-yard on the other side of town. We agreed, mother with the rest of us, that he must not lie beside my sister. It may seem strange to you, but the household appears happier. Father's mind has thrown off a load. And Uncle Clem has been so stimulated that he has filled the stable with horses. He's preparing to drive them to market. Don't be in a hurry about getting up. Just take your time. And I'll go down and have them send you something to eat."

CHAPTER XX.

News came that a minister had preached a sermon upon my devotion to my master and exhorted his hearers to be thus faithful unto their Master, the Lord. This was brought to me by none other than Old Miss herself. I was able to sit with a book upon my lap, and out of respect for her prejudice, I put the volume down as she entered the room, but she bade me keep it. And when she had told me what the preacher said, she added: "You may read all the books you like, for we know now that you cannot be poisoned by them. It was noble of you, Dan."

"Please don't talk that way," I pleaded, my heart smiting me.

"Yes, I will. You tried to throw yourself into my son's place to save him, and I can't say too much in your favor. And you will reap your reward when the time comes. 'Well done, thou good and faithful servant,' can be said of you."

Old Master came in while she was sitting there. He appeared to be pleased with the attention she showed me, or his pleasure might have proceeded from his discovery that her temper was improved. "You'll be all right now pretty soon," he said. "I don't believe that I'd read too much. It isn't well to strain your mind. Has your young master told you that he is preparing himself for examination? He is nearly ready, and will be by the time court meets next week. He's afraid that he won't get through without a bobble, but I think he'll go through like a flash. He has decided to enter old Judge Bruce's office. The old fellow doesn't know much but he is a good palaverer and has a pretty fair practice. He never was a real judge, you know—was a candidate once and came off with the title but missed the office."

As Old Master became warmer toward me, Old Miss grew cooler; her countenance while she talked had been kindly, but now it was veiled with a frown. The prospect of seeing Young Master established as a lawyer lifted my spirits, but the sight of his mother's displeasure toward me threw them down. Old Master observed the change in the atmosphere. "Madam," said he, "I have been thinking that we need a new carpet for the parlor."

"Indeed," she replied, bowing with a mocking grace, "I am delighted to credit your eye-sight with a sudden improvement. I have spoken of the condition of that carpet until I am tired of it. It's the talk of the neighborhood, I'm sure. Mrs. Ramsey turned up her nose at it the other day, and I couldn't help thinking that it was a pretty pass indeed to be humiliated in my own house by such a thing as she is. And it was no longer ago than last fall that her husband had to sell an old negro woman that had been in the family all her life."

"Huh," grunted the old man, winking slyly at me. "Did she turn up her nose very high?" He grabbed out a red handkerchief, snorted into it and sat looking at her with the water of an old mischief standing in his eyes.

"General, don't laugh at me. I am the last person in this world that you should laugh at. Don't you do it!"

"But, madam, you are the first person I should laugh with."

"I don't see how you can laugh at anybody after what we have gone through with lately, blood spattered on our door-sill; but I actually believe that you have been gayer since that awful event." With that remark she flounced out of the room, and the old man sat there, looking out into the blue space of the speck-

less day, silent and absorbed. After a time he turned
his old eyes slowly upon me.

"The youth whose promise in life embraces the
prospect of a broad scope should be taught that at the
end of it all—this alluring rain-bow—lies disappointment. Sometimes when I have seen my men in the
field, with no thought of the morrow and with never
a worry except some trifling physical ill, I have wished
that I was one of them. I started out wrong," he went
on, shaking his head slowly up and down. "Horses
can be called back from a false spurt in the race, and
another start taken, but men must go on. Dan, I have
stood by and seen you trying to educate yourself, and
I have said nothing, although I know that education
is often the sensitizing of a nerve that leads to misery.
To be a gentleman means to possess a large ability to
feel, and to feel is to worry, to brood and to suffer.
Men of the North and gentlemen of the South, the
phrase has gone forth. Our old Virginia blood is
gentle, in society; but alone, it is hot with the lingering
fire of the cavalier. Do you know what I am saying?"
he asked, deepening the wrinkles in his brow.

"No, sir; I don't know that I do."

"I suppose not. I have been beating the devil
around an oratorical stump, sir," he said, his scrawny,

red neck stiffening. "I don't know that I understand myself. Is that Bob or Clem coming up the stairs? It's Bob. Glad to see you doing so well," he added, getting up. And standing for a moment, he put his hand on my head. "You are a noble fellow, even if you are a slave and a negro."

Going out he met Young Master coming in. The young man saluted; the old man gave him a smile and a kindly nod and passed on. Bob spoke to me; said he was glad to see me improving so fast; he sat down and took up his book. He opened it at random, knowing it so well that any place offered an understandable beginning, but he did not read. He turned his eyes toward me and said: "You remember that about two months ago a gentleman named Potter bought the old Jamison place, over on the pike? Mother and I called on the family. And since then I have been over there a number of times, though I have said nothing about it to even you. All my life I have been gazing about to discover a sweet secret, and I think I've found one. Yes—and her name is Jane." At this he laughed, threw down his book, shoved his chair back and put his feet on the table. "The name is well enough, no doubt, but in this part of the country we usually associate it with a black wench, you know; and I was impudent

enough to ask Mrs. Potter why she didn't call her
Jenny, but she shut me up with, 'she was named for
my mother and it is an honorable name, I'm sure.'
And it is, too—it takes on bright colors as I associate
it with her.   But I never thought that I could be
smitten with a girl named Jane.   It struck me that
they had nick-named a rose—said scat to a lily.   Do
you know what she did?   Came over here to see you.
Said she wanted to see a hero.   I brought her up and
she looked upon you as you lay here unconscious.   As
a usual thing, a boy is born in love—falls in love with
his nurse if no one else is handy—but I have escaped
pretty well.   Oh, I did rather love the Webster girl,
and I confess to breathing hard whenever Miss Flem-
ming, the old maid school-teacher, came about; but
I'm sure I never was knocked senseless with a per-
fumed slung-shot until I met Jane.   Well, the name's
all right; is like the finest music—takes you some time
to discover its beauties.   I told her that I was going
to be a lawyer and she said that was charming;
declared that she was coming to hear my first speech.
I wish she would; I could shame Demosthenes."

Not since he was a small boy had I heard him rattle
on so, and it was a delight to me.   Of late his over-
manishness and his abstraction had told of too deep an

absorption in his books, of an impatient ambition gnawing him, and this chaffy talk and the idle light of his countenance relieved a fear that had crept into my mind.

"There is something more than beauty about her," he went on, taking pleasure in the interest I was showing. "She reminds Uncle Clem of a blooded horse, he says. I was inclined to take exceptions at this, but remembered that it was but an expression of real enthusiasm. She steps like a fawn, springs off the turf before she appears to have touched it. My first feeling toward her was one of gladness. I was selfish enough to believe, or to fancy that I believed, she had been created to delight me. And when I removed my eyes from her, I felt sad. Her eyes laughed at me and her lips seemed to say, I have found a fool. At the gate she had jumped off a horse and was in a riding habit when she came running into the room. She was in no wise embarrassed by me. After a while she said that she was hungry and I was startled. I could not conceive of that creature sitting down to vulgar bread, and I was stupid enough to say that I didn't see how she existed in the winter, with the roses all gone. I knew she must eat roses. And she smote me hard by replying that cabbages came on about the time roses gave out. This tickeled her mother immensely and she shook her fat sides and fanned herself with the wing of a guinea hen. I am getting all my visits mixed, perhaps, but I am giving you a collection of impressions. The mother is ignorant and the father is coarse. He made money driving mules to New Orleans and bought the Jamison farm. Yes, her mother and father are plebeian, but the girl is a patrician of the rarest type. She told me that she had just come from school. I asked her if she were sure she had not just come from a gallery of famous portraits. This tickeled her and my blood danced in rhythm with her laugh. Every line of my prose, law, oratory, turned up crackling like drying leaves and was blown away, but all the poetry I had read remained, blooming anew. Now you know how bad off I am, and you may congratulate yourself that you can't follow me into this new domain. Oh, what is so delicious as a fool's love affair! But I wonder if she's going to have fun with me and then tell me to go. No, sir, I'm going to win her love if actions, words and devotion count for anything. Dan, she has given me new blood. Good thing that something has happened, for this quiet, expectant life is almost unbearable."

"What's that?" cried Mr. Clem, stepping into the room. "Quiet life, do I hear? Well, it won't always be this quiet, my son. Lincoln will be nominated for the presidency as sure as you live, and the chances are that he'll get in, and then what? War, my boy; red-whiskered war. The South is as sore as a stone-bruise and won't accept an abolitionist. Our high aristocrats have been hankering a long time for a fight and they are going to get it."

"Let it come," replied Young Master, shoving his hands into his pockets. "It will be a tournament, music, smiles and flowers. Then we'll all eat out of the same bowl."

"Don't you fool yourself!" the old man exclaimed, and I saw that he was deeply in earnest. "It won't be a tournament. It will look more like a butcher's pen."

"But the blood-letting will be good for our swollen pride. It will give us all a chance to strut like a turkey gobbler, and, Uncle Clem, it will bring up the price of horses."

"By the hoofs, I hadn't thought of that. I never saw a young fellow improve as fast as you do, Bob. In the last week or so you have said several pretty good things. You are getting the proper grasp on truth; and if a man has truth in one hand it needn't make any difference what the other fellow has in both hands. Yes, sir, if a war should break out, the horse market would hold up its head and snort. But say, Bob, wasn't there a little love mixed up in what you were saying as I came in?"

"Not a little, uncle. All."

"The girl you've been prancing around with lately?"

"Yes, if you wish to put it that way."

"High stepper, Bobbie; trot a mile in—I mean she's all right. Good nostrils—shapely nose, you understand. Laughs well, teeth all sound, and if I were a young fellow, I'd agree to pay her way into every show that might come along, and make a fire for her every morning. Why, Dan, you appear to be tickled nearly to death. I want to tell you that I found that money on the bed where I dropped it. Talk about your heroes of old, why—"

I interrupted him with a sign of real distress. "I must beg of you and of everyone else, Mr. Clem, not to try to make a hero out of me. But there is a hero under this roof—"

"Dan," Young Master broke in, "I have just sharpened my knife and I am almost tempted to cut off your ears. Of what use is an ear when you turn it from heart-felt praise to catch the unsympathetic tones of average life?   And now when anyone starts to compliment you upon your heroism, I command you to keep your ears open and your mouth shut.   You did act the part of a hero.   Shut up, not a word out of you."

Mr. Clem swore with a horsey oath that I was a hero, and I was compelled to sit there and listen to his extravagant praise.

CHAPTER XXI.

I saw Young Master admitted to the bar. The court-house was crowded, for an exciting trial was on, but a kind-hearted bailiff let me take a seat wherein I could hear every question asked by the committee of examiners. I knew that he could answer them, and I felt not the slightest fear, but my heart stood still as he tripped over a point almost absurdly simple. I noticed that he had just cast his eyes toward the gallery, and looking that way at the instant of his petty stumble, I beheld a tall and graceful girl, standing with her head leaning against a post, looking at him, and I knew that his divinity had confused him. But he recovered himself, and I saw Old Master swell with pride and Old Miss wipe her eyes. I was in hopes that they would give him an opportunity to make a speech after the examination, but there was no occasion for his oratory, so I walked out to wait for him at the door. Old Master and Old Miss came out to wait also, not caring to push themselves behind the bar among the lawyers, and indeed too proud to let

the neighbors presume that there had been any anxiety
concerning the result. Presently Young Master came
out with the girl whom I had seen standing in the
gallery. The old people shook hands with her when
they had shaken hands with him, and upon me the
young woman turned her beautiful eyes. "Oh, this is
your faithful boy," she said, speaking to Bob, but looking at me. "I am glad to see him out and looking so
well."

She had ridden a horse, but Young Master requested
the favor of taking her home in his buggy. She
said that such an arrangement would please her
greatly, and her eyes danced with the delight of the
thought. I brought the buggy and was told to sit on
the shelf seat behind to lead her horse. She bade the
old people an affectionate good-bye, and out the turn-
pike we drove, along the stretches of red clover and
underneath majestic trees. In the distance to her
home, three miles or more, there lay a charm, and
they did not suffer the spirited horse to trot. The day
was warm, the leather curtain raised, and I could hear
distinctly the words that passed between them. I
could see that he had not more than hinted at his love
for her. Her beauty dazzled him and made him afraid.
He would have talked of books, but she leaped lightly

from that subject, and from this I inferred that her mind was not well stored with the knowledge gathered by the busy men of the past. But she was bright and her talk like herself was spirited and pretty, and her observation was minute. She had seen everything about the court-room, an old lawyer with a spot of ink on the sleeve of his linen coat, a tattered book on the floor, a handful of trash swept into a corner.

"The stars shine on all that lies beneath them," said Master, a fine tribute to her eyes, I thought; and she must have thought so, too, for she gave him a laugh that rippled like our creek of a morning when the wind is low. But she protested against his gallantry with a sternness that could not have belonged to her light nature, a plea to him to repeat it, which he did. To his ardent nature, frivolity was a foreign commodity upon which a heavy import tax was laid. He could be argumentative, oratorical, gay, serious and bright for hours at a time, but the silly though pretty chatter which our social life is supposed to dash as spray between the masculine and the feminine mind was far beyond him. In nearly all affairs he was too intense for the perfectly balanced mind. And on this day he strove repeatedly to fasten the young woman down to seriousness, that he might estimate her mental strength, I perceived;

but she flitted about like a humming bird, no sooner attracted by one flower than allured away by another. Still the perfect femininity of her wit, or that which might pass for it, was captivating. A strained and tiresome novelette, now almost forgotten, was then an imported rage, and she had not escaped the infection. She spoke of characters that Bob knew nothing of and was surprised at his frank acknowledgment of ignorance.

"A young man of your standing can't afford not to know that character," she said. "Society demands it of you, and I believe I would pretend to know," she added, laughing.

"We always meet society's demands when we pretend," he replied. "People don't ask us to know a thing but to assume that we know it and not get caught. I haven't had time to sip negus," he went on after a pause; "I have been too busy with drinking a stronger draught. I sit in the glow of the great books, but pass by the little twinkling lights, for I know that soon they must go out."

"Or, in other words," she spoke up, "you tread upon a snow-drop while gazing at a sun-flower."

This remark, and I acknowledge its aptness, was so pleasing to her that she laughed the music of self-

compliment; and the lambs in the grass-land lifted
their noses out of the sweet tangle of clover to look at
her. I was so close that when she leaned back
once a wayward wisp of her hair swept across my face,
more like a breath than a tangible touch, it was so
silken and soft. I studied the almost imperceptible
grain of her pink, plush skin, I was so near her, and
yet to me she was so strangely unreal. To look upon
her surely was a delight, but turning away and shutting my eyes to recall her features, she seemed a
memory far off and shadowy. I could have given her
a sort of worship, the romantic adoration compelled
by a naiad reposing on a moss-bank at the source of a
tinkling stream, but I could not have felt for her the
surging passion of a human love. There was nothing
supernatural in her grace; in her movement there was
the soft and unconscious suppression of a cat's agility;
and her bosom bespoke a strong instinct of mother-
hood, and yet to me she was vaguely unnatural. She
was wanting in heart.

A powerful love looks upon itself as hopeless; upon
it must be thrown that sort of a light, to complete its
deliciousness; and I saw that my master's love was
powerful, but I could not see that it was hopeless.
She might never give him a woman's complete devo-

tion, I argued, for I did not believe that her nature could comprehend his finer forces, but I felt that she would give him her hand and what she supposed to be her heart.

"Do you mean to surrender your life wholly to law books?" she asked, giving him a glance in which I could see a charming fear.

"Oh, no. To my mind a law book without poetry behind it is a heap of helpless dust. At first I must agree to take almost any case that may chance to come along, but after a while I will scorn all but the causes that admit of an orator's effort."

"Oh, that will be lovely!" she cried. "And to think that you entertain yourself and then get pay for it. However, if I were a man, I think I would be a preacher. Preachers are nearly always so nice and clean and they say such pretty things to women."

"It was my mother's ambition that I should be a preacher, and I'm sorry now that I did not gratify it," he said.

"Oh, charming of you to say so, Mr. Gradley. You see I don't let such a compliment get away from me. I might have pretended not to see it, and—and I believe I would if I had thought a moment. Then I could have made you repeat it. But really it is better for you to be a lawyer than a preacher. You have so much fire. Everybody says you are going to make your mark, and when you got into that trouble lately some one said it would ruin you, but father said it wouldn't. He killed a man once. Why, people have to kill men who try to kill them, don't they? But we won't talk about that. Are you going to the pic-nic over at Fletcher's Grove?"

"I hadn't thought about it. Are you going?"

"I don't know, but I'd like to, ever so much."

"Then go with me."

"Oh, that would be delightful, and I will be ready when you call for me. Do you dance?"

"I think," said he, "that I might have courage enough to rob a stage-coach or to fight a duel in a dark room, but I'm afraid that I couldn't summon the nerve to get out before a number of people and try to dance."

"Oh, you wouldn't mind it at all. Just as soon as the music strikes up you forget all about yourself. But isn't it dull about here? Nothing to do but to sit about and wait. Last year I visited an aunt who lives in Connecticut, and I had such a nice time. Everyone there is so active. But, after all, I was kept angry a good deal over the negro question. I never did get so tired of hearing a subject dinged upon. They hate us and can't help showing it; and they actually believe that one of these days they'll come down here, and, as they express it, turn the negroes loose. They believe we keep them chained together all the time; and that hateful book, 'Uncle Tom's Cabin,' is their bible. Have you ever seen it?"

"My uncle brought a copy with him and I read it," Bob answered. "I don't care for its principles, whether they are true or false—literature being its own principle—but to me it bears the mark of a political pamphlet that has happened to make a hit, strong with prejudice but hasty and slip-shod in expression. To me there is no art in it, no imagination but all sermon. The characters are unreal, standing in the light of a red fire; they are talking-machines, grinding out music-box melodies, set homilies; but the subject is powerful and the book needs no art to give it force. And many a year will pass before we hear the last of it."

"Why, Mr. Gradley, you can take an interest in light books after all. I was afraid that you were determined to keep yourself chained to the venerable masters of—of—what shall I say?—venerable masters of profound thought. That will do, won't it?"

"Very appropriate, I assure you, but 'Uncle Tom's Cabin' can scarcely be classed as a light book. It comes in a light garb but its nature is most serious."

The horse shied at a piece of paper fluttering in the road, and with a little scream she seized the lines. He asked her if she would give them back when she should find that no longer was there any danger, and laughing rythmically and with blushes she returned the lines to him.

"No, apology and no embarrassment," said he. "It came of woman's instinctive sense of protection, of her responsibility at a time of peril."

"Now you are making fun of me, Mr. Gradley. Oh, boy (turning to look at me). What's his name? Dan? Oh, yes. How's my horse coming on, Dan? Well, for pity's sake, if he hasn't turned him loose."

The horse was grazing some distance down the road, and without waiting to beg pardon for my stupid neglect of the charge intrusted to me, I jumped down to run after him. Master and the young woman did not wait for me, but drove to Miss Potter's home, now but a short distance away. As I came up leading the horse toward the gate, where master and Miss Potter were standing, old man Potter came walking out. He was effusive in his welcome, swearing upon his life that never was he gladder to see a man. "Ah," he said, looking at me, "and this here is the boy that we all have heard such a good report about. A likely young feller, Mr. Gradley, and I don't reckon you'd care to sell him."

"No, sir," said Bob, assuming to be gentle but looking his contempt for the coarse old fellow. But Mr. Potter could interpret no looks of contempt; he was too busy surveying me from head to foot.

"Yes, reckon you do think a good deal of him, and I wouldn't wonder but it would take a right putty piece of money to buy him."

"I could not be induced to part with him, sir," master replied.

"Yes, sir, got a right to think a good deal of him. Goin' to learn him any sort of trade? Strong enough to make a good blacksmith. Owned one about like him once. Swapped him for a woman and a child."

"Why, father," the daughter spoke up, "Dan is Mr. Gradley's body servant."

"Yes, I know," said the old fellow, his cold and speculative eye still bent upon me, "but it wouldn't be out of the way to learn him how to do something. Comes in mighty handy sometimes and we never can tell what mout happen."

The girl winced at the word "mout," unmistakable symbol of the white trash, and smiling to cut a blush in two, she said: "You observe, Mr. Gradley, that father doesn't care how he talks. He fell into the habit of imitating a queer old fellow who lived near us and now he does it unintentionally. Let us go into the house?"

"Yes, come on," old Potter joined in. "Jest as cheap inside as out, and it ain't as tiresome settin' as standin'. Boy, (giving his eye to me again) go round to the kitchen and tell them to give you something to eat."

"We haven't time to stop," Bob interposed. "We expect several friends at dinner, and—"

"Jest as well eat a snack with us," the old fellow broke in. "Jest as cheap and it won't take nigh so long. I reckon I've got as fine a piece of mutton as you ever set your teeth on—sheep that I didn't want to part with but an infernal dog came along this morning and grabbed him and cut his throat as slick as a whistle—and we know how to cook mutton at our house. Come on."

He continued to urge his hospitality, and to praise the sheep that had been killed by a dog, and the girl pleaded with her eyes; and I thought that Bob would waver, he smiled so and bowed so many times, but in the end he was firm, and bade me turn the buggy around. Even then, with his foot on the step, he lingered to speak another word, though never seeming to utter what came into his mind. At last we drove away, and the moment my back was turned, the girl was only a shadow lying across my memory; and it worried me. I could look at as delicate a thing as a flower and in my mind could reproduce its form and its hue, but that woman was a blur to her own image.

CHAPTER XXII.

"What do you think of her, Dan?" Bob asked as we drove toward home. "Tell me exactly what you think."

"She is beautiful, sir," I replied, "but somehow her features refuse to remain with me."

"They remain with me—black eyes, black hair, rose-leaf ears. She is an oration of the ancients set forth in nineteenth century flesh and blood."

"Yes, sir," I assented, with my mind on the old man, "but I don't think much of her stock, as Mr. Clem might say."

He snatched the lines from me, lashed the horse to a fierce trot, and looked at me as I sat with my hands fallen in idle submission. "Dan, what's the matter with you? You are getting to be a d—— cynic. Don't like her stock! I suppose you mean her father? He has had to work his way, no doubt, and may not have read as many fine books as certain fellows who have been pampered, but he is a gentleman. Do you hear me?" He lashed the horse. "Do you hear what I say?"

"If you say he is a gentleman, he is, Mars. Bob."

"But why the devil don't you make discoveries of your own?"

"I do, but I have not found the North Pole."

"What do you mean by that? Mean that as a gentleman Mr. Potter is a North Pole to you and is therefore beyond your discovery? Is that what you mean?"

At this instant my wretchedness must have smitten him. He pulled the horse back to a walk; he laid his hand upon mine, limp in my lap, and said: "Dan, I was a brute to talk that way when you've been so sick. You are right. The old fellow is as ignorant as a boar but love poured a basket of flowers over him. Please don't try to apologize—I'd rather you'd hit me than to do that. Yes, the old man is ignorant and coarse but the girl is intelligent and refined. Look there," he added, pointing with his buggy whip, "you see a flower with a weed as its parent. The weed has done some good, for it has brought forth the flower, and after all it must have held an unconscious refinement. Here, you take the lines and drive, just as you were doing back there, and don't think of what I said.

Now, you see, we are going along just as if nothing had happened."

The fire and the tenderness of that boy! A passion almost mad, and a gentleness nearly as soft as a young mother's religion, seeking to possess him! I felt even then that he was not fitted to grapple with stern success. Was intuition preparing me for a trial to come, a struggle waiting down the mystic road? Nature may seem to mock her own endeavors, but I believe she creates with a purpose, though the purpose may remain hidden until the end. Nature is pressed upon our many moods, and one mood may strive to pull down the work wrought by another mood. One bent of nature must have had a glorious career marked out for Young Master, though another bent—but of this I will not speak. It is bad enough that it should be told in even the proper place.

That day for dinner there were several guests, among them old 'Squire Boyle, now grown quite feeble. I had been permitted to leave off the service of standing behind Young Master's chair, but on occasions my help was really needed, so I took my old place in the dining-room. It was not expected that even this little gathering could be wholly at peace with itself. There was a rumble, North and South and disputatious vapors floated in the air. And reason, among the party leaders, had given way to fierce gesticulation, and a strife to say something, not to convince but to cut an adversary. I remember that old man Boyle paused with his mouth full of a turkey's white meat to listen to a remark made by Old Master.

"Sir," said the 'squire, after swallowing as if his absorption had dried his throat, "the institutions of this country are tottering, and cool reason alone can prop them."

"And that's exactly what the South won't listen to," Mr. Clem spoke up. "The South wants to block the humane progress of the world. She is not satisfied with her present unhealthful domain, but wants to shove her slave territory into new lands. Reason's voice is but the squeak of a mouse, sir. They can hear nothing but the roar of a lion, and by G——, sir, they want to be the lion."

"Clem," said Old Miss, "you forget where you are. You are not trading horses on the turn-pike, you are seated at my table."

"Hanna, that's a fact, I am at your table; and I reckon that I'm the first one that ever paid his way here."

"Oh, speaking of horses," interrupted the 'squire with a squeak, "reminds me, Clem, that the one I got of you ain't worth his weight in last year's bird-nests."

"What?" Mr. Clem cried, "I am astonished at you."

"Yes, sir, and I was astonished at him; wouldn't pull a settin' turkey off her nest; lies down in the traces like he wants to go to sleep."

"Why, of course," Mr. Clem shouted. "You have profaned a fine saddle horse. He's not intended to pull; he's intended for a gentleman to ride, sir."

"But didn't you tell me that he was a wheel horse and would pull till both eyes popped out?"

"Oh, no; I said I would rather have him than any wheel horse that would pull that blindly. Saddle horses, you know, are of a higher grade."

"I was in hopes so, sir, and I thought I would try to ride this one, but blast me if he didn't try to shake me off him right into the creek!"

"Oh," said Mr. Clem, "I forgot to tell you that he used to travel with a circus. Yes, sir, and an actor used to stand on him to jump headlong into a tank of water, and he was taught to shake himself to announce his readiness for the leap—"

"But he laid down with me, sir."

"Yes, and I was going to say, that a part of his duty

was to go into the tank after the actor. A fact, Bob," he added, nodding at Young Master, who had begun to laugh at him. "Horses, you know, are taught to do most anything. Yes, sir, but getting back to the question of unrest now so strongly marked throughout the country, I want to say that something is going to happen and happen blunt, too. No human government can long stand the internal pullings and haulings that this one is subjected to."

"But what is going to be done?" Old Master cried.

Mr. Clem shrugged his shoulders. "Something is going to pop pretty soon and pop like a whip," said he. "A glass house is going to be broken and hoar frost will gather on leaves never intended for the chill air. The whole trouble comes from slavery and I, for one, am bold enough to say that the end is surely not far off."

"I don't want you to say it at my table, sir," Old Master almost fiercely shouted. "I don't want you to talk treason at my board."

Not in the least was Mr. Clem offended, nor was he at all put out by Old Master's violence. "Guilford," said he, "the trouble is that the South has got the negro mixed up with its religion and with its notion of good government. To own a slave no longer stops at the possession of a piece of property, but becomes so much of a sentiment that the man who does not care to own one is looked upon as an outlaw. And if he declares that he would not own one, that his conscience is against it, he is put down as a traitor to the South, seeking to overturn the American government."

Old Miss threw up her head and sniffed the unsavory air. "Clem," she said, "I don't want you to talk that way in the presence of my son. Why, it wouldn't astonish me to hear you say that a negro is as good as a white man!"

'Squire Boyle listened with his fork raised and his mouth half open. He had long been suspected of holding the views of the abolitionists; it was known that he had favored Henry Clay's scheme for gradual emancipation. He had been studiedly discreet, but being by birth a Northern man, suspicion naturally turned an eye upon him. Sometimes when he must have felt that his silence was eating him like an internal cancer, he had come to Old Master to be bold with healthful utterances, but of late, as the country became more deeply stirred, Old Master warned him to swallow rapidly whenever he felt a strong disposition to talk upon the subject of abolition. And now he swallowed with such vigor and rapidity that a stranger to the precaution placed upon his speech must surely have thought that he was choking to death.

" 'Squire, did you swallow something the wrong way?" Mr. Clem asked, leaning over toward him.

"No, something wants to come up the right way," the 'squire piped, the red Adam's apple at his thin throat dodging like a wood-pecker. "I want to say something, but I won't. But the time will come when I will stand on a hill—I've got it picked out—and bawl what I think. Guilford, you are fixing to scold me, sir, and I must ask you not to say a word."

Old Master laughed at this, the old 'squire's desperate threat of rebellion, and had taken up a bit of bread to roll his customary bolus, when yellow Sam, who had been sent to town, came in with a letter. Old Miss began at once to speculate as to whom it could be from, and Old Master, winking at Bob and looking at her as he wiped his glasses, said that he supposed he could put the letter under his plate and wonder a long time as to the identity of the writer. "But happily," said he, again winking his mischievous eye, "we are provided with means whereby we can cut through all speculation and get at once into the heart and the truth of the subject.   To be brief," he added, "we can open the letter."

"Well, for goodness sake, why don't you?" his wife broke in, as she always did when she saw him indulging a droll humor.   "Give it to me."

"Oh, no," he laughed, putting back her hand. "There may be secrets in this epistle that belong alone to the great free-masonry of men."

"And your organization is shameful enough," she said, not without a show of ill-temper (for any allusion to an understanding in which she was not included always appeared to cut her).   "But I must acknowledge its rare perfection as an organization," she went on.   "Its devotees do not have to be sworn, unless nature swears them at birth."

By this time the single leaf of the letter was shaking under Old Master's gaze.   "Read it," he said huskily, handing it to Bob.   And he bowed his head over the table.   The note was from Miss May.   It told us that her husband was dead, and that she, with her little child, was about to start for home.

CHAPTER XXIII.

Everything was put in order, the house cleaned and the cabins newly whitewashed, to brighten the place for the daughter's return. But the day looked dull when she came with the little child crying in the nurse's arms. There were tears and embraces and tremulous words of love.

On the steps my Young Mistress turned to the nurse and said, "Give her to me, Titine." And at this moment I felt that an arrow from a bow in the sky had shot through me. Titine! I did not know that the world had presumed to hold a beauty and a charm so exquisite. Her complexion was as the richest cream, her hair showed the merest suggestion of a waver rather than a negro kink, her eyes were black-blue, and her lips—Was it Solomon who said "her lips are as a thread of scarlet"? I was a man now, grown to full strength and passion—from the moment I saw that French, Spanish, negro, Anglo-Saxon girl. Never before had I seen anyone to thrill me; surely not a negress, and certainly I had not presumed to acknowledge the charms of a white woman. I did not fall at once in love with Titine; I was too excited, too breathless as I gazed upon her. I reminded myself of an animal, beholding for the first time a female of his own species—and I verily believe that I felt a desire to throw my head up and scream like a panther.

"Dan," Old Miss cried, "why don't you bring in the things? What do you want to stand there for like a chicken with the gapes?"

In this comparison there was something so appropriate that I could not suppress a laugh, though I took care to hide it from Old Miss. Miss May turned to the girl and told her to help me bring in the bags, but Old Miss objected. "Let her rest, May," she said. "Dan hasn't been doing a thing. He's pretty much as you left him—scarcely worth his salt."

This was a fine recommendation to Titine, and I felt the blood mount to my face, as I turned toward the carriage at the gate. But I glanced back and saw the girl following me with her eyes; and I wondered, selfishly enough, why she had not insisted upon helping me, though I needed no assistance, for I was strong enough at that moment to seize all the bags at once and hurl them over the house.

I saw but little of Titine that afternoon (or evening

as we termed it), for the child was fretful and put a claim upon nearly all her time, but I heard her singing in a room down the hall from our "office," and I stepped about, keeping quick time with the tingling leap of my blood.   At the supper hour she came down to stand behind Miss May, and I marched boldly into the dining-room, delighted now to resume a menial service.   I stood beside her, but alas! with what scorn did she look at me.   The child began to cry and she was sent above, and it was then that I began to hear something of her history.   She had belonged to Marston's maiden sister, a peculiar creature who had cared for nothing but Titine and a white woolly dog. The dog died and the mistress, doubling her affection for the girl, sent her to a convent to be educated, greatly to the scandal of her associates.   At the old woman's death, of recent date, the girl had fallen to Marston.   She complained at this transfer, declaring that her mistress had drawn up a paper to set her free, but the paper could not be found, so she was compelled to submit, stubbornly at first, but after a while becoming so much attached to Miss May that she rejoiced in her good fortune.

"She knows as much and is a far better talker than I am," said Miss May.

"Daughter, you must not say that," Old Miss objected. "It cannot be true and it surely is not right."

"Very well, mother, I won't say it again, but you will soon find out for yourself."

Then they all fell into a family talk, the sudden death of Marston and the entanglement in which his affairs were likely to be found. He was not a good manager, never knew what his income was, and was always in debt. But he was so kind-hearted—and here Miss May wept and the subject was changed.

Immediately after supper young master dressed himself to call on Miss Potter, and when he was gone I threw aside my senseless book and went down into the yard, to dodge behind the trees at the corner of the house, hoping to catch sight of Titine on the veranda. At last she came out, with a red cap on her head, and stood with her hands resting on the balustrade, looking far away at the dying pink in the sky. I stepped out boldly and touched my hat. She glanced down at me and tossed her head. But I knew that she was not displeased.

"Beautiful evening," I said.

"Indeed!"

"This is but one of many of our charming sun-sets."

"Ah, then the sun goes down every evening?"

"Y-e-s," I stammered, for she was beginning to make me feel foolish.

"In the same place?" she asked, cutting her eye at me.

"Well, not exactly. But in the West, generally."

"Startling."

"Oh, not when we have accustomed ourselves to it."

"Indeed. But tell me, is salt very high here, or do you use a great deal of it?"

"I don't quite understand you."

"I heard your old mistress say that you were not worth your salt."

"Yes, she would say anything to humiliate me. I inflicted a mortal wound when I began to study with my Young Master."

"Oh, you have studied, have you? That was foolish. I committed the same indiscretion."

"If you have studied, then it was glorious to study."

"It is bad enough not to be worth your salt, but please don't be a fool."

"I can't help it. You would rob a philosopher of his wisdom."

She laughed, and I believe that had a lancet pricked

an artery my blood would have spurted a mile high. I heard a sharp cry from the child, and it smote my heart, not that the little thing might be suffering, but that I was to be robbed. "I must go," she said.

"And shall I stay?"

"Yes, if you sleep standing up, like a horse."

She was gone, and I stood under the trees, gazing at the cabin lights; and I waited there until the lights began to go out, but the girl did not return. I heard Young Master ride up to the gate, and I went out to take his horse. He walked with me to the stable. He said not a word until we were returning, and then, clutching my arm, he told me that Miss Potter had consented to be his wife. "I am the happiest human being on the face of this broad earth," he said, waving his arm so as to take in the entire universe. "And she says that she will wait till I have made myself famous, for I told her I thought that this would be wise, believing with some of the great thinkers, that while marriage might improve a man's judgment, it might also put out a part of his fire. You know I was born with the idea that I was to become an orator, and I have not run against anything to change my opinion. I feel something surging within me, and all I need is a subject. I can be proud of her, Dan; I am proud of her, and I must make myself worthy of her pride. What are you so glum about to-night?"

"You have seen the girl that came with Miss May?"

"Yes, she is a beauty.   And she has caught you? I'm glad of it.   Oh, it seems that old mother Nature is not disposed to let us drift far apart.   In common we felt many an emotion, and love came along to teach one of us what the other did not know.   But you don't mean that you have fallen in love with her so soon?"

"I don't know anything when I think of her, Mars. Bob.   More than half my life seems to be compressed into the few hours she has been under our roof."

It was getting late, and Bob went to bed soon after we reached the room, to dream of a love that had leaped to meet his own; and I lay there listening to the faint cries of a child, and the almost silent sounds of foot-falls on the floor, down the hall.   In the morning I was up before the sun, dodging about among the trees at the east end of the veranda.   At last she came down to freshen her eyes with a glimpse of the dawn-couch, purple with the sun's resurrection.

"I am almost persuaded that you are determined to earn your salt, you are up so early," she said with a smile brighter than the new day.

"Is it because you are from the sugar lands of Louisiana that salt is such a novelty to you?" I asked. She did not reply, but stood looking at the hills, far away.

"I never get tired of them," she said; "they are so strange and new. We have no hills in our country, you know; nothing but a level stretch as far as the eye can see, and we know that beyond this another level stretch lies, and beyond that, still another. But here, I don't know what's beyond. Blue mystery everywhere."

"Some time I will take the buggy and drive you over to the hills," I said, and the light of a new interest flew to her eyes.

"Will you? That will be kind. But will they let you take the buggy?"

"My young master will give me permission, and we can slip off from Old Miss. Let us go Sunday, after dinner?"

This was on a Saturday, and the length of time lying dead between then and Sunday afternoon was to me a sunless, moonless and starless age. But the hour, the minute came, and amidst the half contemptuous titterings and envious glances of the negroes, we drove off from the gate, down a lane, far across two white turn-pikes that streaked a hill and striped a valley, up through a fern cove to a dark, mysterious spring; and here we left the buggy to climb a crag. She had seen red lumps of sand-stone, but never had she touched a living rock, and at the foot of a cliff, moss-grown and vine-strung, she stood with her head bowed and with her red cap in her hand—a goddess in meditation, a nymph at prayer. I stood apart and in deep reverence looked at her, fearful that my nearness might profane her devotions. I had begun to ascribe to her a super-human quality, a beauty belonging not to this world, and a virtue breathed by the ancient maidens who preferred death to a tarnishment of their chastity. Indeed, had there been such an institution as the supreme bench of sentimental idiots, I should surely have been selected to a seat upon it.

"Is it not divine here, in this air, blown fresh from paradise?" I said, lifting my eyes like an ox.

"Yes, and I wish we had brought something to eat," she replied. "This rough climbing has made me hungry."

"You hungry!" I cried. "Impossible."

"Why impossible?" And she put on her red cap and looked at me from head to foot.

"Because your soul—"

"Bosh!" she said and laughed. "All you Kentucky

men are alike, from what I have read and from what I now see.   You try to make love and you declaim like school-boys.   They laugh at such love in New Orleans.   Don't you know that the first step toward making love to a woman is to interest her by something you do or say?"

"And haven't I interested you?" I asked.

"Why, I can't say that you have.   You have been very kind, and attentive, but I haven't seen anything surprising about you.   Ever since I came I have heard how smart you were, and I suppose you must have lorded it over those poor ignorant negroes."

"Miss," said I, "I might be ready to drop at your feet and cover your shoes with kisses, but you musn't talk to me that way.   What little learning I have, has been a source of reproach and trouble to me, and never have I attempted to show it off.   I don't suppose I could say as much if I had been fed upon the hot mush of French romances."

She turned about and sat down, put forth her dainty foot, looked at it and said that hot mush was at all times to be preferred to cold slop.   "Won't you sit down?" she asked, turning her foot over so that I might see the exquisite arch of the instep.   I sat down, though not beside her; and for a time I mused in silence upon the temper, the unhealthful fancy of the old maid who had presided over the mind of this fair creature. I knew that in her selection of a partner she would look high, but I knew also that her actions must ever be subservient to the will of an owner, invested with far more authority than that granted to a husband by our almost mock ceremony of marriage. But how high could she look? Surely no higher than the plane upon which I stood. These reflections threw a dash of old earth into the countenance of my romance, and in bitterness I laughed at myself and at her.

"What has tickled you so?" she asked.

"Two fools," I replied.

"Two fools, or one fool big enough for two?"

"Two fools," I repeated. "We are owned body and soul, and even sentiment, the gift of God, comes to mock us."

In an instant she had planted her feet firmly upon the ground and was standing in front of me. "I can begin to detect a glimmering of sense in you," she said. "In a negro's courtship there can be nothing absurd," she went on, flooding me with the light from her eyes. "An hour's acquaintance is as good as a year's close relationship. He is an animal looking for a mate and he makes his proposal of marriage. He may already have a dozen wives, it makes no difference, for neither law nor society takes any account of his relations with women. My mistress was a sensible woman, and she taught me to hate a negro marriage and I do hate it. I have the instincts of a lady and I refuse to be an animal. I saw at once that you were determined to ask me to be your wife and I am glad you have given me a chance to head you off."

Strange talk for a maiden, there on a hill, under a cliff overlooking broad Kentucky. I might have expected it from a wrinkled hag, a sibyl, but from this ripe and creamy maid it came as a blunt blow upon the head.

"There is truth in what you say," I was forced to admit, "but ours would not be a common negro marriage."

"No, but you are making the courtship characteristically negro. Do you reflect upon how short a time we have known each other?"

"Titine, this suddenness is not negro—it is impulse and romance. How long did Romeo know Juliet?"

"And what came of their love but death? Dan, we can be good friends, brother and sister, but you must not ask me to go through with a mock ceremony, the sentimental joke of a plantation, and pretend that I am your wife. When we reflect upon our condition we must be miserable. Education has made us unhappy, except when we lose our minds in a book; and to unite two miseries, two conditions of helplessness—a crime!" she cried. "Yes, I have read French romances. Year after year I sat beside my mistress and read to her and listened to her remarks upon the phases of life that came under our view. She called me precocious—a reflex of her own mind. My mind was apt and it stored many images and caught many a color from my surroundings, and—but what is the use of talking about myself?"

"Titine, listen to me. Something tells me that the world will not always be thus, holding the worshippers of nature in a grip of bondage—"

"Hush!" she cried, putting her hands to her ears. "When you have changed the subject I will listen to you."

"You will listen now!" I cried, springing to my feet, grasping her hands, holding them tight, bending her backward, gazing into her eyes. "You will listen to me now." Her eyes darted forked tongues at mine, and I liberated her. She smiled and sat down.

"Yes," she said sweetly, her anger vanishing, "I will listen to you now."

"First, let me beg your pardon."

"Oh, another mockery. Let us skip that. Let me hear your speech; you are a lawyer."

"I will not make the speech of a lawyer, but of a lover."

"You can't love. You are a negro." She said this with bitterness and her laugh was cold.

"Titine, even an animal can love."

"Oh, for a season, yes; but nature does not make a mockery of an animal's love. The animal can seize its young and run away, but if the negro runs away to protect his young, he is brought back with the hounds. Dan, I am going to live as my mistress did, and no man shall have a claim on me."

"But Titine, you are a human being, you have passion, the sense of—"

"Sense of justice to myself and to those who might come after me."

"Titine, you are not a girl, you are a beautiful witch. You know too much for one of your age—your shrivelled old mistress left you her mind; and she is now watching you—"

"Ugh!" she cried, putting out her hands, "don't say

that. But if she does watch me she will see that I follow her commands."

"But her commands were against your interests. She would shut you out from all enjoyment, from sentiment and from love. Thank her for her kindness but rebel against her exactions. Be my wife."

"Poor fool," she said, clasping her hands over her knee and gazing at me. "You are not a man to have a wife; you are a piece of property, and no matter how tightly I might cling to you, you could be torn from me and sold, and the howl of the auctioneer, yelling for another animal to be brought forward, would drown my cries of distress. Oh, I have stood in the slave market, and I have seen a child snatched from the arms of its heart-broken mother. Old Mistress used to take me there to show me the bitterness of life. And you would be the father of a stock to be sold! Poor fool, put your foot on such a thought." She rocked herself and laughed, and upon my soul, for a moment I fancied that she was a witch, endowed with a frightful wisdom; but a bough moved, the strong light fell upon her, and she sat there, warm, rich and human.

"Have you given your strange views to Miss May?"

"There are two children in our family and one of them is Miss May," she said.

"But don't you read to her?"

"Yes, the 'Children of the Abbey' and let her cry herself to sleep. She is a child."

"Titine, there is strange blood in you; you are Cleopatra come to earth again; and the serpent of slavery is at your breast."

She shuddered.

"And it may suck out my life, but mine alone," she said.

"Titine, a week ago I could not have believed it possible to be placed in such a position; I could not have believed that a creature like you existed in the world. The knowledge of slavery has always been a burden; you make it a snake and it bites me. But tell me, what are you going to do? Are you going to spend your life in servitude?"

"Who is there to take me away?" she asked, and the look she gave me stilled my blood, but it flowed again with a spurt, and leaping to my feet I ran to the edge of the cliff and looked far below, at the lengthening shadows, the crows sailing round and round, the cattle feeding in a distant meadow. I turned back to her. She did not look at me. I sat down beside her, sought to take her hand, but she moved and motioned me away.

"Titine, once I thought I saw a hangman's rope—the maids have told you a part of the story—and money was thrown at me, but I would not run away so deeply was I devoted to Bob Gradley. I thought that the devil was trying to tempt me, but now I believe that the temptation comes from God."

"You have misunderstood me," she said, and her words were freezing. "I would not suggest a temptation; I would not run away with you. I will be frank—I don't love you, and if I did, I would not run away to be brought back in shame. Let us be fellow servants, Dan?"

"But is there no hope left in the world?"

"Do you read the Bible, and do you find hope there?"

"Come, let us go home," I said.

CHAPTER XXIV.

Now came a political contest to shame the short-sightedness of the wise men who framed our constitution. I do not say this in disparagement of a broad and liberty-loving principle, the Jeffersonian principle that made demagogic men too strong and government too weak, but I do say, as all men now must know, that advantage was taken of the theory of states rights, beast-headed fallacy; and I do aver that Hamilton was the wisest man that saw the birth of our nation. But this is simply seeking to make noon-day clear.

Never was there a campaign of such heat and bitterness. Households were divided and brothers frowned upon one another, and in the distance hovered the vulture-shaped cloud of war. My Young Master supported Kentucky's favorite son, as did Old Master, and for months our house bore the appearance of a committee room. The time came for Bob to display his power as an orator, and never was there a nobler effort. It was in the court-house yard. Great men had spoken before the boy arose to address the crowd.

I was standing near, and I thought that I saw his blood leap; I know that his eye shot fire at me. His first sentence caught the assembly, the lawyers, the doctors and the sturdy yeomen. I cannot recall it; I will not try, but I know that it tingled through me. Since then I have listened to many a speech; I have heard Wendell Phillips and the great men in Congress, but never have I been bound by the spell of such impassioned eloquence. To me his words lost their literal meaning—it was an outpour of passion and emotion. The crowd went wild, and when the orator stepped from the platform, he was borne away on the shoulders of men. Old George D. Prentice, author of an immortal poem, was present with genius shining in his eyes, and the next day his newspaper declared that another great orator had arisen in Kentucky, one to take the place of Henry Clay. It was a glad night at our house. The trees were hung with lanterns, so great was the pressure of people come to congratulate the blue-grass Demosthenes.

Upon all these proceedings, Mr. Clem looked with a quiet smile.

"You made a great speech," he said to Bob, when we had gone to the room, late at night. "Yes, you caught me, but what does it all amount to? I told you

that Lincoln would be nominated, and now I tell you
he will be elected."

"Nonsense," Old Master cried.   He was walking
up and down the room, his head high with pride.
"This country is not yet ready for a revolution."

"That may be, Guilford," said Mr. Clem, "but it is
ready for the election of that man."

"Are you going to support him, sir?" Old Master
demanded.

"Did you ever know me to turn my back upon a
friend?   And he is not only my friend, but the saviour
of this country, the greatest statesman that this republic has seen."

"Clem," said Old Master, pausing and resting his
hand upon a pile of books that lay on Bob's table, "it
is well enough to praise your friend, for he is no doubt
droll and amusing, but when you come to call him a
great statesman, you do injustice to the memory of
Clay and Webster, of Jefferson and Benton."

Mr. Clem laughed.   "Guilford," said he, "you are
misled just as the majority of men suffer themselves to
be misled.   A man brays with the solemnity of an ass
and you think he is great.   Over a vital question he
utters a senseless stupidity and you think he has said a
wise thing.   You don't know that humor is the cream

that rises to the surface of life's wisdom.   Lincoln tells a story and throws a bright light on a truth; he does not invest a subject with a gloom so thick that no eye can penetrate it.   He makes all things plain, and the province of greatness is not to enshroud but to simplify.   But that's neither here nor there; he's going to be elected."

"But can't you understand that the country will not accept him, sir?"

"Not accept him? The people will accept whom the people elect."

"But the South will not accept an abolitionist."

"Then the South will have to make the most of it. Of what good will be her protest? You don't mean that she will secede from the Union?"

"Oh, I hope not," said Old Master. "Surely not," he added. "We cannot afford to throw away the traditions of our fathers."

It was a sore subject to me, and I was glad when they dropped it. I hardly knew why, but my flesh always began to creep when abolition was ventured upon; there was a shudder in it, a threat of trouble, trial and blood.

Bob had shown no interest in the talk; he had sat in a deep muse, his hands listless in his lap, his eyes turned upward; but how handsome was his face, his expression sweetened with success. That day he had been lifted high and given a glimpse, yes a full sight of the heaven his heart so fondly craved; he was to be great and he knew it as he sat there dreaming. Old Master turned to go, and his son came down from the purple clouds. They looked at each other for a moment.

"Bob."

"Yes, sir."

"You have made me the proudest man in the State; you have done what Patrick Henry fired me with an ambition to do. It was denied me, and now I am rejoiced to see it fulfilled in you. The blood of old Kentucky shook your hand to-night. Now give it to me, sir."

Young master arose and they shook hands with solemn ceremony, Bob turning his eyes away. "Your eye, sir," said the old man, and the young man looked into his father's eyes; and they read each other sternly, and with never a sign of flinching, so completely had each mastered himself.

"Father, if I have ability it is indeed the fulfillment of your own ambition, for I felt it as a child, so strongly apart from my own forces that I knew the current must come from you. I have been told by old men that I am a second edition of yourself and—"

"A revised and corrected edition, sir," the old man broke in, still gripping firmly the young fellow's hand.

"But a cheaper edition, I fear," the orator said.

"Enough, captivating flatterer. Good-night."

Old Master strode out, walking hard upon the floor, and Mr. Clem, who with keen amusement had observed this exchange of fine-tempered civility, turned to Bob and said:

"By the flint hoofs, you and that old brother of mine will be snatched out of the sixteenth century before very long. Paw me if I didn't expect one of you to say, 'I come not here to talk, you know too well the story of our thralldom.' Bob, the trouble with the South is the fact that it is not really republican in principle. It is a shapeless aristocracy writhing about to find a head. Tell me, do you believe in a democratic form of government?"

Bob sat down, leaned back and put his feet on the table, leaving Mr. Clem standing behind him; and he glanced back over his shoulder as he replied: "Do I believe in a democracy? I don't believe in the rule of ignorance; I don't believe in a goldocracy, the most insolent and oppressive of all tyrants. I don't believe it just to give to a plebeian mob the right to snatch a brilliant man from public life simply because he refuses to grovel to a vulgar taste; I don't believe—"

"But do you believe in a negro-cracy? Do you believe that the ownership of a hundred slaves should open all doors to a coarse and ignorant man?"

"No, I don't. I would not let ignorance own a slave."

"Ah, but slaves are bought with money, not with intelligence. Bob, you are an orator, but after all you are but a fledgling. Now, I want to ask you a question. What has made this country great, the gentility of Virginia or the dogged industry of New England? To whom do we owe most, the silver buckled gentleman or the steeple-hatted puritan?"

"If you measure greatness by material wealth, Uncle Clem—but there's no use of such an argument. You are too practical for me. You are a Baconian and I would sit at the feet of Socrates. And progress will say that you are right."

"And won't you say so, too?"

"I am not progressive. I worship the utterances of the past; you glory in the achievements of the present. You honor the North because it is rich, and I love the South because it is poetic. So there we are, and it is of no use to argue."

"No, I reckon not. Say, did you notice an old fellow with a white hat, riding a chestnut horse? Didn't get down until you were about half through with your speech, and then he rolled off, turned his horse loose and whooped like an Indian. I kept a weather eye on him, and when the bottom dropped out of the proceedings, I looked him up. Yes, sir, and his horse is out yonder in the stable now, and a glandered nag of mine is missing. The old fellow was so wrought up that he was in no condition to defend himself. So much for oratory. Good-night, lad."

Bob laughed at him as he went out, and remarked to me that the speech had brought good to one man even if it had worked an injury upon another member of the human family. "And," he added, "we can't expect to help more than half of mankind at once. Dan," he said, after a thoughtful moment, "this has been a great day for me. And she was there, sitting in a buggy. And when she took my arm to-night I knew she was proud of me."

I said that her soul must have been filled with an intoxicating joy, and I lied, for I did not believe that she could entertain an exalted pride. I knew that her vanity was flattered, a hard luster in her eye told me that, but I saw that her victory was cold and selfish. I acknowledged to myself that I had surrounded the young woman with a prejudice (and in a prejudice there is always more or less of intuition) and I tried hard to pull it apart that I might see her clearer; but the prejudice was strong and could not be torn asunder.

Bob was undressing when I left him to go out into the yard, to walk among the trees. I loved my master, and his success I felt was my advancement, but with all that I was wretched. To hold aloft a light that I had found was but to illumine a hopelessness.

As I passed out into the hall, I saw Titine step from the door of Miss May's room. She carried a pitcher in her hand and I knew that she was going to the well. I walked slowly behind her until she reached the hall below and then I called her. She stopped and looked back at me.

"What is it?" she asked.

"Going for water at this time of night?"

"When water is wanted, the time of night makes no difference," she said as I joined her to pass out upon the rear veranda. We walked along together toward the well.

"Titine, I don't know you any better now than I did when you first came."

"And I don't know myself any better, and are you presumed to know me better than I know myself?"

"No, I suppose not. But since that day we went to the hills you have never consented to go out alone with me."

"Don't you know why?"

"I can't say that I do."

"Then you are duller than I took you to be."

The moon was shining and the light fell full upon her face, upward turned; she was smiling and her smile was cold. We had now reached the well, and I unwound the chain to let the bucket down. She placed her arms on the curbing and hummed a cool tune of idleness, of a total lack of interest in what I might be doing.

"Yes, I do know," I said.

"Then you are no duller than I thought you were," she ceased humming long enough to say. I drew up the dripping bucket and poured the pitcher full. She reached forth her hand to take it.

"Wait a moment," I pleaded, catching at her hand, but it flew away like a bird.

"Well," she said, straightening up and looking at me.

"Titine, if you and I were free—"

"If I were free I would be a nun," she broke in. "Give me the pitcher."

"Wait just a moment. Let me kiss you."

She shrieked with laughter. "Oh, how blunt you are. Look out, you'll break that pitcher."

"Then I could be classed with Gideon's men. They broke their pitchers before they fought."

"But you are not going to break the pitcher and fight."

"Yes, I'm going to break it and fight for a kiss."

"Oh, what a fool you are. What good would breaking the pitcher do? Give it to me."

She spoke in a tone of such command that I gave her the vessel, but I pleaded with her to stay longer; and now I caught her hand. She struggled to free herself but my grasp was vice-like. "Wait until I have told you something. Nature intended you for me and I am going to have you—"

She spat at me like an angry cat, snatched her hand away, so strong was she, and ran up the path toward the house, the water leaping from the mouth of the pitcher. I caught up with her.

"Are you offended, Titine?"

"Oh, no, it was too good a joke. Nature intended me for you, indeed. Nature doesn't know you, simpleton. If she should meet you in the road she would say, 'who's your master, boy? Oh, young Mr. Gradley, eh? Tell him with my compliments that he possesses a very fine piece of yellow property.' Then what would you do? Tell nature that you wanted to marry another piece of yellow property? She would laugh at you and tell you to black your master's boots.'"

She bounded up the stairway, splashing the water, and at the top she turned to laugh at me.

CHAPTER XXV.

Over events of national importance I am compelled
to pass swiftly, for in no way am I seeking to write
the history of a struggle, and by giving only a glimpse
here and there shall I try to set forth the disaffection
that led to it. Lincoln was elected and for a time the
South stood in dumb surprise, and then she shook
herself and the nation began to go to pieces, crumbling
apart with secession. Further south it was but
natural to expect that all would go one way, but in
Kentucky there were contending factions in almost
every household; and the friendships and affections of
a life-time were torn to shreds. Tennessee, our
respected neighbor on the south, went out of the
Union and beat old drums under a new flag; and it
was expected that Kentucky would follow, but her
grim old leaders set their teeth and swore that the
commonwealth should not budge from her time-
honored allegiance to the government of Washington
and Monroe. Old Master was firm for the Union.
Once he heard a drum beating at midnight and he got

out of his bed and went to town. And when he came back his countenance was sad but hard-set. "They are beating up men for the rebel army," he said. "I raised my hand and in the name of our fathers commanded them to disperse, but they laughed at me. Let them go. The devil is waiting for them."

Within a few days it seemed that every accent of the human voice was a martial tone. There was no talk but of war. Brothers denounced one another in the street, and fathers drove their sons from home. Society was mad. Over line-fences irate neighbors gazed at one another, gun in hand. Day and night the turnpikes resounded with the clatter of galloping hoofs. Brass cannon were dragged by our house; men camped under our trees, without asking permission. Fifes were screaming everywhere, and negro drummers strutted about wearing the cast-off and faded finery of a former war. From the South came the startling report that the conflict was begun. And the drums in Kentucky beat louder.

One evening, just as the family had sat down to supper, Sam came in and said that a man outside wanted to see Old Master. "Tell him to come in here," the old man spoke up. Presently a man entered, dressed and accoutered as a cavalryman. Old

Master glanced at him as he crossed the threshold, and seeing that his uniform was gray, demanded the cause of his visit.

"The government has sent me to buy your crib of corn, sir."

"The government! I don't understand you, sir," Old Master declared, frowning at the man's clothes.

"The Confederate government," the man said.

"Indeed! I didn't know that such a government existed. You may return, sir, and tell the Confederate government to go back to h—, where it belongs."

The man smiled, touched his cap with a military salute and withdrew. He had been a neighbor, but now he was a stranger.

"Guilford," said Mr. Clem, "nearly everybody was surprised when the news went out that you were for the Union. You are so strongly a Southerner and have always tried so hard to justify slavery that—"

"Sir, with me my country is my first consideration," Old Master broke in.

"But I can't, for the life of me, understand why you should deliberately turn your back on your own interests," said Old Miss. "The South is more your country than the North is, and yet you turn against the South."

"Madam, the whole country, the traditions of the American people are mine. And I don't believe that the government will interfere with slavery, but if it should, I say, let it go ahead. The first consideration is to save the country."

Bob had said not a word. Many a time when the drums struck up had he gone out to walk in the woods alone, and I knew that a struggle was raging within his breast, but I asked him no question and he offered not a word. Of late he had gone forth at night, sometimes remaining away until nearly dawn, and in his sleep he had cried sharp words, "right about face," "forward march," "halt!"—

"Bob," said Old Master, "I have waited to hear you express your views; I have given you plenty of time, but you have said nothing. I know without asking, still I would like to hear your say. Which side do you favor? But wait, you needn't answer so foolish a question."

"Father, the question is not foolish. I am raising a company of men for the Confederate army."

It seemed that every dish and cup leaped from the table. Old Master was on his feet, then on his chair, then leaning against the wall, his face hidden. He uttered a cry such as I had never heard, a groan set to the tune of despair. He turned from the wall and looked at his son, now standing with his hands resting on the back of a chair. The young man bowed his head, and I saw the tears trickling down his face. Old Master dragged his feet forward, feeling out with his hands as if to keep from falling. Old Mistress stood with her arms folded and with cold pride on her face. Miss May was pale with an air of fright; and Titine, looking across at me, slowly closed her eyes and smiled.

Old Master reached the table and leaned forward with both hands pressed flat upon it, in the helpless condition of a man hoping and trying not to fall, a man who has received a knock-down blow and who is expecting another. His chin shook and his old lips worked and I thought I heard them rasp like dry corn-blades as he strove to talk. He looked at Mr. Clem as if imploring his help, at his daughter as if to summon strength from her gentle and affectionate nature. His body began to sway like the snag of an old tree about to fall, then stiffened; and now he stood unsupported, straight, head high, in a strength that seemed to turn upon his years and defy them. He spoke and his voice was as clear as the yelp of the hound that leads the pack: "Robert Gradley, your eye, sir."

The young man raised his eyes and they looked at each other, Bob with an expression akin to pleading, Old Master hard and cold.

"Do you mean, sir, to tell me that you are raising a company of men to fight against your country?"

"No, sir, not against my country, but for a principle that some of my countrymen are trying to trample under foot. Instinctively I hate the cold exactions of the Puritan. His aim is not so much to preserve the Union as to humiliate the men who own slaves. For the slave he has no real feeling; to serve his ends he would see the negro drawn and quartered. His hatred of the men of the South is older than the creed of abolition; it began when old Peter Wentworth stood in the English parliament and raised his voice against refinement and gentility. I honor the memory of the men who made our flag the symbol of a mighty nation; but I love poetry more than I do commerce, and a sentiment is stronger with me than a woollen mill. A cold and feelingless duty might call me to the other side, but emotion, stronger than any sense of duty, impells me toward the South. It grieves me to oppose you; it is like boring tender flesh with a red hot iron, and I have wandered up and down the woods at night and in the dawn, praying—"

"Theatrical fool!" the old man shouted.

"No!" Old Mistress cried. I have seen resolute turkey hens turn out their feathers in warning against a trespasser upon the sward where their young ones were squatted. And at this moment Old Mistress reminded me of a turkey hen. "No! he is not a theatrical fool. He has as much right to his convictions as you have to yours. You have taught him to be independent—you sent him from home to school when he was a child to teach him self-reliance; and he found it."

Here Mr. Clem walked round the table and laid his hand upon Old Master's shoulder. "Guilford," said he, "the young fellow is honest, he has evidently suffered over the question, and it is of no use to take bitter issue with him."

"By G——! I'll turn him out of the house!" Old Master shouted, shaking himself free of his brother's touch. "He shan't—"

"Then you turn me out, too!" Old Miss cried.

Miss May ran to her father and put her arms about his neck. "Please don't say anything that you'll be sorry for," she pleaded.

He took her arms from about his neck, but stood holding her hands; and his eyes were not so cold nor did his skin look so dry and harsh. Not in the least was Young Master excited, nor did he appear to be astonished at the denunciations heaped upon him. Indeed, it was clear to me that for months he had been expecting it and was relieved now to think that the blow had fallen. The young man spoke and his voice was soft and musical. "If I were to leave the house before the time comes for me to go, I would but add to an injury which you threaten to inflict upon yourself. You would regret your expulsion of me, and could never forgive yourself if I should be killed. It seems to me now that all my training was to fit me for this step, rather than to equip me for an orator—to stimulate my impulse rather than to train my judgment. I will not say that your cause is unjust, but I must say that I cannot fight with the Puritan. My troop leaves on the day after to-morrow, and until then I will be your obedient son."

Old Master lifted his hand as if his words were to fall as a blow, but Mr. Clem took his arm and eased it down. "Guilford," said he, "the young man has simply gone you one better in his worship of the tinsel of the past. You have taught him that the Southerner is the only real gentleman in this country and you can't blame him for the course he is determined to take."

And now Old Master was surprisingly calm. "But, sir, I never thought to teach him to join in rebellion against his country."

"You didn't measure the extent of your teaching. It went a mile further than your intention. And as it has gone beyond your control, let us make the most of it, or rather the best of it. Let him follow his own bent, let him fight for an aristocracy, and let him go with a blessing rather than with a curse. That's the sensible view to take. I am going to fight for the Union, and I now give him my hand, hoping that one day he may see his error and repent of it."

He stretched forth his hand and Young Master clasped it. "I thank you, Uncle Clem. You have told me how sharp you can be and now you prove how broad and liberal you are."

Old Master reached forth his hand. "It is that you may feel how sore my heart is," said he, as the young man gripped his palm. "You have wounded me and the wound will never heal, but you are my son and I have been proud of you. Not another word," he said, quickly withdrawing his hand and lifting it to enjoin silence. "On this subject no more words shall pass between us; and when the time comes, you may go your way in silence. Daniel," he said, turning to me, "let me see you in the library."

I followed him into the library, and when he had closed the door he said to me. "You know what his intentions were."

"No, sir, he said not a word to me."

"Don't lie to me, Dan."

"As God is my judge, sir, I knew nothing of his plans until he gave them to you."

"And has he said nothing as to what you shall do? Hasn't he told you that you must go with him?"

"I tell you that he has said nothing to me."

"But he will ask you to go with him."

"And I will go, sir."

"What?" I sprang back or I believe he would have leaped upon me. "Come back to me, sir. Don't run away from me. I'll shoot you down like a dog. Come here."

"I am not going to run away from you, Master."

He put his hands behind him, leaned forward and bored me with his eyes. "Some men don't believe it, but I see the end of slavery," said he. "And are you going to assist a cause that is fighting against your own freedom, Dan?" His manner changed and he put his hand on my shoulder. "Don't go away and leave me. I need you—I am a miserable old man, looking about for a prop. Don't leave me."

I dropped upon my knees and bowed my head to the floor, and I heard him sob over me. "I must follow him," I supplicated. "I can't stay behind. He saved my life. Listen to me a moment. I killed Dr. Bates—killed him in the manner my young master described—killed him to save my own life. They would have hanged me, but he took the blood upon himself to save me. And though for months nothing has been said, no one has uttered the doctor's name in his presence, I know that some people look upon him as a slaughterer of his brother, and I know that he has suffered, and for me. Money was offered me and I could have run away, but love, ignorance and superstition held me back, though the rope was ready for my neck. Never but once have I been tempted to leave him, never but once has my heart found a rebellion against him, and that was a woman—"

He put his hands under my arms and bade me arise. I got up and dared not look into his eyes, for I knew they were filled with tears. "Speak not a word of this to a living soul," he said. "Seal your mouth, for they would hang you even now. Go with him."

Old Mistress opened the door, unable longer to bear

the thought that he might be taking me into a confidence, and as she entered, the old man turned wrathfully upon me. "Yau can go to the d——!" he said, his voice high and sharp. "You may go with the rebels and be hanged with them. Madam, this negro boy is going with his master."

"Why, of course," she said with a brightening countenance, and speaking as if I were but to discharge a trivial duty. "He will need someone to wait on him and that's Dan's place, I am sure. And besides, it won't be for long. Everybody knows that it won't be much of a war. The North will soon be compelled to grant every demand made by the South; so for gracious sake, let us not take it so to heart. Come on into the parlor. May will sing an old song for us."

"Madam, I want no song. The rest of you may sing and make merry over the disgrace of my country, but I will not. Good-night."

He strode out, Old Mistress following him, begging him to come back, but he went to his room up stairs and shut the door. Surely no one felt disposed to hear a song, no one except myself, as I listened to the old-time lullaby with which Titine was wont to soothe the little one to sleep.

When I went to my Young Master's room I found

him sitting there alone. His books were put out of sight and a sword lay upon his table. As I entered, he looked up at me and pointed to a chair. "I want to talk to you," he said, and when I had sat down, he continued: "I will not compel you to go with me—"

"I am going Mars. Bob," I broke in. He looked at me with a sad smile.

"Dan, you are a faithful friend."

"I am a grateful slave, sir. And never but once was I ungrateful, and then my heart was on fire and my soul smothered with the smoke that arose. Titine laughed at me when I asked her to be my wife. She said that our marriage would be but a mockery, the multiplication of miseries; and I would have run away with her, but she told me that she did not love me. Don't credit me with more than my due. I am a weak man and under certain conditions might forget a great favor and prove treacherous. Don't trust me too far."

"I would trust you to the end of the earth," he said. "You are a negro, but you are a gentleman. You say Titine doesn't love you?" he continued after pausing to reflect. "What sort of a creature is she? What does she expect?"

"I don't know what she expects, but I believe that

she hopes one day to be a nun. Her old mistress poisoned her."

He reached over, took hold of the sword and drew it part way out of the scabbard. "For a long time I have kept it hidden in my closet," he said, pulling the blade further out and then shoving it back to the hilt. "I was afraid of a sharper and perhaps a juster weapon —my old father's tongue." He got up with a shudder, turned his back upon me and stood at the window. "The time may come when I shall acknowledge that I was bewitched," he said, looking out into the darkness. "But her love and her encouragement urge me on. Dan,"—and now he faced about—"Dan, the woman I love is a champion of the Southern cause. She said that she could not love me if—but it is cruel of me to tell you of love and of smiles. Your heart is sore; I have long known it. But—"

"Master, please don't think of me. Do you need me now?" I asked. "If not, I will go out."

"Go and stay as long as you choose," he said.

Titine was singing to the little child. The door was partly open and I looked into the room. She was bending over the cradle, her long hair hanging loose. I heard Miss May talking in Old Master's room.

"Titine."

"What do you want?" she asked, looking at me.

"Is the child asleep?"

"What is that to you?"

"Please don't snap at me that way. I want to talk to you—in the yard alone."

"I know what you would say, and you needn't say it."

"No, you don't. I have something to tell you that I never told before. I am going away and I want to talk to you."

"Oh, going with your master? Poor fool, to fight against your own interest, but you can't help it—You are a piece of yellow property."

"So is gold," I declared.

"Yes, so is gold, a piece of yellow property."

"But will you come down?"

"What is the use? You have already told me."

"And have you said all that you could say?"

"Yes, you are a poor fool."

"Your frankness will become insulting, the first thing you know."

"Indeed! Shut the door, please."

"Are you a human being?"

"No."

"I believe you are but a beautiful witch."

"Thank you. Even witches like a compliment. Shut the door, please."

I shut the door with a slam and I heard the child crying as I strode down the stairs.

CHAPTER XXVI.

My Master's troop was composed for the most part
of young men who had struggled with principle and
with family opposition and who regarded it wise to
meet in secret to prepare themselves for battle.   In
many families the dividing line ran as in our house,
across the dinner table.   Sometimes a "Confederate"
and a "Federal" company would go through with their
maneuvers in the same wood pasture; and on such
occasions the strictest dignity and decorum were
maintained, with never a jeer or idle word passing
from one side to the other.   The quarreling was
indulged by older men and irresolute persons who had
great bitterness, but not enough nerve to impel them
into the ranks.   From the moment when Young Master was forced openly to take his stand, his spirits
seemed to rise, though my accustomed eye could
sometimes see a sadness striving to pull his gayety
down, as when he heard Old Master's voice or met
him unexpectedly.   Sometimes they saluted each
other coldly as they passed, but often they appeared

almost to forget the difference lying like a shrouded corpse between them. One cool morning they met in the yard. By a silent agreement they no longer sat together at the table.

"A crisp and beautiful day," said the old man, bowing. "By such a day I am always reminded of a shaggy dog we used to own—we called him Wolf. Do you remember him?"

"Yes," Young Master answered, his countenance illumined with a sudden light. "One of his eyes was brown and the other blue. He must have died long ago, for he seems now to trot around the outer rim of my recollection."

At this figure the old man was so much pleased that he laughed. "You were very young," he said, "but little taller than old Wolf's back;" and here he fell into a meditation, leaning against a locust tree. The dog was still in his mind when he spoke again. "On a frosty day he was always frisky. He believed that the chill in the air foretold a rabbit hunt; and frequently it did. He used to come to my door early at morning and scratch to awake me. And I think he treed the first 'possum you ever saw. Old Simon brought the 'possum to the house, and you asked him why there was no hair on his tail. This gave him an opportunity to tell a story that I heard when I was a boy and which has been told in every negro cabin. The Lord made a raccoon and the devil was so taken with the work that he was resolved to imitate it. Well, he made a thing as near like a coon as he could, but was so disgusted at the appearance of the result that he seized the animal by the tail and swung him round to dash his brains out against the jamb, but the hair slipped off, the animal escaped with his life but with a hairless tail. Yes, sir, and I believed the story until I was nearly grown."

"I remember the story," said Bob, "though I don't recall the one particular 'possum used by Simon as an illustration. But I remember that Simon took me on his back one night, out into the woods where the dogs had treed one. It must have been long after Simon told the 'possum story, for I don't think that old Wolf went with us. He must have been dead."

"Yes, he was," the old man agreed. "I recollect the night. A coon was treed in an enormous oak, and the boys were a long time in cutting it down. Do you remember, Dan?"

"Yes, sir," I spoke up. "It was the night that Mr. Bill Putney was killed in town by Mr. Tom Ellis Gray."

"That's a fact," said the old man. "But how do you happen to associate the two events?"

"Why, when we came back to the house, a boy was waiting for you. They wanted you to come to town and go on a bond."

"But that couldn't have fastened it on your mind. What else was there? Out with it, sir."

"Why, Old Miss got mad at me for coming through the hall and slapped me off the front steps."

"Ah, that was it," he said, musing. "And it seems long ago, even to me, much longer than happenings thirty years before."

"Dan," said Young Master, "get my horse. But wait a moment. You may hitch up the buggy if you want to go over to Potter's with me."

"I don't care to go unless you would much rather have me," I replied.

"All right, then; saddle the horse."

"He has a love affair of his own, I am inclined to think," the old gentleman said, talking to Bob, but winking at me. "How about it, Dan?"

I had turned to go, but had halted and faced about. "A very empty love affair I am afraid, Master."

"Tut, sir, tut. There is no such thing as an empty

love affair if it's managed rightly. You are too faint-hearted. Do you remember what the poet said?"

This was the first time that he had addressed himself to what I conceived to be my learning, and I was flattered.

"You mean Pope's master, sir."

"Hang the scoundrel, to talk about Pope's master. He had no master, or if he had, he bought his freedom with his genius."

I was still flattered and I made bold to venture upon a criticism. "Not with his genius, but with his pains and his polish."

"Confound you, sir, go on and get that horse, you yellow scoundrel."

When I had led the horse round to the gate, Bob and the old man came out talking in easy good-humor.

"Your mother is mightily tickled," said Old Master. "She thinks you have drawn a prize. And so do I. She's a charming young woman, sir. But you have said nothing as to when the wedding is to take place."

Bob had put his foot in the stirrup to mount, but he took it out and stood there irresolute, as if he knew not what to do or say.

"You haven't said a word as to the time set for the marriage," Old Master repeated.

"No, sir. She is to wait—wait until I come home."

A dark shadow fell upon the old man's face, and without another word, he wheeled about and strode into the yard.

Old Miss came to the door and commanded me to bring a stick of wood to mend the parlor fire. When I went in with a log on my shoulder, I found Titine sitting by the fire, trying to amuse the little girl.

"Get out of the way, Jessie," she cried. "Dan, let me help you ease it down."

I was strong enough to have tossed the log in the air but I told her yes, and I caught at her hand as she stood close to lend her aid. She laughed and stepping back declared that I might help myself. I put the log into the fire-place and stood on the hearth to brush my coat.

"You ought to be proud of your strength," she said.

"That may be, and I ought to deplore my weakness."

"Yes, you ought. Jessie, don't go near the fire."

"And I do."

"Then you are climbing toward firmer ground. Put down the tongs, Jessie."

"The ground may be firm and yet slippery."

"If salt were given in exchange for words, you

might have enough to sell.   Jessie, put down the cat; you'll get all covered with fleas."

"Titine, I believe that hateful and unjust remark made by Old Miss has set you against me.   You cleave to it as if it were a piece of wisdom inspired of the Lord."

"But wasn't it the truth?   And isn't there wisdom in all truth?"

"No, it was not the truth.   It was spite.   She hates me and you ought to have sense enough to see it.   But if truth were a diamond and sparkled in my favor, you would shut your eyes to it.   I came to you with the devotion of a strong man.   I showed you my heart. I threw it at your feet and let it flutter there, and so far from taking it up out of the dirt, you did not even look down upon it.   You have no heart.   An old woman killed it and left a senseless whim to vibrate in your breast.   You could have made of me—"

"Nothing," she broke in.   "How could I make anything of a thing that could never belong to me? Jessie, you'll fall out of that rocking chair if you don't mind.   I once told you that I have the instincts of a lady, and I have, and I will not turn upon those instincts and mock them."

"But if you would only acknowledge that you care

for me," I pleaded; "if you would only light a candle, call it hope and hold it aloft, no matter how far down the road, I could keep my eyes fastened upon it and live on faith."

She looked at me, whether in pity or in scorn I could not tell. But I could gather no comfort from her words. "Flies scorch their wings in the candle lighted down the road," she said.

At this moment Old Miss came into the room. "Why, gracious alive, why do you let that fire smoke so?" she cried. "Shove that log further back. I never saw as worthless a negro as you are. To bring a log in and throw it down right in front of the fire where it can do nothing but smoke! Go out. It makes me weary to look at you."

She had not the opportunity much longer to look at me, for on the morrow, Young Master's troop, now but a play-thing, was to become a part of the great machinery of war. It was known that we were going, but at the supper table not a word bearing upon that subject was uttered by Old Miss, Mr. Clem or Miss May. We heard Old Master walking up and down the hall. At night Mr. Clem came to the room.

"Well, you march to-morrow, I suppose," said he.

"Yes," Young Master replied, "we go, rain or shine."

"And I go very soon. I am waiting for my commission. Having once been a soldier gives me some little importance."

"Uncle Clem, do you think we can get through within ninety days?"

"Get through what?"

"Do you think that the war will be over within that time?"

"Yes, if the South lays down her arms."

"She won't do that."

"Then the war will last until she does. You people have a peculiar idea of this government. Do you think we are going to suffer it to go to pieces, that we will submit to disruption as long as there is an arm to strike? Why, the women in this community, your mother included, look upon it as a pic-nic excursion. Dan?"

"Yes, sir."

"Are you going to shoot at the men who would free you?"

"I am going with Young Master, sir, to do as he bids me."

"He is not going as a soldier, but as a servant, Uncle Clem."

"Same thing, Bob. The teamster is as much of a

soldier, when results are estimated, as the man who carries a gun. But it is all right, Dan. No one can hold you responsible. Bob, old Potter is a hot rebel, isn't he?"

"Rampageous; and his daughter is making a Confederate flag—for me. We'll stop there and get it as we pass to-morrow."

Early the next morning our troop was marshalled on the turn-pike about a mile from the house. From the rear veranda Old Master could see the flashing of their steel. He stood there gazing until Bob came out from breakfast.

"One moment," said the old man, stepping into the hall. "You do not go with my curse, but with my wounded love. There, sir, not a word from you."

They shook hands, but did not look into each other's eyes. Old Miss, Miss May and Mr. Clem walked with him to the gate. The parting was not sad, for no one of us, except Mr. Clem, attached much importance to the war cry, the bugle and the drum. Young Master mounted first, and then, turning to me, said: "Dan, I have forgotten something. Run up stairs and get my Horace. You can overtake me."

When I came down, Titine was standing alone at

the gate. "They are about to leave you," she said, laughing.

"It would delight me to be left if I thought you—"

"Too late for nonsense, now, Dan."

"You have made it too late for sense, Titine."

"Of course you blame me with everything."

"No, but I blame you with one thing, which, after all, is nearly everything—the death of my heart. But why talk of heart to a heartless creature—Titine, let me kiss you."

"Go away!" she cried, waving me off. But I seized her in my arms, kissed her and sprang upon my horse. And she threw a stone at me as I galloped away.

CHAPTER XXVII.

How sadly were dashed the hopes of the husband and the lover who had expected not a war, but a military demonstration to last but a few days. The cheerful party of decorated pleasure seekers soon became a sober army, stripped of feathers, bent upon the shedding of blood. I may be pardoned this egotism, but it seemed that the South, more Anglo-Saxon, more American, fought with brighter fire and bravery than the miscellaneous nationalities gathered in the North. I know one thing, that the Southern soldier held the foreigner in contempt. He had, however, to face too much of his own blood. But I am going to follow the fortunes of no campaign; I am going to be as brief as possible. My Master was promoted for gallantry, and soon was placed at the head of a regiment of cavalry. I rode by his side, and I knew that beyond that blue line, away over yonder, my freedom and the freedom of my down-trodden race was lying, but I was true to him, and was proud of him.

Letters from home were very irregular. Old Mas-

ter did not write. Old Miss wrote; but never came
there a word for me. I wrote to Titine, but no answer
reached me. Sometimes, at night, alone in the tent,
master would read aloud Miss Potter's letter, and
though the words were affectionate, they appeared to
me to be mechanical and meaningless. But to him
each sentence was a string of pearls.

For a time the Confederate arms were so successful
that it looked as if the war might soon close, with victory for the South. But a change came. The old Puritan stock, the old blood that humbled a king and cut
off his head, gathered in solemn and God-serving
force. We had chaplains and held services; we prayed
to God to bless our cause, but the Puritan mixed
prayer with his powder and brightened his sword with
a scriptural text.

We went with Bragg's invasion into Kentucky.
How joyous it was again to turn our faces toward
home. We did not think of the blood that was to flow
at Perryville. One day we halted within fifteen miles
of Old Master's house. And Young Master received
permission to visit his home. We set out at night.
First we were to go to Potter's. We were cautioned
to be back by day-light, to overtake the army at a
place called Elwood. The night was moon-flooded.

The turn-pike looked an endless strip of light. How delightful to see the first familiar object, an old mill where Bob and I had caught many a sun-fish. Now we were but a short distance from Potter's. We passed the toll-gate. The bar was up and no one came out. We met an old negro and he told us that the people had nearly all flocked to town, that they had been ordered in as a battle was expected.

"Here we are!" Bob cried, and he jumped from his horse in front of Potter's house. A dog barked, but there was no light. He went to the front door and the sharp fall of the brass knocker resounded afar off, throughout the stillness of the night. He called me and I went to him.

"I believe they are gone, too," he said, his voice choking with disappointment. "Let us go around and see if we can find anyone."

We went to the cabins in the rear of the house. All was dark. We mounted and rode on toward home, silent, desolate with the realization of war's uncompromising demands. I heard the creek and my heart leaped. We turned into the lane. The gate was down and heavy artillery had cut the road into deep ruts, here where Dr. Bates had lain under the eye of the law.

"They are all gone, too," said master, "negroes and all."

"No," I cried, "there's a light in your room."

We put spurs and dashed up to the gate. The front door stood ajar. There was no light in the hall. "Easy," said Bob, and we tip-toed up the stairs. A light streamed under the door of our "office." We did not knock, but Bob shoved the door open. Then he sprang back with pistol in hand.

"Why, helloa!" a voice cried. It was Mr. Clem. "Come in, boys."

He stood there in the uniform of a Federal colonel, his sword on the table. We shook hands and the greeting was one of unaffected warmth. We sat down, though not yet over our surprise. "How on earth did you get here?" Colonel Clem asked. "The country is full of our troops. You took a big risk. Sorry the folks are not here. Had hard work in driving Brother Guilford in. Swore he'd stay here and let them knock the house about his ears. But, how well you're looking, my boy. Make a nice prisoner for me to take in, eh?"

Bob touched the butt of his revolver and smiled. Colonel Clem nodded goodhumoredly. "Bobbie, so far as we are now concerned," said he, "there is no war. But haven't we had a time? Told you it wouldn't be a picnic. Come, don't be sad."

"When did 'she' go to town?"

"To-day," the colonel answered. "I saw her about noon-time. She is more beautiful than ever; said she had a charming letter from you not long ago. I have been over in Missouri a good deal of the time lately," he added with a strange smile. "Had a piece of the past thrust into my face while I was there. A fellow had been court-martialed and sentenced to be hanged. I met the guards as they were taking him out. My old-time negro-trader, the man that robbed me years ago. It was hardly the same sort of court that he had escaped from in Illinois. What did I do? I ordered them to halt—I ran to the commander and begged him to let me have that fellow. I wanted to kill him with my sword. But they wouldn't let me, so I had to content myself with seeing him hanged. What sort of stock are you boys riding? Now, I've got a good mare here that I think would just suit you, Bob. But I don't want any Confederate money. Come down and let's see what can be done."

Bob shook his head and laughed. "I am to get back to my command by daylight, Uncle Clem," said he, "and I know that if I should trade horses with you, I'd have to walk."

"What nonsense. I want to see you on a good horse. Come on."

"No, I thank you."

"Let me show you the mare."

"Don't want to see her."

"She's a beauty—got her from General Buell."

"Take her back to him. I don't want her."

"All right," he said, with a loud laugh. "Got your eye teeth, haven't you. Well—what was that? A bugle."

"Come," said Bob, starting toward the door. But he halted. "Uncle Clem, give my love to them all. Tell the old man that I love him."

CHAPTER XXVIII.

The days fell dark for the Confederacy. It seemed
that the whole world had sprung up in arms against
the South. Stronghold after stronghold was taken,
and Richmond itself was threatened. No hope was left
to illumine the soldier's heart; he had followed a bright
phantom, year after year, expecting it to lead him out
of the wilderness, but he was becoming deeper and
more darkly involved in the thicket, and now the
phantom was fading. In his haversack, he carried
roasted acorns and pieces of sugar-cane, and his
enemies, in blood his brothers, shook their heads and
marveled at his courage, for he was just as ready to
fight as he had been on the morning after Bull Run.
To face death at morning, to shed his blood at noon,
to lie down supperless upon the wet ground at night,
was a duty that he was not there to question, but to
discharge.

One night my master and I occupied a room in a
deserted farm-house near Richmond. About us lay a

broken army and the scattered fragments of a civilization.

"A few more days will settle it, I think, Dan," he
said. Sitting on a box, with one leg drawn up and
with his hands clasped over his knee, he was gazing
at the lightwood sputtering in the fire-place, and upon
his thoughtful countenance a black shadow and a
yellow light alternately arose and fell. "Only a few
more days and most of us may be shot or permitted
to go home. Who would have believed that we could
have gone through such a time since Jane stood on
the stile-block waving the silk flag she had made for
me. And I can't carry even a scrap of it back to her.
Do you know one thing that I'm going to do if I'm
permitted to go home?" he asked, his face brightening. "I am going to acknowledge to father that I was
wrong, not in fighting so hard after I got in, but in permitting a glamour to blind me in the first place. The
most gigantic mistake of the age. I was like you,
Dan. I followed my heart rather than my judgment.
But you are free. I am your master no longer. Don't
turn away. I don't reproach you; I congratulate you.
If any man deserves freedom, you do. Better spread
the blankets and let's try to get a little sleep. We

need no alarm clock to wake us up. Brother Ulysses with his cannon will see to that."

And with his cannon he did see to it. We were aroused before the break of day, and by the time the sun came up we were in the thick of a fight. There came a charge—a wild rush, sword, pistol, bayonet—and when it had swept past, I was on the ground beside the man whose fortunes I had followed. He was desperately wounded. The farm-house was turned into a hospital and I took him to the room which we had occupied the night before. The weak remnant of our army was crushed. We were prisoners.

The hour was late. Precaution no longer was necessary and camp-fires were burning everywhere. A surgeon told me that Master could not live until morning. And this was to be his end, in an old house, a prisoner, the hungry dogs howling on the hill.

"Dan," he called. I was bending over him, my face close to his. "Are you here, Dan?"

"Yes, Mars. Bob."

"It's all over, Dan. And I don't see how it could have been otherwise. I seem to have been born for this hour. Dan, I want to be buried where I fell. And tell them not to disturb me, but to let me sleep there. Bury her letters with me. Tell the old man that I love him."

Early in the morning, with the tears falling upon him, I folded his arms on his breast; and I heard a glad shout and the cry that the war was done. From an officer in command, once a neighbor, I obtained permission to bury my poor Master under an apple-tree shading the spot where he had fallen; and assisted by an old negro, I laid him to rest. My heart was so heavy that I cared not what might become of me. Judgment day had come and I was branded a sinner.

I built a fire near the grave and watched beside it a whole night, wretched, struggling with myself, feeling that I could not leave him lying there alone. In the morning I was ordered to mount a mule and drive a wagon into Richmond. As I drove along I scribbled a note to Old Master, not knowing how long I might be held, and gave it to a neighbor to give to him. Now I was in the service of the North, driving a team of mules into the city that I had striven to defend. But I liked it not. I was heart-sore to hear the babble of our creek and to look upon the colts in the pasture. And after two days of enforced labor I was permitted to turn my face homeward. I was now even worse off than the regular rebel soldier. I was looked upon with suspicion. I had no means of transportation and therefore was compelled to walk. I slept in the woods or on the road-side. Once when I went up to a house to buy food, an old man set his dog after me. My money gave out (I had started with but a few dollars, the amount earned by driving the government wagon) and now I was reduced almost to starvation. The country was destitute. Everyone looked to the army for food, and supplies were delayed. At last, after days of tramping and nights of sleepless hunger, I crossed the Kentucky line. Two more days and I should be at home.

But how cold and distant had begun to sound the word home. How time must have transformed the old place. And all the negroes were free. I scarcely could realize it. I wondered what they would do with their freedom, if they knew how to act. They could not support themselves by standing about and proclaiming themselves free. They must work and after all their liberty was to be tinged with slavery. Thus I mused as I moved with sore tread along the hard turn-pike, slowly entering the domain of my boyhood, growing heavier and sadder with the sight of each familiar object. I came to the old mill, gray and green, with roof fallen in, with cap-stones pulled down by the wanton hands that reach out to destroy when a war-storm has swept over the land. The creek sang to me, not as of yore, a sweet and poetic tune, but a sorrowful and hollow-sounding dirge.

Onward I strode, limping now, for my shoes were worn through and my feet were bleeding. The day was closing. The shadow of the trumpet vine, clustered high on the top rail of the fence, fell dark athwart the white and ghastly pike. Another rise of ground and Potter's house was thrown into view, red in the setting sun. I had to halt to calm the tumultuous beating of my heart. I wondered if the news had reached her. Surely word must have been sent from Old Master's house. But it was my duty to stop and repeat his last words, to tell her that I had buried her letters with him. I dreaded the look she would give me, the tone of her voice. Now I could see that she had been passionately fond of him. I thought of the sentence I had passed upon her nature, the complaint that I could not hold her clear in my mental gaze, and I repented of this dark injustice. Onward again I limped, my eyes low upon the white pebbles; and I did not look up until abreast of the gate. Then I found myself among a number of carriages and buggies. A score of horses were tied to the fence. An old man stood by the road-side and I addressed a question to him.

"What means all this?"

He nodded his head toward the house and thus he answered me: "Miss Jane Potter has just married a Yankee general."

I tried to run, when it seemed that I had grabbed myself up from falling, and I stumbled away down the pike. In a corner of the fence I dropped upon my knees and cried aloud. Merciful God, was the whole world false! Long I knelt there in agony, reviewing my pitiable life, with my master's image and his blood vivid before me. Merry laughter startled me to my feet. A carriage, followed by other vehicles and horses, passed briskly along; and fiercely I shook my fist at the carriage in front, and bitterly I wished for a gun, a cannon, that I might be avenged upon a black and traitorous heart.

Homeward now I turned, chilled to the core, prepared for anything. Over a fence I climbed and took a shorter way across the pastureland. Darkness had fallen and I heard old Stephen calling the sheep, to be housed for the night, safe from the ravages of prowling dogs. I came upon the little creek, weaker than far below at the old mill, but chanting the same hollow dirge. I stood upon the rock where Mr. Clem had found me with his shrewd temptation; and a little further on I came to the deep hole wherein Bob and I had sworn to drown ourselves. Here I stopped and bathed my face and hands, lingering, dreading to meet Old Master's grief-chilled eye. Fire-light came from some of the cabins, feeling its way and trembling through the darkness; but for the most part the negro quarter appeared deserted.

The door of the "big house" stood open and the hall lamp was burning. With dragging feet I climbed the steps and raised the brass knocker, the familiar old dragon's head, but did not let it fall; so much was I in dread of its startling alarm. I stepped back to go round to the rear veranda, when Old Miss came out of the library. She saw me and her cry pierced my heart. Oh, how wretched she looked and how feeble! And how weak was that cry, a mere whisper; but it rang in my ears night and day for many a month. I believe she would have fallen, I thought she was falling and I put out my hands and caught her, eased her upon the hall settee and fanned her with my hat.

"Go," she said, motioning me away, "go to your Old Master. He is dying in his room up stairs. Wait, let me send him word. He was afraid you wouldn't get here. May, May!" she called, "go and tell him Dan has come."

Miss May, pale and tear-stricken, had stepped out of the parlor. She grasped my hand and then hastened up the stairs.

"Elliot brought the news," said Old Miss, leaning back against the wall. "And May went over—over to tell 'her.' Infamous creature, she was making preparations for her wedding. Oh, this world, this world! Oh, my son, if I could only call him back!" She looked at me with her head turned to listen for Miss May's footsteps. "I have been the most miserable woman in the world, and a thousand times I have prayed for death." Her eyes grew brighter. She straightened up with pride. "But he died like a hero. Tell me about him."

I told her how he had fallen; and when I mentioned the letters that were put into the grave with him, she cleared her throat with the old dry rasp.

"How long has Master been sick?" I asked, wishing to change the subject.

"A long time, but the doctors did not give him up until the day before yesterday. They might have known at first that there was no hope for him. Why should there be any hope for him or for anyone?

Why can't we all get out of this miserable world and be done with it?"

"Have many of the negroes gone away?" I asked.

"No, not many. We have hired most of them to work the land. I don't see much difference in them. They are as near no account as they can be."

"It will take them some time to adjust themselves to their freedom," I remarked.

"Freedom!" she repeated with a sneer. "They can never adjust themselves to it. They think it means a privilege to take whatever they can lay hands on."

Titine was in my mind, but I was afraid to ask about her. She had treated me with scorn when I was well dressed, and now I must be far below her contempt.

"Do you want me to remain and take charge of things about the place?"

"No," she said, with sharp emphasis, "you must go away and let me die in peace, or as near in peace as possible, for I shall never know a moment's ease. Looking back, it seems that I was born wretched; and yet I know that I was happy until treachery—but I will say nothing. Oh, this miserable world!" She swayed herself to and fro, her lips tightly drawn, her eyes hard-set. "But an end of it all will come sooner or later, and then we can say that it all amounted to nothing—that it was all a nightmare. Here comes your Miss May."

"Walk as softly as you can," Miss May said to me, and then looking down, she added: "Poor fellow, you couldn't make a noise with those tattered feet."

I followed her up the stairs, through the hall where so often I had found the old man walking in the dead silence of the night—followed her into the room opposite our "office." At a glance I saw my young master's canopied bed; and upon it lay the old man, propped high with pillows.

"Come here, Dan," he commanded. His voice was weak, but I was surprised at its clearness. "May, leave us alone, please."

I knelt beside the bed. I took one of his hands and he gave me the other, looking at me with an ashen smile. "Dan, I was determined not to die until I had seen you and I have compelled them to leave me alone most of the time. I was afraid of company—afraid that it might lead my mind off and let death sneak up and master me. I was so determined to live, that nothing but my own mind could have killed me."

How changed he was, even aside from the ravages of disease. His hair was perfectly white and his teeth were gone. His eyes were sunken, but they were still sharp.

"I did not believe he would ever come home, Dan. Something kept on telling me that he would not, morning, noon and night. When we knew that the war could certainly last but a few days more, I took hope; but that something was louder than ever, dinging my boy's death in my ears. So I was not greatly surprised when Elliot came with the news. He gave me your note and told me how he died—like a Gradley and a man. In your note you said—I have it under my pillow—that he told you to say that he loved me. God bless him."

"Master, he told me more than the note contained. He said that if he lived to get home, he would acknowledge to you that he was wrong."

He broke down at this and I wiped the tears out of his eyes.

"He didn't owe me any apology; he had as much right to his opinion as I had to mine. Some of the noblest minds and kindest hearts in the country went wrong. Don't tell me anything he said that bordered on an apology. He should not have apologized. In my heart I forgave him a thousand times; and, night after night, I sat in his room, reading his books.

When I was taken down I had them bring his bed in here that I might die on it. Yes, we were all wrong," he said, pressing my hands. "Dan, lean over." My face was almost touching his, and I trembled violently. "You know the hoof-marks on the stairs—you know that I killed Solomon Putnam. But you never knew why."

"No, sir; no one ever told me."

"No one knew. Dan, your mother was a beautiful woman. Titine reminds me of her. Did anyone ever tell you that your mother was handsome?"

"Yes, sir, an old negro man, a long time ago."

"Dan, that scoundrel offered to buy your mother. I scorned his money and he poisoned her. And I sent him word that I would kill him on sight; and he rode up the stairs, drunk, to kill me in my bed. I raised myself up and shot him—Dan, lean over further. My life has been miserable and I am—I am the author of all your misery. There, don't pull away from me. Put your head on this old breast for a moment. My poor boy—I have been a disgrace unto myself and the cause of your humiliation. But I have loved you and have shown it whenever I could without bringing a cruelty down upon your head. My poor wife—God forgive me—always strongly suspected, but she did not know. She hated you and who could blame her? That scoundrel Bates kept her mind on fire with insinuations—He was afraid to tell her outright. A thousand times I have been tempted to tell her and beg her forgiveness, but the quality of forgiveness was always a stranger to her heart. She has had enough to harden her against the world and I am going to beg her for mercy as I would beg at the Judgment seat. Dan, I have no money to leave you. The farm is mortgaged. All I can leave is the love and the blessing of a wretched old man, a sinner. Is that someone at the door?"

I opened the door. Old Miss and Miss May came in. They drew near to the bedside and stood there, seeing that the hour of parting was not far off.

"I was afraid of some sudden shock," said the old woman, and she looked hard at me. "Shall we go out again?" she asked, smoothing back Old Master's white hair.

"No," he said, his voice feebler than when he had spoken last. He motioned to her and she sat down beside him. Miss May was at the foot of the bed with her face buried in the covers. A few moments passed and he strove to talk, but the power of speech was gone. Several of the neighbors had come to see him, and they were admitted to the death-room, though the old man had passed beyond the border line of consciousness. His breathing grew heavier and, toward dawn, he fell asleep. I stood and gazed upon him with a new reverence, a strange and half fright-ened affection. The revelation did not come to me as a great surprise; it was as plain to me as to the reader who has followed me through these memoirs; but I had not permitted myself to muse upon it; there was always something so startling in the thought.

I turned to go and Old Miss followed me down the stairs, and in the hall she bade me wait a moment. I stood near the door, in the gray light, she halting near me; and her eyes were dry.

"What did he tell you?" she asked.

"Madam, for mercy sake don't ask me to repeat it."

"Madam!" she said bitterly. "You are drinking your freedom fast. But have you lost your sense of obedience, and at such a time as this?"

"I would rather not tell you."

"But I command you."

"Then you shall know. He told me that he was my father."

It seemed a long time before she spoke again. She stood looking at me. "You have been the humiliation and the bitterness of my life," she said. "The first sight of you gave me a shudder, and never since then have I known a moment of peace. I brooded in a doubt worse than a certainty—I could not find out the truth. And but for my children I would have drowned myself. Yes, you have been the humiliation and the bitterness of my life. Now go."

"Yes, I will go—But did you ever stop to reflect that while I might have been a humiliation and a bitterness, it was not my fault?"

"I thought of nothing but my own shame and my own bitterness. Go, and I hope never to see you again."

"Just one moment. There is something that I ought to tell you. I told Old Master before I went into the army. Young master did not kill Dr. Bates. I killed him to save my own life, and Master, knowing that they would hang me, took the blood upon himself."

"Then you shall be tried for murder!" the old woman said. "I will go and have you arrested," She turned her back upon me. "Sam," she called. "Sam, where are you?"

"Wait a moment before you send for an officer," said I. She faced me again, frowning. "You must know," said I, speaking as kindly as I could, "that you have no law to take hold of me now. The strong arm of the North has freed me, though I opposed it, and now it declares me the equal of any man before the law. It says that if I am innocent I shall be protected, and I am innocent. You could not have me arrested in the first place, and, even if you could, it would not be in good taste at this time. You have told me of the bitterness of your life, but I have not told you of the misery of mine. You—but I will charge my misery to nature. Good-bye, and in all truth I hope that God may bless you."

I stepped out upon the portico; and—and there in the growing light stood Titine. My breath came with a gasp as I beheld her. She looked at me, looked at my tattered feet and covered her face with her hands.

"Titine, I must now say good-bye forever."

She looked up. There was heaven in her eyes. "No," she said. "No, you are not to say good-bye. I am going with you."

"What!" I cried, almost choking with emotion.

"I am going with you. I would rather go to perdition with you than to be separated from you again." She caught my hand and held it and I stood there trembling. "You told me of your love and now I am going to tell you of mine," she said. "My soul has wept over you, and in the night my heart has cried aloud. I am going with you."

I put my arms about her, thanking God that I was alive, but almost unable to believe my senses. And then my condition smote me. "But I am a pauper, Titine. I am a penniless tramp and the dogs bark at me."

"You are not a pauper," she said. "Wait a moment."

She ran up the stairs and soon returned with a pocket-book.

"Take it," she said, handing it to me. "I have saved it for you. And now, let us go away from this desolate place—away off somewhere into the world of freedom and love."

And with my arm about her, we stepped forth into the light of a new day, our faces turned toward the rising sun.

*   *   *   *   *

I sit here to-night in my Ohio home, and I look at a portrait on the wall, enlarged from a powder-blackened photograph that I brought with me, when foot-sore and heart-heavy, I walked from Richmond to my desolate birth-place in Kentucky. And here beside the portrait is the picture of a monument and an apple-tree. I hear my daughter at the piano, and I hear Titine singing a mellow song of the long ago. It has been a night of company at my house, and some of the younger guests have lingered into this late hour, for the occasion is one of exceeding cheer. Early in the evening a committee called to inform me of what I knew full well, my re-election to Congress.

THE END.